MORE ZOMBIES THAN BULLETS

CARL R. CART

SEVERED PRESS
HOBART TASMANIA

MORE ZOMBIES THAN BULLETS

WWW.SEVEREDPRESS.COM

ISBN: 978-1-925493-43-6

Other Books By This Author:

ROTTERS

ROTTERS: BRAVO COMPANY

ROTTERS: ALPHA CONTACT

DWARFS OF THE DEAD

DETOUR 366

ACKNOWLEDGEMENTS

This book sprang full blown into my head one mean and grisly day, when the skies were grey and blood was on the wind. I take the blame for most of this one. Still, some thanks are in order, as always. My most sincere thanks to:

My friend Captain Dave. Dave and I discussed the QZ at great length. As always, he was the initial sounding board for the rough draft, and I am in his debt. Every story that Dave hears comes away better.

My friend Tony Bobo, who always proofreads and critiques my stories; as with Dave, his input is always welcome and enjoyed. One of us once said to the other, "I will always listen to your good ideas and then not use them."

My friends Matt Bliss and Mark Robinson, who generously provide their military expertise to my stories.

To my friend Jamey Aebersold, who always generously helps me with formatting and proofreading.

To my friend Kelly Pitt, who always lends me his printing expertise and assistance with first runs and draft copies, and who did the original cover art.

My wife Jennifer, who has to listen to my ideas and stories over and over to the point of numbness. At this point, I can safely say she hates zombies.

Finally, my thanks to the most excellent band Rammstein. Their music has fueled many of my more productive writing days, and I highly recommend them to any zombie fanatic!

I would also like to take the opportunity to explain my use of place names in the book. Many of the purely fictional locations are based upon real road maps of the great states of Missouri and Kansas, and street maps from the cities of Saint Louis and Kansas City. If I have included a facsimile of your home town in my narrative, please forgive me. This is a work of fiction and I mean no disparagement or offense. I don't really mean to imply that there are zombies in your neck of the woods. I believe most of them are here in Indiana. My place names are made up, totally fictional. As to the military installations, and especially Fort Riley, Fort Leavenworth, and Smokey Hill, those places and the people there, especially active duty military, have only my deepest respect and admiration. The book is dedicated to you and your service to our country. Those locations as depicted in the book are also fictional. Imaginary places from the mind of the author. There is no secret research Lab Three at Fort Riley, and no secret Cold War storage facility located there. I made all that stuff up: all fictional, period. We all know that zombies aren't real, right?

Finally, all of the people depicted in the narrative are fictional characters. Any resemblance to any person, living or dead is purely unintentional and coincidental.

MORE ZOMBIES THAN BULLETS

Fort Riley - Kansas

The four-point-two earthquake that shook Central Kansas on that hot summer day, the day we now call Z Day, didn't really do much damage. A few farm houses shifted on their foundations. They felt it in Junction City and Manhattan Kansas. There were no injuries. No one died, just then. That would come later, in spades. They did feel it at Fort Riley. Not so much at the surface, but deep underground in Research Lab Three, they really felt it. A huge fissure split Research Lab Three apart. The lab's triple redundant biological seals suffered a catastrophic failure. A four-foot crack split open right down the center of the facility, a crack that ran all the way to the surface. The engineers who had designed the biological research facility had never imagined an earthquake of that magnitude being centered directly on the storage areas. Everyone in the vicinity of Lab Three died. The earthquake killed some of them and the virus got the rest. Karma is a bitch.

Main Gate - Fort Riley - Kansas

Specialist Matt Brewer loved his job. He was the guard at the main gate. He was the man. No motherfucker got onto the base without his permission.

Before he had joined the Army, things had been bad. He had been picked on quite a bit in school. Growing up had been a little rough for Matt. But none of that mattered now. Now he had the power.

Anyone who tried to come on post that he didn't like, for any reason, was going to get the business. Specialist Brewer loved fucking with people. It was his turn to be the bully.

1

He was busy being a total prick to some poor bastard when the earthquake shook him. All of a sudden there was a lot of chatter on his radio, but everything looked normal at the main gate. Brewer frowned; the pussies on the base were wetting their panties over nothing, just like always. He didn't know about Lab Three. He held up his hand and stopped the incoming traffic. He couldn't make out what was being said on the radio, everyone was talking all at once.

The virus drifted past him on the gentle Kansas breeze. Specialist Brewer breathed the virus deep into his lungs. He coughed and then he choked. He collapsed to his hands and knees. His spittle ran freely from his gasping mouth onto the concrete walkway. Brewer pitched face forward. He turned purple, and then black, and then he died. Twenty minutes later, he got up and walked away.

North Perimeter Fence - Fort Riley - Kansas

"Watch out!" Sergeant Kane bellowed. He yanked the bucking jeep's steering wheel back to the right, away from the fence. The jeep's driver, Specialist Dee Taft hit the brakes, bringing the vehicle to a stop. The earthquake ended as fast as it had begun.

"What the fuck was that?" Taft asked.

"Earthquake," Kane responded tersely.

Sergeant Kane keyed his radio. "This is Alpha Two. I'm reporting a strong tremor on the northern perimeter. Do you copy, Control?"

"Affirmative, Alpha Two," a voice replied. "We just had an earthquake, check your patrol sector for damage."

"Copy that," Kane answered. He pointed down the perimeter fence row, "Let's roll."

The jeep rolled slowly east down the dirt road that paralleled the perimeter fence for three miles with no sign of damage before Kane spotted any problems. A thin wisp of smoke rose into the sky just to the south of them. Kane directed Taft towards it.

The jeep cut cross country through the tall grass, towards a pair of metal buildings a quarter mile away. As they approached, Kane had Taft slow the jeep. "Take it slow," Kane instructed his driver.

"What's up?" Taft asked.

"Nothing," Kane replied. "This part of the base used to be a storage area during the eighties. I've heard tell there's some pretty nasty shit stored up here, that's all."

"What?" Taft stammered. "Nobody said anything about that."

"Just pull up short until I scope it out," Kane ordered. Taft pulled the jeep to a stop, and shut off the engine.

Sergeant Kane uncased his binoculars and scanned the buildings. Both of them were heavily damaged, and smoke rose skyward from the furthest one. A dirt road led back south to the center of the base, away from a small parking lot nearby. Roughly a dozen cars and trucks were parked there. Kane grunted as he slowly scanned the area.

"What is it, Sarge?" Taft asked.

"Casualties," Kane responded.

"Where?" Taft inquired.

"Just in front of the far building," Kane replied. He handed the binoculars to his partner. Taft eagerly scanned the area until he found the bodies.

"Shit," he whistled. "Do you think they're dead?"

"They probably ain't napping," Kane quipped back.

Taft started the jeep. "Let's go check it out," he said.

Kane reached over and shut the jeep back off. "We aren't goin' down there without chem gear, you moron," he responded. The sergeant keyed the radio mic again. "Control, we've got casualties and heavy damage at the northern storage area. Do you copy, Control?"

There was no response.

Kane keyed the mic again. "Control, do you copy?" He looked at Taft. "Base Command, do you copy?" he spoke. Only static came back through the radio. "Shit, this ain't good at all," he growled.

Taft shifted nervously in his seat, "What's wrong, Sarge?"

"Damned if I know," Kane replied. "But nobody's on the fucking radios, and I don't think the equipment is down. Does anybody copy?" he spoke into the microphone.

"Affirmative," replied a voice through the radio. "This is Delta One."

"What's your present location, Delta One?" Sergeant Kane asked tersely.

"Western perimeter patrol," came the reply. "We're at the old pump house, copy?"

"Who is this?" Kane asked.

"Specialist Jackson," the voice replied. "I've got Mason riding shotgun."

"This is Sergeant Kane. We've lost contact with Control and Base Command. I'm setting up a mobile command post at my location. Proceed along the north fence road until you see smoke, and then proceed south towards the old storage buildings and rendezvous at my location. Stay on the perimeter road until you are directly north of my twenty. We have casualties and damage. The quake may have caused a chemical leak from the old storage areas. Do you copy, Delta?"

"Affirmative," Jackson answered.

"Get your asses over here pronto; we've got a situation here," Kane ordered. He depressed the mic button again. "Does anyone else copy me?" He heard only silence.

Specialist Taft continued to scan the damage through the field glasses. Kane pulled out his cell phone and flipped it open. He used the phone's internet connection to pull up the number for the Smoke Hill Air National Guard Range. They were the closest military asset he could think of. He identified himself and asked to speak to the base commander.

Taft pushed Kane's arm, "Hey look, Sarge, those guys are getting up. They're not dead after all!"

Keets - Kansas

Fort Riley's eight-foot security fence whizzed by on the left-hand side of Erick Buckman's beater pickup; there were only weeds on the right. He flew down the country road at eighty miles an hour; he could see everything for miles. He turned the car radio's dial from left to right, desperately hoping for anything but country or gospel music. Sometimes he could pick up a rap station out of Kansas City.

He looked up just in time to swerve around the girl in the yellow sundress walking down the center of the dirt road. Erick stood on the brake with both feet, and the truck spun to a stop in a cloud of brown dust.

"Crazy cunt," Erick cursed. The truck tried to stall. He gingerly gave it gas, turned around, and slowly drove back the way he had come. As the dust cleared, he could see the girl staggering away from him. He gunned the car and then slowed to a crawl behind her. From behind, she looked pretty damn good. The girl had a nice ass and long legs that he could see silhouetted through her dress. She also had long blonde hair. Erick loved blondes. The problem was that blood was running slowly down her right arm, it spattered from her fingertips onto the dusty road. Her yellow dress was blood-stained, dirty and torn. Erick realized that she must be in shock.

He stopped the pickup and blew the horn. The girl slowed to a stop and stood in the road, but she didn't turn around. Erick opened his door and walked towards her.

"Hey, are you okay?" he stammered. The girl teetered, and slowly began to fall. He grasped her waist as she collapsed into his arms. She grabbed him and pulled his face towards hers. Erick's concern turned to alarm. The girl's face was a mask of blood, and black froth flew from her lips as she writhed in his arms, grasping at his shirt.

"Get the fuck off me!" he screamed. He pushed the struggling girl away, but she clung to his legs, tripping him. They rolled together across the hard packed road. Erick pinned her beneath him. In a blind panic, he punched her face. His fist rose and fell like a mallet, again and again, until her features were a pulped, broken mass. She only moved feebly now; Erick brushed away her bloody hands and staggered upright. He flexed his cut and bleeding fingers. Now it was Erick's blood that spattered onto the road. He stumbled slowly back towards his truck, then stiffened and collapsed.

Rands - Kansas

Michelle Turner led her second-grade class outside to the playground. A dozen eight year-olds were a lot to handle, and some days she hated the little monsters. They had been pretty good today though, even she had to admit. She turned them loose inside the fenced in playground.

"Go on and play," she said distractedly. She sighed and wished for the day to be over. She just wanted to go home and read a romance novel, drink some red wine, relax, maybe break out her vibrator, anything but babysit a dozen screaming kids.

As if on cue, half of the kids began to scream all at once. They did that a lot, but somehow Michelle knew this wasn't right. She snapped out of her daydream in alarm.

Billy Trew took two stumbling steps and fell to his knees. Snot was flowing freely down his face. He was choking on something. Before she could take three steps toward him, three more of the children had collapsed, vomiting and choking.

Michelle looked around in absolute horror. Every child in her care was either convulsing on the ground or choking to death before her eyes. She took in a breath to scream; then her hands flew to her throat. Her lungs were on fire, and her throat had totally constricted. She dropped to her knees and crawled painfully towards the closest child. Streamers of snot and spittle ran freely from her mouth and nose; they jerked grotesquely as she convulsed. Finally, she collapsed face forward onto the hot pavement and was mercifully still.

Intersection - State Highway 99 - Interstate 70 - Kansas

"I repeat, it looks like everyone down there is dead," Captain Glen Switzer said calmly into his radio mic. He banked the OH-58 Scout helicopter into a tight turn and circled the intersection again. The captain and his co-pilot were both wearing MOPP-4 chemical-biological protective suits. It made flying the small chopper that much more difficult, but Switzer was pretty sure they would be dead now without them.

"Copy that," came a voice through his headset, "Proceed due east on 70 and give us an estimate on the outbreak's progress."

"Affirmative, Command," the captain replied. He banked the chopper to the east and followed the highway towards Topeka.

"What the fuck is going on?" his co-pilot yelled. His voice was muffled by the protective gear.

"This shit came out of a stockpile at Riley!" Switzer yelled back. "No one knows what it is yet!"

The OH-58 sped east over the interstate. Below them, the

roadway was a mass of burning wrecks and overturned cars and trucks. Bodies lay strewn randomly about like a child's discarded dolls. They flew seven miles before they saw traffic moving again. The captain brought the chopper to a hover. A few cars were still driving in the westbound lanes, towards the destruction waiting there. As Switzer watched, two of them veered off the road and crashed. One simply came to a smoothly controlled stop. Its driver stepped out and collapsed onto the pavement. Within seconds, a speeding truck ran over his still-convulsing body and smashed into a delivery van, which flipped and burst into flames. More and more cars and trucks approached the line of the virus' eastward movement.

"Control, this is Yellow Bird Six. The present line of contagion is approximately eight miles east of Highway 99. Do you copy?" Switzer reported.

More vehicles approached their position. Some simply stopped as they approached the stalled vehicles in the roadway, others crashed and burst into flames.

"I think I'm going to be sick," his co-pilot complained.

"Affirmative, Yellow Bird Six," the voice broke through on the radio again. "Return to base."

"Copy that," Switzer replied.

"That shit is going to hit Topeka, isn't it?" his co-pilot asked calmly.

"Probably within an hour or two," the captain replied.

He turned the bird west and flew back the way they had come. Four miles west of the Highway 99 intersection, Switzer noticed movement on the highway below them.

"Look at that!" Switzer yelled, jabbing his co-pilot in the arm. "There are survivors down there!" As the captain slowed the helicopter, they could see more survivors moving among the wrecks below them on the roadway. Some of them were obviously injured.

"Control, this is Yellow Bird Six!" Switzer shouted into the microphone. "We have survivors west of 99! The toxin must be an incapacitation agent!" he shouted.

"Repeat that Yellow Bird Six," came the command through the radio.

"I've got survivors," Switzer replied. "We're going in to take a closer look."

He slowly circled and descended to a landing on the interstate. Wounded survivors slowly approached the men from all sides of the helicopter.

Captain Switzer jerked his head from side to side in disbelief.

"Are you seeing this shit?" his co-pilot sputtered.

Almost all of the approaching civilians had suffered horrible, debilitating, obviously fatal wounds. The closest casualty had been burned beyond recognition, his skin had peeled away to reveal bone and charred muscle tissue, yet he was still slowly limping towards the helicopter. Two of the civilians had been totally disemboweled. None of them could still possibly be alive.

Switzer twisted the cyclic without thought. The helicopter rose into the air, away from the horrors below on the highway.

"Control, we are inbound," Switzer spoke woodenly into the microphone. "You guys aren't gonna' believe my report."

"Can you confirm survivors at your location?" the voice on the radio inquired.

"Negative," the captain answered. "I was mistaken. There are no survivors."

Murdock -Kansas

Colonel Jim Warren was having a really bad day, but he figured pretty much everyone east and south of the fly-speck town of Murdock was too. The shit had hit the fan, and just his luck, he was the one who had to sort it out.

"This is close enough," he barked. Warren could see civilians moving on the roadway ahead.

His driver pulled their Humvee off the state road and pulled to the shoulder. The colonel deployed his five-man fire team across the roadway, behind cover. They were just outside the town. Each of his men was wearing MOPP-4 protective gear and carrying an M-4 rifle and one hundred and twenty rounds of ammunition, the standard issue. He rechecked the chemical test strip attached to the vehicle's windshield. It still read negative to any chemical agents. At least they had got that one right.

Warren had been dispatched from the Wichita National Guard headquarters to verify the stories of reanimated victims of a supposed viral outbreak from Fort Riley. No one really seemed to know what had happened. He thought the whole thing was bullshit, but someone had to check it out. Something very bad was happening in Kansas today; that much he definitely believed. People were dying out here.

Warren heard a siren's wail, and then a Kansas State police cruiser came into view, sirens blaring and lights flashing. The colonel waved his men back. The car sped past at seventy miles an hour, veering around the milling civilians and disappeared into the town. The sound of its siren slowly faded away into the distance.

"What do we do, sir?" PFC Duncan shouted to him.

Warren cursed under his breath. He didn't want to expose his unit, but waiting here wasn't getting the job done either.

"Walk up the road and see if you can get those people's attention," he replied. "We'll cover you. Don't get too close; just see if you can get them to follow you back here."

PFC Duncan rose and slowly moved down the road. He looked back occasionally. Colonel Warren watched intently. Duncan stopped midway between his position and the closest civilian. He waved his arms and shouted. The effect was immediate. The civilians began to move slowly towards him. Duncan turned and ran. He slid back into his position and readied his rifle.

"They're coming, sir!" he shouted.

"I can see that, Duncan," Warren replied. "Good work."

Colonel Warren studied the approaching civilians with the critical eye of a combat veteran. Something was very wrong with them. All of them were limping, or more closely jerking, as they walked. As they drew closer, he could see that many of them were injured, some critically. He observed obvious high-caliber gunshot wounds and severed limbs, wounds that he considered mortal or at least incapacitating. Some of the approaching civilians were unmarked, but all moved with that unsteady, jerking gait. His men began to mutter and grow uneasy.

"Hold fast!" Warren commanded.

The civilians were almost on top of their position. He could clearly see now that these people were not alive. He was either hallucinating or the reports of reanimation were correct.

Warren knew there was one way to find out what was up. "Open fire!" he screamed.

CIA Operations - The Pentagon

Deputy Director Jamie Schissler had just sat down with her second cup of coffee when the phone on her desk rang. It was a secure land line, and Jamie knew it wasn't going to be good news. She hesitated for just a second, then picked it up and held it to her ear.

"Director Schissler," she identified herself.

"This is General Roberts, SAC-NORAD," a voice spoke through the phone. "We have a confirmed accidental release of a viral agent from a storage facility at Fort Riley, Kansas."

"Do you have casualties?" Schissler asked tersely.

"Affirmative," the general replied. "This is a bad one."

"Are you positive it is viral?" she demanded. She quickly accessed her computer, and began to pull up classified storage data records.

"Yes," the general responded.

Schissler accessed the records for Fort Riley's Top Secret research facilities. She quickly scanned through the listings. Everything there was decades old, she wasn't familiar with any of the agents listed. She had never heard about a research facility at Riley before.

"Can you forward all the information you have to my station?" Schissler asked.

"I'm doing that now," the general replied. "Can you tell me what we are dealing with?" the officer requested.

"I honestly don't know," Schissler retorted. "There are over thirty viral projects listed for that facility, and they all date back to the Cold War era. All of that stuff should have been destroyed over twenty years ago." She paused for a few seconds. "You said it was bad. How bad? Do we have a major dispersion?"

"The agent is an aerosol. It is estimated to have reached Topeka and Wichita, and is spreading. Casualties reports vary, but seem to be in the ninety plus percentile range," the officer reported.

Director Schissler gasped, "That's impossible."

"It gets worse," General Roberts added.

The War Room - The White House -Washington, DC

CIA Director Carlton Lindsey walked calmly into the War Room, the report file in its plain manila envelope tucked under his left arm. He crossed the carpet and sat down quietly with the others at the big oval table. The president looked up as Lindsey sat down.

"Well?" the president asked tersely.

Lindsey tapped the report as he spoke. "It has been confirmed. It is out, sir. I am truly sorry."

"That's it?" the president screamed in rage. "You mother-fuckers run this project without my knowledge, and then when it goes to hell, you dump it in my lap?"

"Sir…" Lindsey began.

The president interrupted him with a growl, "I swear, Lindsey, if you say it was on a need to know basis, I will have you shot, right here, right now!" The Secret Service men behind him shifted.

"Please, Mr. President; this project predates your administration by a good thirty years. This was a Cold War development, it was doomsday scenario stuff. It should have been disposed of a long time ago. But it's out, and we have to act quickly to minimize the damage. Operation Tourniquet will work," Lindsey countered confidently. "Containment is our only viable option."

"You call that an option?" the president asked. He covered his eyes with his hand and shook his head.

"Wait a minute!" the secretary of the interior demanded. "If this virus is airborne then this plan is insane! A quarantine line won't work. The winds will carry it across the entire eastern seaboard."

"We took that into consideration," Lindsey explained. "The virus was designed to have a limited lifespan outside a human host, but it is incredibly contagious once it establishes itself within densely populated areas. Not only does the virus kill its target, but then the human victim becomes the transmission vehicle. This virus was brilliant; it could have ended the Cold War."

"Or life on this planet," the president added grimly.

Everyone was silent for a long moment.

The chief of staff spoke up, "We will do this thing together, sir, it's too much for one man to bear."

"Set it in motion," the president whispered. "God save us all."

Eisenhower Memorial Tunnel - Interstate 70 - Colorado

PFC Benny Sullivan pulled his uniform sleeve across his forehead. Cold sweat ran down his back and across his clammy stomach. His M-4 rifle was slippery in his hand. Directly behind him, a squad of combat engineers was connecting the detonators to the last few blocks of C-4 explosives. Sullivan had stood guard as two truckloads of the stuff had been driven into the tunnel and rigged to explode. He desperately wanted to be anywhere but here.

"We're hot!" one of the engineers finally yelled.

"Everybody out!" a burly NCO shouted. The trucks raced past him, and PFC Sullivan ran after them down the deserted interstate.

A quarter mile away the Commanding Officer, General Bob Feldman, knelt behind a Bradley fighting vehicle. The senior engineer squatted down beside him, a radio detonator in his hand. "What the fuck is going on, sir? Are we really going to blow the Eisenhower Tunnel?"

"I guess we are," the general replied.

The last of the men ran past and took cover. General Feldman looked back at the tunnel and then down at his watch.

"Everyone is clear, sir," the engineer reported.

"On my command," the general intoned. "Blow the tunnel."

Tyndal Air Force Base - Florida

"Attention!" came the command. Captain Tom 'Tinker' Redding stood up and came to attention along with his wingman Captain Sam Hurly and the rest of the combat squadron's fighter pilots.

The squadron's Commanding Officer, Colonel Abe Aaron, walked forward to the map board and turned to face his men.

"At ease!" he barked. The pilots sat back down. He slowly looked at their faces. Most of them were excited; a couple of the older pilots looked worried. They should be, he thought. He certainly was.

"Men, it has been my privilege and honor to lead you," the colonel began. "You will remember that you are officers of the United States Air Force, and you will do your duty. You will carry out your orders without question, and without hesitation."

He pointed to the oversized road map on the map board. "Our mission is to destroy all bridges in the greater Saint Louis area. Targets are assigned as follows. Captain Redding, you will destroy the Martin Luther King and Eads bridges. Captain Hurly, you will destroy the I-64 and Mac Arthur bridges. Redding and Hurley are first group. Lieutenants Chance and Black will be second group on standby in case first group fails to destroy their targets."

Captain Redding leaned forward in his chair and whispered, "Holy shit."

West Quincy - Illinois

Army Reserve Sergeant Jim Kline slammed on the brakes of his Humvee and cut traffic off in the east bound lanes at the approach to the I-24 bridge. Civilian vehicles stopped and horns began to blow. The sergeant deployed his four-man fire team across the lane and began to move back away from the bridge, clearing each vehicle as they went. He approached a minivan with a female driver and her two kids. He gave her the 'roll the window down' hand sign and stepped up as the driver's door window came down.

"Please step out and remove your children from the vehicle, miss," he commanded sternly.

"What the hell is going on?" the woman asked.

Sergeant Kline knew he was going to hear that one a lot today. "Bomb threat on the bridge," he replied. "Don't panic, just walk back towards town."

To his relief, the woman grabbed her kids and ran back down the on-ramp. He approached the next car.

Chamberino - New Mexico

"You have got to be fucking kidding me," someone groaned

from the line of assembled men.

"I am not fucking kidding!" Sergeant Eddie Torres yelled back. "Get to it, get it done, ladies!" he screamed as he ran up and down the row of New Mexico National Guardsmen assembled at attention.

The men broke up and grabbed shovels and picks. They were quickly detailed into work groups and began to dig foxholes along the west bank of the Rio Grande River, approximately 100 yards apart. Two of the younger guardsmen began to lug heavy ammo boxes into position.

Sergeant Torres paced back and forth, supervising the work and gauging the terrain. "I want the 50 cal. right here," he commanded, pointing to a hole that covered a bend in the river. "And set up the mortar right behind it. Bring down all the fucking ammo we have with us and then go back to town for the rest of it!"

One of his men paused to lean on his shovel. "What is going on, Sarge? That's U.S. territory across the river there. This doesn't make any sense, us setting up defensive positions here!"

Sergeant Torres didn't know what was going on, but he didn't like it. "I don't know, I'll tell you as soon as the brass cares enough to enlighten my ass! Now get back to work, you worthless fuck!"

East Lake Street Bridge - Minneapolis, Minnesota

Robin Bishop looked at his wrist watch for the tenth time. Traffic had come to a complete stop everywhere in the city this morning. He had diverted to a side street in hopes of avoiding the worst of it, but traffic had snarled just ahead of him on the approach to the bridge. He had been stuck in the same spot for almost half an hour now; nothing was moving. Most of the radio stations reported the same thing; all of the bridges were closed. One of the broadcasts had mentioned that the military was involved. People were leaving their cars and walking up the road to see what had happened. He was going to be very late for his meeting in Chicago if things didn't move really quickly.

"Fuck it," he muttered. He opened the door of his rental car and stepped out onto the pavement. He walked alongside the parked cars until he had joined the other stranded motorists.

A pair of military Humvees was parked across the highway, and ten armed men in Army uniforms were standing between them and the milling civilians.

A woman was arguing with one of them. "You can't just close down a bridge like this," she insisted. "I have to get to work!"

"No one can drive across!" the man shouted back. "This bridge is closed to all vehicles."

"Well, I'm walking across then," she replied. The woman stepped over the guardrail and onto the pedestrian walkway.

"Captain, are we letting people walk across?" the grunt shouted.

An officer near the Humvees looked around. "You people are crossing at your own risk!" he yelled to the woman.

"Hey, you can't just leave your car!" a man shouted. The woman kept going.

"How long is the bridge going to be closed?" someone yelled.

"We don't know," the grunt replied. "Could be indefinitely."

Three more people jumped to the walkway and began to cross.

"I'm going to regret this," Bishop groaned. He jumped the rail and started walking across the Mississippi River.

St. Joseph - Missouri

Brother Raymond pulled the microphone closer and dropped his voice to his most prophetic bass. "I'm telling you, Brothers and Sisters, this is the Lord's work. His day is upon us!"

His voice quickly climbed back up the scale to a falsetto shriek. "Repent! This is just one of the signs! I'm talking about these reports comin' out of Kansas of the dead walkin' the Earth. Don't discount them! Oh, they're not zombies." Brother Raymond stopped preaching long enough to laugh.

"Hell, everybody knows there is no such thing as zombies. They are the dead, our dead loved ones, coming back to life because the Day of Judgment is at hand." He really drove those last words home. "The cities are dens of sin and filth. They are going to be cleansed! The wicked will be punished. Death walks the land. But be not afraid all ye of the faith. The Rapture will take us from this place, far from the sin, far from the dead." He laughed again.

"So you had better get things right, repent of your sins. Don't be left behind, don't be a sinner. This ain't the time to be a sinner. You know why? Listen up, you sinners; the dead are a comin' to get ya."

Press Room - The White House - Washington, DC

The cameras switched to a view of the podium with the seal of the United States, and the flag in the background. The president walked onto the stage. He looked haggard. He paused for a few seconds, and then he began to speak.

"My fellow Americans, a time of great crisis has befallen us. Over the last two days, I have had to make some very hard decisions, decisions that will affect each and every one of us for all the days to come. Remember that now is not the time for recriminations, we are being put to the test, to see if this great nation will survive. We must work together through the dark days ahead, we must unite as Americans."

As he spoke, he began to sob, and tears ran freely down his face. "A deadly virus has been unleashed upon the American heartland. We do not know at this time if this is the work of terrorists, or accidental. This virus is highly contagious, and has spread with great rapidity. I have mobilized the entire United States military and all National Guard units in an attempt to contain it. A quarantine zone has been established along the line of the Rocky Mountains to the west, and the Mississippi River to the east. The entirety of the country between these two natural boundaries has been declared a quarantine zone. No one may enter, or leave this zone until further notice. A state of martial law has been declared for the entire United States. All travel, by land, sea, and air has been stopped until further notice. I have ordered that all bridges along the Mississippi River be destroyed. Army, Navy, and Air Force units have been deployed along the entire length of both borders, and no one may enter, or leave the zone. I have issued a shoot-to-kill order. Anyone attempting to break the quarantine boundary will be shot on sight."

The president paused to let this sink in. "I know that almost everyone in our great country will be affected by this order. We all have loved ones within the zone, but we must all accept the fact that those loved ones are now gone. The virus must not be allowed to spread beyond the boundaries I have established, or every single American, indeed everyone in the entire world, will perish. I did not make this decision easily, and I know many of you will hate me for it. I have condemned over one hundred million of my fellow Americans to a horrible death, and I will carry the weight of my decision to the grave. I take full responsibility for the actions of all of our military men and women; they are following my orders, and I ask that you forgive them for what they must do. Hold instead your hatred for those responsible for this horrible crime, or if you must, blame me."

The president slowly walked away from the podium and the entire press room disintegrated into pure chaos. Secret Service members rushed the president out, and for several minutes, the journalists fought with security and the officials present until someone fired a gun to restore order. A member of the president's cabinet took the podium, and tried to explain what was going on over the shouted questions from the press corps.

At 12:01 PM Eastern, the quarantine went into effect. The mother-fucking quarantine. If you were on the right side of the line, it saved your life. If you weren't, it was a death sentence. It was Z-Day, the end of the mother-fucking world for everyone inside.

In order to contain the viral outbreak, the country was divided into three zones. The eastern border of the QZ was set along the Mississippi River. All of the bridges that spanned the river were destroyed almost simultaneously. National Guard units stopped traffic, and the Air Force launched bombing strikes against all the bridges. From Minnesota to Louisiana, everything was hit. Before the burning rubble even stopped smoking, Naval and Coast Guard patrol boats stopped all commercial river traffic and escorted them to the eastern side, where the crews were put ashore. Every single civilian boat on the river was sunk. Sometimes, the naval crews were able to let the civilians abandon ship, but there wasn't always time to explain the situation and people died. National Guard and local police helped to destroy smaller boats docked or in storage along the river. Everything that could float was sunk, burned or shot full of holes. There were a lot of casualties; not everyone cooperated.

In the west, the border was set along the line of the Rocky Mountains to the north and along the Rio Grande River to the south. Regular Army and Guard units were deployed to form a continuous line from Canada to Mexico, where they linked up with Army units from those two countries. Engineers immediately began construction of a permanent quarantine zone, or as it came to be known, the QZ, to contain the unfortunates trapped inside.

The states in between became the Quarantine Zone. No one was allowed to leave and no one was allowed to enter; period. A no-fly zone was established. All military units outside the zone were issued shoot-to-kill orders. They had their hands full for quite a while. Desperate people tried to break the line from both directions at once. It was pure chaos. Orders were issued to military and police personnel inside the zone to assist in the enforcement of the quarantine. To their credit, some of them actually followed the orders. Most of them didn't. Full-scale warfare erupted along the line, especially in the west. The line would have failed, but eighty percent of the Air Force's assets had been shifted outside, and non-stop air strikes broke up all the organized attempts to break out. All civilian aircraft attempting to fly out were shot down.

Approximately one-fourth of the United States' population was abandoned to die.

South Pass - Wyoming

Private Dan James ducked as another round ricocheted from the rocks near his head. He cursed under his breath. He looked over at Sergeant Daniels and cursed again. Daniels had a neat half-inch hole right above his left eye. Blood was still feebly oozing from it onto the rock under his head. The surprised look on his face was almost funny, but the bullet hole kind of killed the comic aspect of the whole thing.

"Keep him talking," his squad leader urged.

James raised his head up just a tiny bit and yelled to the unseen sniper, "Hold your fire, asshole!"

His opponent laughed harshly in the distance. "Fuck you, you

Nazi faggot! You got no right to keep me and my family in here with these fucking zombies! I'm an American citizen, you son-of-a-bitch!" He punctuated the last remark with another round of rifle fire. The bullet struck the rocks inches above James' helmet.

James scrunched even lower into his foxhole. "You crazy red-neck bastard, you know the score!" James screamed back. "I'm just doing my job, so fuck off yourself! Nobody can leave the Quarantine Zone!"

James lowered his voice, "Somebody do something!" he urged.

"Keep talking to him, I've got inbound air support," his squad leader replied quietly.

Private James raised his head up just a tiny bit. He yelled, "Hey buddy, what's got eight hundred legs and four teeth? The line for corn dogs at the Wyoming state fair. Get it?"

"You're real fuckin' funny! Just come up outta' your hole and I'll give you something to laugh about!" the sniper yelled back.

"Incoming!" the squad leader shrieked.

James pulled himself into a ball and prayed the pilot didn't miss. The roar of the F-4 Phantom's engines washed over their position and then James was pounded by the shock waves of two five-hundred-pound bombs. Once the dust settled, he cautiously peered over the rim of his foxhole. Nothing remained of the rock-strewn hillside where the sniper had been except two huge smoking craters.

Raystown - Kansas

Arguing with her mother was about to drive Natalie Clark insane. They were both nearly hysterical, but Natalie was trying to hold it together.

"Mom, we have to leave, we have to get to some place safe!" she insisted.

"The television said to stay inside," her mother countered.

"Mom, they said that over three days ago," Natalie shot back with a sob.

They had been trapped inside their suburban home for a solid week now, and neither one of them had ventured outside. Natalie was sure that was the only reason they were still alive. The outbreak had swept over them so quickly.

Natalie didn't know what had happened, but she knew that it was bad. School had been dismissed, and she had been instructed to go home. She had driven home through a surreal landscape of urban chaos. No one knew what was happening. Her favorite radio station had reported a chemical leak and mandatory shelter in place order. Natalie arrived at home to find her mother already there, but she knew only as much as Natalie. The power had gone out almost immediately, and the cell phone service had been interrupted.

They had no way to learn what was happening. A police car had driven through their neighborhood, instructing everyone on loud speakers to stay indoors and to close all windows and doors, and to shut off all air conditioning units. Natalie had filled the tub and all the empty pots and pans with water. Her mother had objected, but luckily Natalie had done it anyway. The faucets had lost water pressure on the second day. They also began to hear sporadic gunfire, and it had continued for the next two days. Eventually, the shooting stopped.

Natalie had wanted to check on the neighbors, but her mother hadn't allowed it. She was glad now that she hadn't. On the morning of the fourth day, Natalie noticed that almost all of their neighbors were outside, walking around the street. She had almost gone outside before she noticed that something was horribly wrong with them.

Natalie was peering through the front window blinds.

"Mom, come and look at this," she whispered.

Her mother joined her. They stared in horror at the morbid parade on their street. All of their neighbors were dead. They had been dead for days. They were bloated and bloody. Their clothes were fouled with dirt, blood, and feces. Some of them had horrible wounds, some had been burned alive. Many of them bore ragged, gaping gunshot wounds. That was bad, but their eyes were the worst. Their eyes were glazed, milky white, and utterly dead. They stared, unseeing. All of their neighbors were dead, but they were just outside.

Natalie and her mother held each other and cried.

Dillion - Colorado

"Civvies in the wire!" someone yelled from down the line.

Sherriff's Deputy Ed Townsend flipped the safety of his AR-15 to the three-round burst position. He looked up and down the barbed wire, but only the corpses of his previous kills were visible in the gloom. His eyesight wasn't as good as it used to be, especially at dusk. Then he caught movement to his left. A young woman emerged from the darkness, carrying a baby and leading a small child. She ran up to the wire and pulled up short as she discovered the rotting bodies.

"Don't shoot!" she screamed. "I have a baby, we're not sick, I swear it!"

Ed turned his baseball cap around backwards on his head and settled down behind the rifle. The woman began to push her way into the wire, holding the baby before her. She pulled the screaming child along behind her. Ed took his time lining up the shot.

Sometimes the civilians came to the line purposely for a bullet. It was a lot cleaner death than being eaten alive by the Zeds. He didn't think this woman was one of those, but he had to end her just the same.

His first burst took the baby and the woman both through the chest. The woman fell forward onto the wire, the baby pinned beneath her. The wire made a weird metallic stretching noise as the woman twitched and kicked. He dropped his aim down to the now-screaming child. He didn't close his eyes the way he had the first time he had been forced to shoot a kid. He had screwed that up, and the memory still haunted him. Better a clean shot. The rifle barked a second time, and then silence fell back over the barricade.

The Quarantine Zone

Armed civilians gave battle up and down the borders for weeks, and casualties were high. Eventually, the virus stopped all attempts to break the boundaries from the inside, and everyone within was legally declared dead. That was the government's official position, but we all knew there were survivors still trapped inside.

No one was really certain what was going on inside the zone. No news coverage was allowed to report on what was happening there.

The government shut down all phone and computer communications with anyone inside. They had to in order to stop the rescue attempts. For weeks after the boundaries were established, people attempted to break into the zone and rescue family members trapped there. All transportation was temporarily halted, and roads were closed to civilian traffic. Anyone caught driving was arrested, and if they resisted, they were shot. Although this discouraged rescue attempts, they didn't actually stop until the government cut off gasoline supplies to civilian outlets. Everything ground down to a halt. Even then, people walked to the borders, and attempted to break through. They were shot. The news coverage did show a lot of civilians being executed, in order to discourage more attempts to break the quarantine. Over and over it was repeated that everyone inside the zone was dead. Eventually, I believed it too.

I didn't give up hope for a long time. My ex-wife, Alice, and my fourteen-year-old-daughter, Natalie, were inside the zone. They lived in a nice house in the safe little suburb of Raystown, on the outskirts of Kansas City. My ex had grown up there. I was originally from California, and I worked as a computer programmer. My job had kept me away from home a lot. That was a big part of our problems. I would call every night if I was on the road, and talk to Alice. Sometimes, I would talk to Natalie, but more often than not, she would just send me a text or an e-mail. We had a cute little code word to let each other know we were okay, and that everything was normal. I would get a one-word text, just the word TAG. Things are good. Tag, you're it, Dad, and I would send it back. Sometimes, I would add, miss you, or love you. Natalie was a natural hacker on the computer, and I taught her some code basics. She was one smart kid.

After Z-Day, I never heard from them again. I crossed the bridge, and I walked down the ramp on the Wisconsin side. The Army had set up a roadblock across the westbound lanes too, and cars were backed up for miles. There wasn't any traffic on the eastbound side of the highway, and I just walked away from the bridge. The first thing I noticed was that the cell phones were down. I placed a call to my boss, but it dropped before I could even explain what was going on. After that, the phone was useless. I was still trying to get the damn thing to work when everything went down.

I heard the jets approaching. I remember thinking that they were flying really low. Then this tiny pair of black dots separated from one of the jets. The plane went into a steep climb and then the bridge just exploded. I felt the concussion through my feet on the blacktop. The bridge suspension tilted at this crazy angle, and the whole center span fell over into the river. A huge cloud of dust rose into the sky. I just stood there with my mouth open. I couldn't believe it. Then, to my amazement, it happened again. Another jet came screaming down and bombed the next bridge down river. It was quiet for a moment then all Hell started to break loose. Horns, sirens, and screams, everything got loud and stayed that way. Once I was sure that the planes were gone, I walked back towards the bridge. People started to climb up onto the interstate and wandered along with me. No one knew what was going on. I figured that the bombing had to be the act of terrorists, but it didn't make much sense. The Army had shut the bridge down before it was destroyed. They had to have been warned it was going to happen. I stood and stared at the bombed out bridges for a while. It was pretty scary, and I knew deep down that things were going to be bad.

Eventually, I wandered down into town and tried to find a phone. No one had cell service and the land lines were jammed. It was pure bedlam. I walked into a bar, and the rebroadcast of the presidential address was on the television. Of course, everyone in the place was talking at once, but after I watched it for the third time, I got the message. The shit had hit the fan, and I knew that I had to get back to my family.

For about a week, I wandered up and down the east bank of the Mississippi River, desperately trying to find a way across. I wasn't alone. Hundreds of desperate people were doing the same thing. There were all these wild rumors about what was going on inside the quarantine zone; stories about riots, sickness, mass shootings, and even zombies. Everyone you talked to had a different story or theory, and the speculation on what had caused the mess was just as varied. Army patrols were everywhere along the river. They would drive us away, warning us that any attempt to cross the river would be met with lethal force. I didn't sleep or eat much. There wasn't any way to cross. I saw two men try to swim the river. Snipers got them before they even made it half way across. The Mississippi was full of corpses, and gunshots rang out continuously. Occasionally, I would see a Navy patrol boat cruise by, staying close to the eastern shore.

For a long time, I just sat in the woods on the Wisconsin side, crying, hugging my knees, trying desperately to think of a way to get back home. I just wanted to be there with my family, even if it meant my death. I knew they were probably already gone, but not knowing was even worse. Eventually, I fell asleep, too exhausted to care anymore. When I awoke, I felt much more clear-headed.

I couldn't go home, but I realized there might be another way. My job had brought me into contact with a lot of people. Someone I knew might still be in the loop. One of my old friends from high school, Brad Fuchs, was an Air Force Reserve officer. He might be able to help me. A little light came on. I pushed my grief aside and started walking towards Chicago.

Fort Leavenworth Military Prison - Kansas

Doctor Jace Cooper picked up the phone and placed the call. After being transferred several times, a secretary for the joint chiefs of staff put him through on speaker. "Hello, can you hear me?" the doctor asked.

"Yes, Doctor Cooper," one of the cabinet members replied. "Can you describe what is occurring there?"

"Yes, I can," the doctor replied. "A fast-acting virus of some sort has infected the entire prison population." Doctor Cooper paused to cough. "I estimate that over eighty percent of the prisoners are dead already," he continued.

"What would you estimate the time from initial infection until death to be?" the staffer asked.

"It varies. Some of the prisoners died within minutes, others are still alive over twenty-four hours later, but very sick. It is my opinion that a previously healthy individual will last longer, although death and reanimation are unavoidable after contact with the virus," the doctor concluded.

There was a moment of confused conversation on the other end of the line. "Doctor Cooper, can you confirm the reanimation?" the staffer demanded.

"Yes, I can," Doctor Cooper confirmed. "As hard as it is to believe, the dead reanimate after a short period of time following death by the virus. I have confirmed this under laboratory conditions. As of yet, I can provide no explanation, but I am still working on the problem. I am suffering from no shortage of volunteers here." He laughed grimly.

"Is there anything you wish to share with me?" the doctor queried.

"I'm sorry, information about the virus is classified," the staffer replied.

"I thought so much," Doctor Cooper said. "Well, I have sent you my analysis on video. I apologize for the video quality. I had to shoot it with my cell phone."

"Thank you, Doctor, we have your number." The staffer ended the call.

"Wait, what about rescue ?" The doctor realized he was speaking to a dead line. "Bureaucratic mother-fuckers," he cursed.

Raystown - Kansas

Natalie knew that if they stayed inside one more day, they both would die. She had tried desperately to shake her mother out of her deepening depression, but nothing seemed to help. The zombies outside appeared to somehow sense them, even though they were careful not to make any noise. They pressed against the windows and doors, moaning and constantly attempting to batter their way inside. The noise was maddening. Worse still, there seemed to be more of them every day. Hundreds of them were just outside, the house was totally surrounded.

Things had become desperate. They were almost out of water, and very low on food. Natalie's mother had turned to pills to deal with the horrors they faced, leaving her daughter to fend for herself. Because of this, Natalie had found a new sense of self-reliance, and taken matters into her own hands.

The only luck they had was her father's old muscle car. Her mom's sedan was parked outside in the driveway. It might just as well been on the moon. Dozens of zombies surrounded it.

After her parents' divorce, her father had left his 67 Mustang convertible in the garage. He had been in the process of restoring it when he and her mother had separated. Although the car was in primer, her father had always been meticulous about keeping the battery charged and occasionally starting the car. Natalie had suspected that the Mustang would eventually be a gift for her. Now, it was her only hope.

She had placed what little food they had into a backpack, and loaded it in the car. They had two full gallon jugs of water; they went in too. Natalie desperately wished she had a gun, but her mother had always hated them, and wouldn't allow her father to keep one in the house. She had carefully gone through the garage, looking for things she might need; they couldn't come back for anything once they left. Natalie had loaded a folding ladder, a spare gas can, and a first-aid kit into the back seat. She carefully placed her old softball bat between the front seats, close at hand. It was her only weapon. Once the car was loaded, she went inside and roused her mother. Natalie helped her through the garage and into the car. She carefully strapped her mother into the front seat, and got into the car.

Natalie stroked the lucky rabbit's foot that hung from the keychain. She steeled herself and turned the key over in the ignition. The car's starter turned over three times before the big V-8 caught, and the Mustang came to life with a throaty roar. The zombies outside the garage door surged against the thin steel. Natalie hit the garage door opener and revved the engine, her hand poised on the shifter. The zombies pushed forward as the door climbed open, shoving against each other and the door. Natalie only waited until it was high enough for the Mustang to slip through. She slammed the shifter into drive and jammed the gas pedal to the floor. The Mustang roared, its rear wheels smoked and slid on the slick concrete, until it caught and shot forward. The car crashed through the zombies like a shot from a gun. The closest undead were crushed, the others were sent flying like tenpins. Natalie screamed as two zombies slid across the crumpled hood and off the windshield, leaving a trail of black and green gore behind on the fractured glass. The Mustang was beaten and battered as it struck zombie after zombie, but it lunged forward, an unstoppable engine of destruction. Natalie held the accelerator to the floor. The muscle car responded with gusto, snarling in mechanical defiance at the frail human bodies between it and the street. As Natalie spun the steering wheel, the Mustang flattened the last zombie between her and escape. The car roared away from the pursuing horde of undead, Natalie still screaming at the wheel.

Laundo - Arkansas

Jed Hobsen looked back over his shoulder, but he didn't need to see the zombies to know they were still pursuing him. He could hear them moaning in the distance. The sound echoed through the swamp, and they sounded like the lost souls that they were. Jed cursed himself and wished he still had the faith to pray. His legs were giving out, and his left knee felt like someone was slowly twisting a red-hot poker into his tortured kneecap. He had gotten fat and lazy over the years, and now he was paying the price.

He stopped for a moment and leaned against a pine tree, trying in vain to catch his breath. Jed coughed until he was hoarse, and tried to ignore the specks of blood on his hands. Cigarettes had fucked his lungs over a long time ago, and he was pretty sure the bastard zombies were going to catch up to him. He was about two miles from the road, and any chance of finding help. There was nobody out here but him and the undead.

Jed stood up stiffly and checked his jacket pockets, hoping he might have missed a cigarette. He only found his lighter and the last shell for his shotgun. The groans were much closer now. Jed didn't have any more running in him; it wasn't how he wanted to go out anyway. Those cannibalistic fuckers could eat him cold.

He broke down his old shotgun, and carefully pushed the shell into the barrel. Jed gently snapped the action shut and pulled back the hammer. He carefully stretched out his arm until the business end of the barrel rested against his head, just behind his right eye. Grimly, he reflected that he couldn't mess this up. Jed stuck his thumb through the trigger guard and pushed back hard. The shot rang out through the swamp.

Greenfield - Nebraska

Everything was ready, he couldn't wait any longer. Mike Renwick heaved the heavy steel trap door of his storm cellar open. Its rusty hinges groaned in protest, but that was the only sound Mike heard. He waited for his eyes to adjust to the bright sunlight. Mike had been down in that dark, stinking hole for eight straight days. He figured that was long enough. There were zombies out there, and Mike had shit to do. He had lived and breathed zombies since he watched his first Romero movie as a kid. He had read every zombie book and comic, and owned every zombie movie. His dearest dream had finally come true. A zombie virus had been unleashed, and he had survived it.

Mike didn't know a lot about viruses, but he did know they couldn't survive indefinitely without a host. He was betting that the air outside was safe to breathe. Mike stepped out into the sunlight and looked around. There were no zombies in sight. Of course, he lived in a rural area, so that was no surprise. He took in a deep breath of the fresh Nebraska air and slowly exhaled it. Mike felt fine. This was going to be a great day; his time had finally come.

He had carefully stockpiled weapons and ammunition for the zombie apocalypse. Mike lugged up two spare ammo cans full of 7.62x39 millimeter ammunition for his automatic AK-47 and carried them to his pickup truck. He reverently removed the Russian assault rifle from its case and carried it out into the sunlight. After checking the action on the rifle to be sure there was a round in the receiver, he flipped the safety off. Mike stuffed eight thirty-round magazines into his BDU jacket pockets and climbed into the truck. He fired up the engine and drove towards the small town of Greenfield. The town was going to be his for the taking. He was going to shoot zombies until his trigger finger fell off and he couldn't shoot anymore. Then he was going to loot the liquor store and find himself a smoking hot cheerleader to rescue.

The road to town was deserted; he passed only three abandoned vehicles. Mike pulled into the tiny town and parked in front of the deserted gas station. The station's front door was wide open, but there was no one in sight. Mike knew the zombies were here, he could literally smell them. He laid on the truck's horn and stepped out into the street.

Mike raised the rifle to his shoulder and assumed a combat

stance, just like the characters in his favorite video game. The zombies didn't keep him waiting.

Three of the living dead lumbered up the street towards him. Mike fired off his entire magazine on full auto. The first zombie took eight rounds in the chest, and went down like a cheap hooker. Mike walked the fire into the second zombie. The gun barrel lifted as the rounds went off, and his target's head exploded like a meat-filled water balloon. The remaining rounds missed the third zombie completely as the gun climbed. The AK-47's bolt locked back as the last round fired, the smoking gun was empty.

Mike had shot lots of cans and bottles, but he had never fired the rifle at a moving target before. He let out a war whoop and quickly slammed in a fresh magazine. He nervously pulled and released the bolt as the zombie he had missed reached out to grasp the barrel. The zombie's fingers disappeared as Mike pulled the trigger. Mike jerked the bucking gun to the left and down. The heavy rounds blew out the zombie's guts and broke its spine. It collapsed at his feet, still grasping at his leg with its one remaining hand. The first zombie he had shot was dragging itself towards him, leaving a bloody trail of rotten meat on the pavement.

Mike fumbled to put in a fresh magazine, dropping one of his spares into a bloody hole in the struggling corpse at his feet. He finally got a magazine into the gun and threw the bolt. Four more zombies were coming across the street towards him. As he lifted the gun to fire, he heard a noise behind him. He jerked his head around just in time to see another of the undead stumble out of the gas station, only ten feet away.

Mike screamed and fired the gun blindly all around him. Glass shattered in the nearby buildings and a tire on Mike's truck noisily deflated, but no zombies were harmed. The bolt locked back as the gun emptied itself. He stared at the still-approaching zombies in disbelief; this wasn't supposed to happen.

The zombie at his feet bit through his calf, and the monster behind him clamped its rotten arms around him, dragging his gun arm down. Mike struggled to free himself and reload the gun. Suddenly, blackened teeth sank into his shoulder. Mike's screams echoed through the empty streets as the other zombies reached him and joined in the eating. His empty gun fell to the pavement.

Kansas City - Missouri

Natalie drove the battered Mustang through the back streets and alleys at a reckless speed. There were zombies everywhere. They were drawn to the sound of the car's engine, and she was afraid to hit anymore of them. The Mustang's entire front end was crumpled and damaged, and the fan was making a horrible rattling noise. The temperature gauge was climbing into the red, Natalie knew she didn't have much time. She flew down a side street and turned into the park. She hoped there would be fewer zombies there.

Natalie had thought long and hard about where she should go. She turned onto the service road that led to the Kansas City Zoo. She had decided that she needed a place with a strong security fence. The zoo was the only place she could think of that was close enough to reach. The entire place was surrounded by an eight-foot security fence, designed to both keep the animals in and people out. There were also strong cages and buildings inside that would provide further protection. She drove to the far side of the mostly deserted parking lot and parked the Mustang. She roused her mother.

"Come on, Mom," she pleaded.

Her mother responded groggily, "Where are we?"

"We are at the zoo, Mom. Come on, we have to get inside," Natalie prompted. She hoped her mother would cooperate.

Her mother wandered over to the fence and looked inside. "Why are we here, Nat?" she asked. She linked her fingers through the fence and pulled against it.

Natalie quickly pulled out the folding ladder and set it carefully against the fence. She looked around for zombies, but there were none in sight. She knew her luck could only hold for so long.

"We have to get over the fence, Mom, we'll be safe from the zombies inside," she patiently explained.

"That's illegal, Natalie," her mother complained.

"Mom, that doesn't matter anymore," Natalie sighed. She carefully climbed the ladder and dropped her meager supplies over the fence. From the top of the ladder, she could see into the zoo. The winding pathways seemed deserted, but she could hear various animal noises. She turned on the ladder and scanned the parking lot. Natalie cursed as she spotted a pair of shambling figures slowly crossing the lot from the direction they had come. The zombies had found them.

Natalie quickly climbed down. "Come on, Mom!" she prodded. She pushed her mother to the base of the ladder.

"I'm not climbing that thing," her mother whined.

"Mom, we have to," Natalie calmly explained. She pointed to the approaching zombies.

Her mother began to snivel, but she slowly climbed the ladder. Natalie came up behind her. Once she reached the top, she held onto her mother's arm and helped her drop into the park. Her mother landed roughly and began to cry.

"Natalie," her mother sobbed.

Natalie hung precariously from the top of the fence. She pushed the ladder over with her leg, and then dropped to the inside. She collected their food and water and gripped her softball bat. The zombies approached the fence.

"Don't look at them, Mom," she grated. Natalie turned her mother around and led her into the zoo.

Shreveport - Louisiana

A random bullet struck Maria Lopez in the lower abdomen. She slowly sank down on the pavement in shock. It didn't hurt too badly, that was how she knew it was serious. Blood seeped slowly through her fingers and stained her blouse and jeans. No one stopped to help her. People ran past her on all sides, and a speeding truck almost crushed her. Death and chaos had come to Shreveport.

The power had gone out and cell phone service had been cut, but still the word had spread. A fast-moving virus was on its way to the city, and everyone there was doomed. The federal government in Washington had deserted them to their fate and no help would come. The tenuous veneer of civilization had been torn away, and it was every man and woman for himself. The city had erupted into an orgy of looting, rape, and murder. The civil authorities could not stop the massive outbreaks of violence that swept through the metropolis. Although the virus had yet to arrive, Armageddon had come.

Numbness crept through Maria behind a slow wave of pain and cold. She knew she was dying, but she wasn't afraid. Maria knew now that there were worse things than death. The screams, the gunfire, the sounds of breaking glass and violence, they all faded away.

Aberdeen - South Dakota

The F-16 Falcon shuddered slightly as its last missile shrieked away in a blast of white exhaust gasses. Lieutenant Adam Pullen watched the air-to-ground missile as it pulled away and dropped to its target. The cell tower on the ridgeline below him erupted into flaming pieces of scrap metal, and then his bird was beyond visual range to the target.

The lieutenant knew full well that his missions against civilian targets were blatantly unconstitutional, but he didn't give a rat's ass. He just loved blowing shit up, and he had flown more missions in the last week than he had ever hoped for. He just wished he had more missiles.

He keyed his mic, "Cutter Two to base, mission accomplished, all designated targets destroyed."

His controller responded on the radio, "Roger that, Cutter Two, return to base."

Pullen banked the F-16 to the east and hit the afterburner just for shits and giggles. The aircraft roared and pushed him back into the seat. The pilot climbed slightly and scanned the ground below him for any activity. Suddenly, he jerked his head to the left. A pair of cargo trucks was driving along Highway 12, on his nine. From his altitude, they were just two tiny black dots, but the movement had caught his eye.

"Base, this is Cutter Two, I've got unauthorized movement on the highway," he spoke into his mic. "Permission to engage targets?"

There was a pause, "Negative, Cutter Two. Return to base."

"Affirmative, Base," Pullen sighed. He eased his finger off the gun trigger and pulled back on the stick. He craned his neck to look down at the fleeing trucks. "Next time," he whispered.

Chicago - Illinois

The one thing the Feds got right after Z-Day was the Displaced Persons Program. Thousands of people were displaced or stuck with no way home, if they had a home left to go back to. The administration set up a free shuttle service to transport people displaced by the quarantine, and I traveled to Chicago on a government bus. My company had an office downtown and I often worked there. It was the closest thing I had left to a home.

I immediately began to contact people I knew, anyone who might be able to help me. I was desperate for any intel about what was happening in Kansas. Information leaked out, just rumors really, nothing specific, but none of it sounded good. The virus had originated from somewhere in Kansas, and spread outwards very quickly until the quarantine lines stopped it. Casualties were estimated to be in the millions. Everyone inside the QZ was considered dead. There were no survivors. The government did everything it could to foster and reinforce that concept, in order to quell attempts to break the quarantine. The major cities were said to be completely overrun with zombies and the dead. I didn't believe the zombie stories, few people did, but they persisted. I assumed they were just another lie fabricated by the government.

The internet was still operating on a limited basis, but had been badly disrupted. I hacked into a Department of Defense site and searched desperately through the satellite photos of the area around Kansas City. It was horrible for me to look through them, searching for some sign of my daughter, some small spark to keep my hope alive. There was nothing there.

Kansas City Zoo - Missouri

Natalie pulled her mother along behind her like a petulant child. She didn't like this role reversal, but there wasn't much she could do about it. She knew the zoo's layout well, and it only took a few minutes to figure out where they were. Natalie had a plan. She was going to scout the main paths to make sure the fences had held, and that the zoo wasn't full of zombies. Then if everything was okay, she was going to hit the zoo's small restaurant and snack bar to restock their meager food supply. Natalie didn't think that water would be a problem here; she knew that the individual animal cages had pools and external water tanks. Finally, she planned to hide out in the Reptile House. The building was made of stone, and it was very defensible. It had been designed to keep the exhibit reptiles inside, but it would also serve to keep the zombies out, if they got past the fences.

Natalie led her mother through the twisting pathways. She could hear animal noises all around her. Some of the cages exploded with activity as she passed them. She suddenly realized that many of the animals hadn't been fed in days. Some of the cages were empty, their doors open. Natalie decided she would skirt the big cats and bears. The main path made a rough circle through the grounds.

Zombies wandered the perimeter just outside the fence, and had gathered in hundreds outside the main gate, but they encountered no undead inside. Natalie did find old blood stains in several places. She proceeded carefully to the snack bar.

As they approached the small building, Natalie could hear voices. They seemed to be arguing. Natalie quietly led her mother forward and slowly slid around the building until she could see the food court. Three men and two women were standing there. They were definitely having an altercation. One of the men had a steel pipe in his hand; he menaced the others with it. As she watched, a young man in a wheelchair rolled himself between them, pleading for calm.

Natalie stepped out into the open.

Everyone froze and turned to look at her. The man with the pipe approached menacingly. "How did you get in here?" he yelled. The man stepped closer. "Did you open a gate?" he screamed, raising the pipe.

Natalie's mother thrust herself between them, "Leave her alone!" she screamed.

"We climbed the fence with a ladder!" Natalie explained quickly. "No zombies came in with us! I knocked the ladder down," she added.

The man lowered the pipe. "You have to leave, we only have enough food for ourselves," he growled.

"But we don't have much to eat," Natalie explained.

"That's tough, kid," he growled, raising the pipe again. "Now get the fuck gone!"

Natalie's mother pushed her back, away from the man. She began to cry again.

"Wait a minute!" the boy in the wheelchair shouted. He pushed himself forward. "I'm sorry," he offered. "Everyone here is just scared and hungry," he explained. "My name is Nicky." He held out his hand. Natalie pushed forward to grasp it.

"Hey Gimp, you can go with them!" the man shouted. He pushed the boy's chair violently.

Nicky spun in his seat. "Maybe I will," he spat. "It stinks around here anyway." The boy angrily wheeled his chair away down the path.

"Go!" the man urged violently. He pointed after the departing boy with the pipe.

Natalie and her mother dejectedly followed him. The boy stopped after a while and turned his chair to face them. Natalie introduced herself and her mother. The boy was obviously still angry.

"Where are you going?" she asked.

"I don't know," Nicky answered.

"We were planning to go to the Reptile House," Natalie offered. "Why don't you go with us?"

"Sure," Nicky agreed.

They found the Reptile House deserted except for a few snakes and turtles. Natalie secured the doors and windows, and sat down on the floor. Nicky rolled over and looked down at her. "I'm glad you guys came," he said.

Natalie began to cry. He clumsily moved closer and put an arm around her. "Hey, it will be okay," he suggested.

"No, I don't think it will," Natalie laughed bitterly.

Natalie and Nicky quickly became good friends. As Natalie confided more in Nicky, her mother became more and more withdrawn. Natalie couldn't help but like the good-natured boy, they made each other laugh. The circumstances drove them together.

They had water in abundance, and Natalie was able to take a bath for the first time in over a week. She felt so much better after the bath that she almost cried again. The food situation was not so good. After sharing their meager supplies with Nicky and making two meals, they were out of food. A search of the Reptile House provided nothing edible. They discussed their situation grimly.

"We have to contact someone before we starve," Natalie complained bitterly. "No one can rescue us if they don't know we are here."

Nicky laughed softly and shook his head. "No one is coming," he stated. "Don't you know about the QZ?" He explained the quarantine to her.

Natalie was nonplussed, "My dad would rescue us if we could let him know where we are," she stated confidently. "He was a security specialist."

"Even if we could reach your dad, we're trapped in here," Nicky sighed. "The government has written us off as dead, and they want us to stay that way."

"You don't know my dad," Natalie countered.

"I've still got my laptop, but the battery is dead," Nicky suggested. "We could try to upload a virus through the zoo's satellite dish. There's an emergency generator, but it's out of gas."

"I left a gas can at the fence when we came in!" Natalie declared excitedly. "Can you really hack in a virus?" Natalie asked.

"Dude, I'm a cripple," Nicky stated. "All I did before this shit was hack computer programs. Get me power, and I'll get a message to everybody on the eastern seaboard. The only problem is the message will have to be really short, it can't be much at all."

"I know just the thing!" Natalie squealed.

Chicago - Illinois

My company put me back to work, and even found me a room in a small boarding house. I went back to my vocation, but my heart wasn't in it. People started to act almost normal again. The government had counseling programs for people like me, but I didn't want to forget. Everything was purposely designed to make you think things had returned to the ordinary, and that the center of the United States, the QZ, wasn't there. The government treated it like a radiation leak. We could go back there once it cooled off, once the virus and all the zombies were gone. Unfortunately, everyone inside was dead, period, end of story. But I knew it was all bullshit.

After this had gone on for quite a while, I began to grow despondent. I started drinking. I would drink myself into oblivion. The numbness was better than my new reality. I really didn't want to start over. I found a guy in a bar who traded me some meds I had for a gun. It wasn't anything fancy, just an old government model 1911 pistol. I would sit in my little room on my cot and take out the gun. Looking down the barrel of that handgun was like looking into a black hole. It was great comfort to me to know there was a way out. I would rack the slide and push the barrel against my temple. All I had to do was pull the trigger, and I would be back together with my wife and daughter. I didn't care whether we were reunited in Heaven or in Hell. I was already in Hell.

Somehow, I just couldn't ever work up the nerve to pull the trigger. Then it happened. I was sitting on the floor with the pistol in my lap. I was drinking whiskey and searching through my laptop for any new information. My e-mail icon popped up and began to flash. You've got mail. I opened my inbox and there was a new message that simply said, "Open Me." My finger hovered over the delete button for a moment; then I changed my mind. I opened the e-mail. A virus infected my computer's hard drive before I could react, and then it was gone. Before my computer crashed, a single word had filled the screen over and over, TAG.

Joliet Park Airfield

"Damn it, Brad, you have to get me in there!" I pleaded. My friend held up his hands in exasperation.

"It isn't that easy, Robin," he replied. "To begin with, I don't fly the planes, and that is a pretty big favor for me to ask of a pilot. Kansas City is about three hundred miles inside the QZ. If a plane goes down in there, or a pilot has to bail out, he is listed as KIA. They don't even send in an observation plane to see what happened," he added.

"You guys still fly over the Quarantine Zone," I demanded.

"True," Brad retorted. "But only on specific missions, and you don't even know for sure that Natalie sent that e-mail."

"It was her, Brad," I countered. "I know it was her. She's still alive in there, and I have a pretty good idea where she is."

"You aren't thinking this through," Brad insisted. "Even if you get to her, you'll just be stuck in there with her. Think about what is best for Natalie. How is that helping her?"

"I need to be with my daughter," I maintained. "I don't care about anything else."

Brad shook his head. "Let's go outside for a smoke," he suggested.

We walked outside, and he led me behind one of the older hangers. He pulled out a pack of smokes and lit one. He looked around and then began to speak. "Listen, Robin, you didn't hear this from me, I'll deny ever speaking about it."

"Go on," I prodded.

Brad looked at me narrowly. "There are people who still travel into and out of the QZ," he declared.

"I knew it," I spat. "You military fuckers are blowing this shit all out of proportion. I knew it wasn't that dangerous."

"You're wrong about that," Brad shot back. "If anything, it is more dangerous than you imagine. No regular military personnel are allowed to travel into the QZ, just like I told you. I've heard that some volunteers have gone in on a one-way ticket, but that's not what I'm talking about."

"What then?" I asked.

Brad hesitated. "There are civilian raiders who cross into the QZ to grab loot and then sell the stuff on the black market," he replied.

I was stunned by this news. "What?" I countered. "How is that even possible?"

"Someone on the military side is being paid to look the other way," he concluded as he ground out his cigarette.

"You knew about this, and you didn't tell me?" I shouted in his face.

"Back off, Bishop," Brad growled. "I've heard rumors; that's all. I didn't want to tell you, but then you dropped this e-mail shit in my lap. If there is any chance that Natalie is still alive, then I'm going to help you out. I can only do so much with air assets; you're going to have to handle the stuff on the ground. I care about her too, you know." He gripped my shoulder.

"I'm sorry," I offered.

"Forget it," he muttered.

"So what do we do?" I asked. "Can you get in touch with these guys?" We walked back towards his office.

"I can't," he replied. "But I know someone who might be able to."

It cost me everything I had left to get a name and a meeting with a fence. One of Brad's crew chiefs knew a guy from Chicago who was connected to the underground. Chicago had been divided into smaller areas under the control of different gangs and ethnic groups before Z-Day, now it was even more pronounced. Some parts of the city were so dangerous that the police and military didn't even enter them. I had to walk to the bar where I was supposed to meet the fence. No one robbed me, I didn't have anything to steal or lose, and I looked like it. The bar was a dive called aptly enough the Robber's Roost. I stepped inside and looked around. The interior was dark and dirty. It smelled like stale beer and old urine. A few locals were seated at the bar, aside from that the place was empty. The bartender looked up as I approached, but he didn't say anything.

"I'm looking for the Rooster," I said hopefully. Someone at the bar laughed.

The bartender replied, "Never heard of 'em. If you're not drinkin' then get the fuck out." He pulled a baseball bat out from underneath the bar.

"I'm broke," I replied. "But I'm not leaving until I talk to him."

A very muscular hand grabbed me by the nape of my neck and slammed my face into the bar. I could see what looked like a broken tooth lying inches from my face. Someone with incredibly bad breath hissed into my ear, "Maybe I'll just cut you here." I felt something sharp and pointy poke me just below my ribs. I tried to remain calm and still.

"Let him go, Mal," a voice ordered. My captor released me. I stood up slowly and turned to see a very large Hispanic woman with a stiletto backing away. She pointed the knife at me.

"You very lucky," she suggested.

A swarthy man in a hooded sweatshirt motioned me to a booth nearby. I slid into the seat opposite him. "Thanks, I guess," I offered.

"Don't mind Mallory," he laughed. "She just doesn't like strangers."

I rubbed my neck. "Are you the Rooster?" I asked.

"The people I choose to do business with call me that," he replied as he critically looked me over. "You said you were broke, how are we supposed to do a deal?"

I sat up straighter in the seat. "I trade in information," I retorted.

"What's your name?" he asked.

"You can call me Bishop," I informed him.

"Are you a Fed, Bishop?" he asked.

"No," I replied calmly. We sat and sized each other up for a moment. I wasn't going anywhere.

Rooster leaned in towards me. "What do you want?" he finally growled.

"I want to go inside the QZ," I answered. "I need to talk to a driver."

The Rooster leaned back and smiled a crooked smile. "Shit man, you know that ain't going to happen," he said shaking his head. He started to get up.

"Wait!" I barked, grabbing at his arm. He frowned and looked calmly down at my hand. I released him quickly. "I have a line on some pharmaceuticals," I offered.

The Rooster slowly slid back into his seat. "I'm listening," he said.

Now I leaned forward. "I can help a driver get to a lot of scripts," I added.

"What kind of scripts?" he asked.

"Painkillers," I replied. Prescription painkillers were in high demand on the black market. Currently, they were in very short supply. I had to set my hook with the right bait; I would only get one shot at this.

"I might know someone," the Rooster whispered. "You give me the info and I'll set up a meet."

I shook my head in the negative. "I meet with the driver, set up the deal, and you get a straight ten percent of my cut, in drugs," I concluded.

He licked his lips. "Come back tonight at ten," he ordered.

"I'll wait here," I stated. "I don't want to be outside after dark."

The Rooster laughed. "Give this motherfucker whatever he wants, on my tab," he shouted to the bartender. "And don't kick his ass out until I get back."

He slid out of the booth. "If this is bullshit, Bishop, I'm giving you to Mallory." He walked away laughing.

I sat in the booth and tried to appear inconspicuous. The bartender brought me a sandwich and a beer. Eventually, I slid back into the corner and fell asleep. I awoke with a start as Rooster slid back into the booth next to me. Another man and woman sat down opposite us. The man was slender but muscular, and appeared to be ex-military by his bearing. His hair was dark and cut very short. He wore faded blue jeans and a plain black shirt. The woman was a slim blonde with Eurasian features. She was dressed in black leathers and looked dangerous. I could see the butt of an automatic pistol in a shoulder holster jutting out from under her jacket.

"Bishop, this is Simon and Oksana," Rooster explained. He motioned to the bartender who brought us another round of drinks. They sat and looked me over for a moment.

"He doesn't feel like a Fed," Simon said bluntly.

"I checked around," Rooster replied. "He seems legit."

They were looking at me but discussed me as if I wasn't there. I stayed quiet.

"He looks like shit is more like it," Oksana surmised. "He smells like shit too."

Simon addressed me. "The Rooster here tells me you need a driver to fetch back some merchandise from the QZ."

I shook my head no. "That's incorrect. I need a driver to take me into the QZ," I replied.

Oksana tensed and sat down her drink. Her hands disappeared under the table.

Simon calmly sipped his drink. "I don't run a fucking taxi service for suicides," he stated flatly. "If you want inside, pay off a pilot, or bribe a border guard. You're wasting my time."

"Wait," I implored. "At least hear me out. The drugs are there." Simon relaxed a little, Oksana did not. She made me edgy as hell.

"You come in here with no introduction, nobody knows you here. How do I know you're legit? Why should I believe your story?" Simon inquired.

I threw my old security pass on the table. It had my name and picture on it. Simon picked it up and looked it over.

"I used to work for one of the big software companies, before the shit," I explained. "I still do some work for them. I'm tied into a lot of computer security operations."

Simon considered this. "Where, exactly, are we talking about going to?" he asked.

I knew this would be the hard part of the sell. "Kansas City," I replied.

For a few seconds, everyone was dead quiet; then they all started laughing. The laughter died away as they realized I was serious.

"The KC, you've either got suicide on the brain or you're fucking retarded," Simon pronounced with a laugh.

The Rooster frowned at me. "I'm sorry, Simon," he said. "I didn't know this guy was that stupid."

"What is so special about Kansas City?" I asked.

Simon looked up at the ceiling in exasperation and sighed loudly. "Look, Bishop," he began. "We raid into the QZ about seventy-five miles or so, then we turn and burn out of there. That's our max range."

I shook my head, "Why just seventy-five miles?" I asked perplexed.

Simon replied slowly, "That is the car's maximum range."

I still didn't understand. "I can get you gasoline," I suggested.

Simon looked at me and frowned. Oksana began to laugh again. She picked up her drink and tossed it down. "This asshole knows zip," she quipped. "And I thought you might be dangerous," she laughed again.

"I'll break it down for you," Simon began. "Then I'm going to kick your ass for dragging me down here for nothing."

I wasn't sure if he was serious or not.

"The Feds fly helicopter patrols over the QZ, not too deep inside, say the first forty miles or so. Attack helicopters, usually Apaches, sometimes Marine Super-Cobras, but all equipped with infrared sensors and air-to-ground missiles, not to mention mini-guns. You can't drive a combustion engine vehicle inside the QZ. Even shielded, the engine produces a lot of heat. They stand out like a red flag on infrared. The Feds are riding shotgun constantly, and they'll spot you. If the choppers don't see you, the satellites or the spotter planes will, and they guide the choppers in for the kill. We used to be able to slip through in the beginning, but not anymore."

He paused to take a drink. "Now we use custom-designed electric cars, and we only move at night. They're invisible to infrared sensors. It's still dangerous as hell. The car's range is roughly one hundred and fifty miles on a charge. Seventy-five in and seventy-five out. That's it, so as you can see, a run to the KC is out of the question, no matter what you may think is still there. It is about three hundred miles from the closest entry point on our side of the world to the Kansas state line. Do the fucking math," he concluded.

Everyone looked at me. I hadn't anticipated this.

"Plus, you've still got to deal with the Zeds," Simon continued. "Let's see, the Kansas City metro should have around two million plus zombies packed in there about now." He shrugged his shoulders, "We stick to small towns and industrial areas that were lightly populated before Z-Day. We can only carry so much fucking ammo. Once you are inside the QZ, there are literally more zombies than bullets."

"But the zombie stories aren't real," I countered.

"The hell they're not," Simon growled.

Oksana snatched me by my shirt and pulled me halfway across the table. "The zombies are real, you fuck!" she spat into my face.

"Easy," Simon interceded. "Let him go." Oksana reluctantly pushed me away. "No deal," Simon declared.

My mind raced desperately as I sought a solution. Then I remembered Brad. "What if I could have supplies airdropped ahead of us, into the QZ, closer to Kansas City, or half way there? Ammo. Even batteries for your car?" I asked.

"You don't have that kind of juice," Simon suggested.

"Actually, I do," I responded. "I have an old friend in the Air Force. We go way back before the shit."

Simon looked at me closely. He slowly twirled his drink in lazy circles. "Tell me about the drugs," he prompted.

"I have the location of a Wheeler Pharmaceuticals warehouse. According to the invoice I hacked, there are thousands of pounds of painkillers there. I can guide you right to it," I explained.

"How do you know that the goods are still there?" Oksana asked.

"The receiving date was the day before Z-Day," I replied. "And the satellite photographs show that the warehouse is still intact," I finished.

Rooster whistled through his teeth.

"I'll take you to the drugs on two conditions," I offered.

Simon shook his head in the negative, "I don't do conditions," he growled.

I continued, "Just hear me out, please." Simon didn't speak so I pressed my luck. "I don't want any of the drugs, you guys can have my share, all of it, whatever. I have to go with you. My daughter is there in Kansas City. She's still alive. I want you to take me there and bring us both out. I want you to help me rescue my daughter."

Kansas City Zoo - Missouri

Natalie and Nicky fell into a daily pattern of things they needed to do in order to survive. Water wasn't a problem, the Reptile House had pools and tanks for the aquatic animals that had been on display there. Even without power and water pressure, there was enough water there to last for months. Food was another matter; there simply wasn't any. Every day, Natalie would push Nicky out into the zoo in search of something, anything to eat. Even though they knew that food was nearby, they stayed clear of the other survivors. Natalie was tempted to sneak into the restaurant, but she felt responsible for Nicky and her mother, and she was sure that the man with the pipe would hurt her if he caught her.

At first, they scavenged uneaten food from the cages and storage sheds, but the rotten fruit and vegetables were soon gone, and most of the remaining food was not fit for human consumption. They turned to eating the animals that had starved in their cages. This sickened Natalie at first, but she had to eat. Nicky had freed many of the birds and small animals soon after his arrival, rather than see them starve. Natalie was glad he had, even though it meant they had less to eat now.

Finally, they killed and ate the remaining snakes and turtles in the Reptile House. The creatures were starving anyway. Once they were gone, Natalie took to hunting for birds and squirrels. Her only weapons were large rocks, and she missed far more often than she brought down any game. As the days passed into weeks, she began to lose weight, and feel more and more lethargic.

Her mother became very sickly, and complained bitterly about everything. She became dangerously detached from reality, and was convinced that they should return to their home in Raystown. Natalie had to watch her constantly for fear she would wander away.

Finally, that happened. Natalie and Nicky awoke one morning to find her mother gone. They searched the zoo in vain for hours, even approaching the other survivors who drove them away with curses and threats, but Natalie's mother had vanished.

Natalie was inconsolable for days. Only her sense of responsibility for Nicky kept her from despair and suicide. Finally, she decided to live, which she found ironic considering the fact that they were slowly starving to death. Her dirty clothes hung loosely on her emaciated frame, and Nicky resembled a starving skeleton in his chair. His upper body wasted away until it matched his emaciated legs. Natalie couldn't look at him without crying. Finally, they were too weak to go outside anymore.

Natalie clung to the hope that her father would find them, but she was pretty sure that she was going to starve to death first.

Chicago - Illinois

It wasn't that easy to convince Simon to do what I wanted. Oksana actually had more pull than I did. She made up her mind in favor of the job and convinced Simon for me. The greedy bitch calculated the street value of a successful run at around two hundred million; give or take a million. They walked away from the table and argued for a full fifteen minutes before Simon gave in. Of course, Simon tried to talk me into staying behind, telling me how I was jeopardizing the chances of a successful rescue, whatever he could think of, but I wasn't having any of it. Either I went, or the whole thing was off.

Finally, he relented. I went along with them when they left the bar. Of course, I pushed for speed, but Simon pointed out that he would need at least two days to prep, and that I would have to set up the airdrops. I knew my daughter could die during those two days, but I didn't really have a choice.

Simon had an old warehouse on the north side of Chicago, in a bad neighborhood. It wasn't bad for him, the local thieves and criminals were on his payroll, and they helped him move reclaimed property he brought in on his raids. No one stole from him; in fact, they helped protect him. I had to admit, he had a pretty smooth set up.

We took the subway to the north side of town and walked the last mile and a half. The area had settled into serious urban decay before Z-Day and consisted of rows of abandoned and decaying warehouses. Simon's building didn't look much better from the outside.

Two heavily armed men opened the warehouse bay door and let us in. The front of the building was stuffed with various piles of contraband on pallets or loose on the floor. I saw everything from cases of ammunition to scotch, motor oil, toilet paper, clothes, and caviar. A row of brand new BMW motorcycles were parked against one wall, and buried under tarps and cases of whiskey was an Abrams tank.

I stopped to stare. "Is there anything you don't have in here?" I asked in amazement.

Simon laughed. "This is just the tip of the iceberg; the really good stuff is in the back. Come on, I'll show you." He led me through the piles of contraband to the back of the warehouse. I noticed the windows had been bricked shut.

We emerged into the rear of the building. It resembled a small nightclub, complete with a fully stocked bar and two pool tables. A jukebox stood against one wall.

"This where I do most of my work," Simon explained.

Oksana stepped behind the bar and poured us drinks.

"I'll need a computer," I suggested.

"You can use one of the computers in the warehouse," Simon stated. "They're brand new. The whole building has Wi-Fi. Oksana will take you wherever you need to go tomorrow, and help you with any technical specifications for the car."

"Is the car here?" I asked.

Simon looked at me over his glass. "Yes, would you like to see it?" he asked.

I was very curious. "I would," I replied.

"Then follow me," Simon said. He led me even further into the warehouse. Against the furthest wall were two steel doors on tracks. Simon produced a key and unlocked the door on the left. He pushed against the door, and it rolled aside to reveal a large mechanic's bay. Overhead lights came on as we entered. Tools and spare parts littered the workbenches along the far wall. At the bay's center was a large vehicle, covered with a tarp. Simon walked towards it. Oksana followed us into the bay; then leaned against the doorframe. She kept one eye on me.

"Allow me to introduce the Nachtpanzer," Simon announced as he pulled aside the tarp.

The thing was huge. I had expected a small electric car. It resembled a light cargo truck that had been partially smashed flat. The tires were oversized, but the car hugged the ground. Every surface of the car was rounded; it seemed to blend together at all the joints. I didn't see any doors. The entire vehicle was painted in a black tar-like substance, and the small rectangular windows were also tinted black. Simon ran his hand across the rounded front of the car. It sported a stout push bar partially recessed into the vehicle's body.

"The entire car is armored with a mixed-medium, Kevlar titanium ceramic plating, over a high-density poly-monofilament exoskeleton." Simon rapped on the car's armor with a knuckle. "The car is made of plastic. All of the armor is sloped, every surface is curved. There isn't a single flat surface on the entire vehicle. The windows are bulletproof. It carries a crew of four; the driver and navigator in the front, a gunner in the top turret, and a loader in the cargo bay. The car can be configured to carry a variety of weapons packages, depending on the specific mission."

I walked around the car and examined it as Simon continued to talk.

"The car is powered by an electrical hydrogen battery array that is entirely modular. The batteries are quite heavy, but they can be exchanged in less than five minutes by an experienced crew. The car also employs KER technology, allowing the car to recharge itself in a coast condition. As you can see, the vehicle is still quite heavy, and every ounce of weight is calculated to allow for the maximum recoverable cargo payload. All of the vehicle's weapons utilize caseless high-density plastic ammunition, and are jettison-capable. The car is equipped with an onboard computer and infrared camera array; the driver can literally see in the dark. The navigator has full access to the net and GPS systems, low-frequency short-range radar, and can monitor all channels of military communications."

I stopped as I came full circle around the car.

"This bitch is bad news. It's a prototype, one of a kind. I had it custom built for runs into the QZ," Simon concluded.

"How do you move this thing around without attracting attention?" I asked.

"You're not the only one with friends in the military," Simon replied. He thumped his hand against the car's front armor. "The car will be in position tomorrow night, then it's up to us and luck."

Simon led me back to the bar. He showed me to a cot with a sleeping bag near the bathrooms. A computer sat nearby on a pair of boxes. "That's the guest room," he explained. "Don't wander around, it's dangerous."

They left me there and disappeared into the warehouse.

I hadn't slept well in days. The next thing I knew, Oksana was kicking my cot.

"Get up, asshole," she growled.

I could smell something cooking, and I realized I was ravenous. I followed her groggily back to the bar. Simon was there drinking coffee. The bar top was covered with road maps and breakfast. Simon poured me a cup and pushed a bagel and some bacon at me.

"Okay, Bishop, listen carefully to me. I've planned our route, and started things in motion."

He turned a dog-eared road atlas towards me and pointed to the open page as he spoke. "This is the wonderful state of Missouri. We have to cross the Mississippi at the closest point available to our objective. Our timing is bad and things are really hot down there right now. I would suggest we wait until things cool off, but I know that's not an option for you, so the only place I can get us across is at East Saint Louis." He paused and looked up from the map.

Oksana snarled, "You can't be serious!"

Simon remained calm. "I knew you wouldn't like it, but there are a lot of things about this run you're not going to like."

Oksana paced back and forth like a caged tiger. "How can you be so stupid?" she barked.

"May I remind you that this run was your idea; I didn't want to do it," Simon replied.

Oksana whirled towards the bar; her right foot shot out in a snap kick. Simon caught it in mid-strike and grabbed her by the hair. He slammed her into the bar and forced her slowly backwards until she was pinned against it.

"You're my bodyguard, not my boss," he whispered into her ear. "I run the show, I decide the routes, got it?"

She snarled defiance. "I won't go back there."

Simon released her and stepped away. He turned and retrieved his coffee cup. "You don't have to," he explained.

"What do you mean?" Oksana barked.

"Bishop will ride navigator on this run, we can only take four so you are out," Simon replied. "You're staying here."

Oksana stared daggers at me and Simon. She turned without a word and stalked away.

Simon poured himself more coffee. "Wow, she is really mad," he stated. "She actually didn't talk back, that's a first."

I reached across for the coffee carafe and queried, "I know I sound like an idiot, but what's so bad about Saint Louis?"

Simon shook his head and sat down at the bar. "We tried a run into Saint Louis once before. It went badly. We lost the car and the cargo. The gunner and the loader died. The Zeds got 'em. It was messy, real messy. They were good friends of mine. Oksana and I barely got away. We had to swim the river." He laughed quietly. "Oksana doesn't swim. She nearly drowned us both before I could pull her across. She never got over it."

He thumped his finger down on the map. "Saint Louis has more zombies per square foot that any other piece of real estate in the QZ. Before the outbreak, there were like two-point-eight million people there. Most of them are zombies now. Nobody goes there anymore, period. The Feds don't have to patrol it because no one tries to cross there, it's suicide. All we have to do is time our crossing to avoid the naval patrol boats and we can get through. They'll never expect it," he concluded.

"Okay," I replied dubiously.

"Assuming we get through Saint Louis, we will run State Road 30 to the southwest." He followed the road with his finger. "It links up with Highway 50, and that will take us west towards the KC. I need to check the aerial photos of the highways to make sure we can get through on the route I've planned. I always got a back-up route in mind, but the primary has to be clear, or at least passable. I'll want you to use your assets to double check the route. Got it?" he inquired.

I nodded in agreement.

"The first airdrop has to be made at the Jefferson City Airport. It's roughly half way," he explained. "The second drop has to be at Lee's Summit Municipal Airfield. That is just to the south of Kansas City." He pointed out each airfield on the map. "We're still going to be cutting it close, the distance of each leg is just inside the Nachtpanzer's range."

"Why don't you just carry spare batteries with you, especially on the trip out?" I asked.

Simon shook his head. "Leave the technical shit to me, Bishop," he replied with an annoyed sigh. "The batteries are heavy, if we carry spares, it reduces our range, and we can't carry both spare batteries and cargo. My crew is putting the drop packages together now. They have to be on target, and we have to make sure that the airfields are still accessible, and that there aren't any crazy surprises waiting for us," he directed.

"Oksana will go with you to make sure the Air Force will play ball. She has to be satisfied with the arrangements, or the run is off," he warned.

"Great," I replied. "I'm pretty sure she hates me already."

Simon nodded in agreement. "She hates your guts, she's told me so. That's how I operate. Checks and balances. I can't afford mistakes during prep." He closed the atlas. "I'm going to patch things up with Oksana, you take a shower. I sat out a clean uniform and some boots for you." He walked away.

After I had gotten cleaned up and dressed, Oksana came to collect me. We walked outside. Simon's men were loading the battery arrays and other equipment into a pair of Army trucks. Oksana stood to one side watching them. I noticed she was also scanning the area around us, and she occasionally looked up at the sky. I tried to stay out of the way. I walked a little closer to her. She looked up as I approached.

"I'm sorry if I'm causing problems for you," I suggested. "But I will do whatever I have to do to save my daughter."

She laughed harshly. "Fuck you and your brat daughter, Bishop. We aren't going to be friends, so you can stop trying to make me feel sorry for you." She stepped closer to me and looked straight into my eyes.

"If anything goes wrong with this trip, I'll kill you myself. You are on my shit list, permanently. The only thing I care about is the drugs. If you are wrong about them, you better stay out there with the zombies; it'll be safer for you." She walked away.

I didn't try to stop her. I figured the psychopathic bitch meant what she said.

Once the trucks were loaded, we rode in silence through the deserted streets, out of old Chicago and through the countryside along Highway 55. We arrived at Joliet Park Airfield and drove directly to an open hanger where Brad was waiting for us. He waved us inside and had his men take over the unloading operations. Once this was underway, he joined Oksana and me. I introduced them.

Oksana and Brad looked at each other warily.

"What are this piece of shit and his daughter to you?" Oksana asked.

Brad grinned back at her and answered, "Robin and I are old friends. We grew up together. Natalie is like a daughter to me. She calls me Uncle Brad."

Oksana was gauging his sincerity; she was testing him, looking for a lie, a falsehood, some reason to scrap the mission. She moved in very close to Brad. "You are willing to risk imprisonment for her, maybe even death?" she asked.

"Yes," Brad replied.

Oksana stepped back. "I believe you," she stated. "But know this. If you don't deliver, or the resupply gets fucked up, I will hold you personally responsible. I will kill you."

Brad didn't back down. "Fair enough," he shot back. "You can try."

Oksana laughed at him. "You should have chosen your friends more wisely."

"The packages will be where they are supposed to be," Brad concluded. "Just get Natalie back safely."

Oksana turned and walked away.

Brad checked out her backside. "That bitch is hot," he observed. "I'd like to hit that."

"It would be safer to screw a meat grinder," I retorted.

The trucks had been unloaded, and one was waiting to take us back to the warehouse. Oksana stood impatiently beside them. She waved me over.

"Looks like it's time for me to go," I said. "I don't know how to thank you."

Brad took me aside for a moment. "Do you trust these people?" he asked. "Because you shouldn't."

"What choice do I have?" I retorted.

"Just watch your back," he suggested. "Once they have the drugs, they won't need you or Natalie anymore. Keep a gun handy. Look for the double cross, it will happen," he finished.

Oksana shouted at me, "Come on, Bishop. Let's roll!"

I shook hands with Brad and walked to the waiting truck.

Simon had been busy while we were gone. A small convoy was assembled in front of the warehouse awaiting our return. The Nachtpanzer was loaded on a flatbed tractor-trailer rig under a camo tarp. Two Humvees would provide escort and transport for us. A pair of men in urban camouflage uniforms stood near the car, rechecking the straps and rigging.

Simon walked over to greet us. He leaned in to kiss Oksana. "Everything copasetic with the drops?" he inquired.

"Yes," she affirmed. "But I still think I should go along."

Simon smiled at her. "No room, babe; and I need you to watch my back here."

Simon guided me over to the car and introduced me to the other two crewmen.

"Bishop, this crazy asshole is Steven Stone. Stone is our gunner." Stone was a handsome, muscular man with curly brown hair and a friendly disposition. He smiled and shook hands with me.

"This other old fucker is Thumper, he's our loader." Thumper was a thick, mean-looking older man with a crew cut and a scarred face. He spit on the ground between us and grunted.

Simon continued, "Guys, this is Bishop. He's going to make us all rich. Oksana says he's okay."

"He's a pussy and a piece of shit!" Oksana countered. "He'll run as soon as he sees a zombie."

Stone and Thumper laughed.

"Don't mind Oksana," Stone suggested. "She doesn't even like Simon, and he's fucking her."

"Fuck you, Stone," Oksana growled.

Stone laughed good-naturedly and shot her the bird.

Simon laughed. "Let's get this abortion on the road. Bishop, you're with me." He hugged Oksana and kissed her good-bye. They whispered something to each other, but I couldn't hear them.

Simon and I climbed up onto the back of the trailer and into the Nachtpanzer. We had a five-hour trip to East Saint Louis. Simon wanted to use the time to teach me the basics of the navigator seat in the car. The convoy pulled away from the warehouse. Simon didn't look back.

Simon threw the front upper hatches open. They let in enough light to see. I climbed into the passenger seat, and Simon sat down on the edge of the driver's seat. He powered up the car's electrical system. The screens and control panels illuminated, filling the interior with a dim green glow. The navigator's position was equipped with three monitor screens. The left, and smallest screen, was the standard computer monitor. It utilized a touch screen, and a standard keypad. It was linked to the net. The center screen was the largest, and was used to monitor the low-frequency short-range radar. Simon quickly explained its operation to me. The radar was almost completely computer automated. It could identify almost any target it acquired, and pass the information to the crew through the car's weapons systems and Simon's heads-up display. The third screen was the mapping monitor, and was used to display the car's position on the map generated by the GPS system. Two radio sets were positioned directly below the screens. One was a scanner that could be used to monitor military and police frequencies. The other set was a standard CB radio for emergencies only. Simon had me practice with the equipment just long enough to familiarize myself with it; then he shut everything back down.

He looked at me. "You got this, Bishop?" he asked.

"I got it," I replied.

"You'd better," he shot back. "Nobody knows how they are going to respond to combat until they actually experience it. Just remember what's at stake, try not to panic."

When he was satisfied, we both sat back for a moment. I looked around at the vehicles interior. It didn't seem cramped, but there wasn't a lot of extra room inside. The car had been designed to utilize all the available interior space. The rear of the vehicle was just an empty shell for cargo. Several crates of spare ammo and extra rockets were stowed there, along with some food and water. The gunner's seat and the 50 caliber mini-gun hung down into the cargo bay on the car's right side. Once the hatch was open, the seat and gun could be pushed up into position inside the turret. The main cargo door was on the left. Two large control buttons, one green, one red, were located on the bulkhead just beside the door. Emergency supplies, some tools, a twelve-gauge assault shotgun, a machine gun and a rocket launcher were stowed between the door and the driver's seat.

I looked over at the driver's position. The vehicle's basic controls were laid out much like a standard car. The accelerator and brake pedals were as I had expected them to be. The steering wheel, however, was obviously designed to control the car's weapons systems. It resembled a thick U-shaped oval that terminated in a pair of pistol grips. A firing trigger was positioned on each side, and I noticed a thumb button atop each grip. A long panel of rocker switches was situated on the roof panel just over the driver's right shoulder, and the dash was filled with gauges and indicators of various shapes and sizes. I realized the vehicle was much more complex than I had imagined.

Simon noticed my examination of the car's controls. "I could show you how to operate the car's controls and weapons systems, but then I would have to kill you," he stated.

I laughed halfheartedly until I realized he wasn't kidding.

He continued, "The car was custom designed for me, I'm the only one who ever drives it. The power array is equipped with a lockout key code that will shut the car down permanently until it is reset." He tapped a keypad under his left hand. "A reset requires the dismantling of the entire cockpit, and only I know the code," he added.

"What if something happens to you?" I asked.

"You might want to make sure that doesn't happen," he replied. "In my line of work, it is important that my safety be a priority. I trust the people I work with, Bishop, but only to a certain point. We pull out millions of dollars of pharmaceuticals on every trip. There is always the temptation for someone to take the whole package. The people I deal with are thieves or worse."

"You're not talking about Stone and Thumper, are you?" I asked quietly.

Simon laughed. "No, not in particular. I meant everyone. I have made it a point to spread the word that the car is keyed to me. I also have taken pains to spread the wealth around. Happy mother-fuckers are friendly mother-fuckers. Not that we can't handle ourselves. This car is loaded for bear. Do you know anything about weapons, Bishop?"

"Not really," I answered.

"Since our business involves dispatching zombies, almost all the weaponry we carry is anti-personnel; munitions designed solely to kill and maim people," Simon explained. "The car is currently loaded with its maximum capacity anti-zombie weapons package. We are carrying twelve short-range high-explosive missiles, two forward-firing 30 caliber mini-guns and the 50 caliber mini-gun in the roof turret. The guns all use caseless ammunition with plastic projectiles to save weight. There are also point mounted anti-personnel mines on the exterior armor, roughly six to a side, four to the front and rear. All of the weapons are linked to a heads-up display here on my position and the steering wheel fire controls."

"Why didn't you use voice-activated controls?" I asked.

"I don't like them," Simon answered. "Call me old-fashioned."

"Anything else I should know about?" I inquired.

"Just know that I always keep an ace up my sleeve," Simon said as he pulled a wicked-looking knife from a hidden sheath under the steering column, and slowly slid it back.

"I'll try to keep that in mind," I replied.

When we stopped to refuel, Simon and I climbed out of the Nachtpanzer and moved to the rear Humvee. Our driver was a regular Army sergeant. He didn't talk to us.

The sun set as we traveled south on Highway 55. Traffic was light, and no one questioned our passage; we looked like just another military convoy. Simon went over a set of maps and looked at a couple of aerial photos. Finally, he put them away. We rode along in silence for a few moments.

The Humvee's tires were loud on the pavement. "Damn, these things are noisy," Simon stated. He twisted around to look at me in his seat. "Bishop, I need you to think about something," he stated. "You are the weak link in this whole operation. I've shown you how to run the nav equipment, I'm not too worried about that, and you're a computer guy. But a crew trains to work together, and you haven't had any of that. If I tell you to do something, you have to do it without thinking about it. You just do exactly what I say, got it?" he asked.

"That's going to be hard for me," I admitted.

"Just remember your daughter's life will depend on it," Simon expounded. "What is she like, this daughter of yours?"

I pulled a picture of Natalie and me from my wallet and handed it to Simon. Someone had taken it at a fourth of July picnic. It was faded and torn; I had looked at many times.

"She got her looks from her mom," I explained. "But she's got my brains. I taught her how to write code and hack, but she had a lot of natural talent."

"She's got to be pretty smart if she stayed alive this long in Kansas City," Simon suggested. "Not to mention getting a message out in a virus."

"Yeah, she's smart, and pretty," I added. "I'll have my hands full in a couple of years, once she starts dating."

"Are you certain she's at this zoo you told me about?" Simon asked.

"It's the only place that makes any sense," I replied. "She loved that place, and they had everything there, food and water, defensible buildings, emergency generators, everything she needed. The place was pretty solid. It has an eight-foot perimeter fence. Her favorite place in the world was the Reptile House. The zoo is only two miles from our house. I used to take her there a lot after the divorce." I trailed off into silence.

It took us five hours to drive to the outskirts of East Saint Louis. We took an off ramp and drove into what looked like a Third World war zone. Stripped, abandoned vehicles and burned-out, vandalized buildings stretched out in every direction around us. Our convoy slowed to a halt. Simon directed the nervous driver to take point. We drove around the transport and switched places with the other Humvee. We slowly picked our way through the debris-filled streets, occasionally pushing a wreck aside in the roadway. Glass crunched under the Humvee's tires as we slowly moved towards the Mississippi River. We came to an unmarked intersection.

"Turn left here," Simon instructed the driver. We slowly rolled forward between two abandoned warehouses. The Humvee's headlights illuminated a garbage truck parked across the narrow roadway ahead of us.

"Sir…" the sergeant began.

"This is far enough," Simon instructed. "Stop here." Simon opened his door and stepped out into the street.

The distinct sound of a dozen rifle bolts being thrown echoed down the alleyway.

"Freeze motherfucker," a gruff voice shouted from the darkness. Simon held his open hands before him, and slowly turned in a circle.

"It's Simon," he responded.

"Do you have the shit?" the voice inquired.

"Of course, as we agreed. Caviar, cigarettes, and Scotch," Simon replied.

"And the ammo?"

"Nine mil and forty," Simon suggested.

Dark figures emerged from the shadows and approached the trailer. Simon pointed out the items, and they were quickly carried away. The garbage truck started up.

"Are we good?" Simon shouted.

"This time," the voice responded.

The garbage truck rolled out of the alley. Simon ducked back into the Humvee.

"Drive," Simon urged. The convoy pulled through the industrial area and emerged at a loading dock on the Mississippi River. A pair of derelict barges lay half-submerged against the rotting river piers. Simon checked his watch. "We have about twenty minutes to unload," he urged. "Let's get to it."

"What can I do?" I asked.

"Watch the river for patrol boats, stay low and quiet," Simon instructed.

The Nachtpanzer was quickly cut loose from the trailer as the loading ramps were put into place. Simon climbed into the vehicle. The big electric car slid smoothly down off the trailer and onto the dock. Stone and Thumper moved quickly to stow their personal gear and weapons on board. The sergeant approached the car as Simon emerged through the loader's door. Simon gave him a thumbs up, and the sergeant quickly returned to the Humvee. The military vehicles drove away into the darkness, and silence reclaimed the riverside. Once they were gone, I realized how dark it was. There was no moon, and I could barely see my hand in front of my face.

"Two minutes people," Simon warned. "Bishop, get inside the car," he urged. I climbed inside and sat down in the passenger seat. Stone clambered into the Nachtpanzer's gun turret and quietly readied the car's mini-gun. He peered over the rim of the turret. Thumper knelt beside the car's nose, the machine gun in hand. Simon looked at his watch and then at the river.

"No noise," he whispered.

A light stabbed out of the darkness and played along the western shore, illuminating the Saint Louis riverside. The massive buildings had been invisible in the darkness, but now stood out in stark relief as the searchlight played across them. The light was reflected back from the shards of thousands of broken windows. They gleamed in the darkness like wicked teeth in a skeletal framework face. Many of the buildings were fire-blackened, burned-out shells. The level of destruction was beyond anything I had imagined.

"Is Kansas City like that?" I whispered.

"Probably," Simon answered. "But I haven't seen it myself, no one has."

I involuntarily shrank down in my seat as the light switched to our side of the river and flashed across the car's windshield.

"Relax," Simon whispered. "They can't see us; we just look like more blackness to them."

The searchlight played back and forth over the docks as the patrol boat slowly moved past our position. I could see the cone of light as they moved gradually downriver, then it disappeared as the boat rounded a bend.

"Our ride should be here in a minute," Simon explained.

Thumper moved to the dock's edge with a small flashlight. Within seconds, a dim red light flashed from the darkness on the river. Thumper flashed his light twice in reply. A faint shudder ran through the car as a barge pushed its prow against the dock. Men in black uniforms leaped ashore, and quickly secured the barge. Thumper walked back and forth, checking the junction between the barge's prow and the dock with his light. He waved the light to signal the car ahead. Simon slowly edged the car forward onto the barge. I clinched my seat as the weight of the car settled the barge's nose lower into the water. The dock groaned in protest as its forward edge crumpled under the weight. Simon goosed the car's throttle. It shot forward onto the barge and just as suddenly stopped as Simon applied the brakes with both feet. I was thrown violently against the instrument panel.

"Was that necessary?" I asked, rubbing my bruised arm.

"Unless you wanted a submarine ride," Simon shot back.

Thumper banged twice on the car's side armor, and Simon visibly relaxed. The barge's crew cut the boat loose, and its engines let out a muffled rumble as the pilot smoothly backed the barge away from the docks and spun it around to face the western shore. The craft fought against the sluggish current and slowly moved along the edge of old Saint Louis, away from the patrol boat.

Simon stretched out in his seat and put his hands behind his head.

"Enjoy the ride while you can," he suggested. "Because as soon as we unload in Saint Louis, the shit is going to hit the fan."

I was pretty nervous about going into Saint Louis after everything I had heard about it, and seeing it in person had made it much worse.

The barge made slow progress, but within a few minutes, the engines were cut, and we turned towards shore. A crewman directed the pilot towards a concrete pier with a small flashlight. Thumper climbed inside and secured the cargo door. Simon tersely watched the view screen linked to the car's infrared backup cameras, his hands played nervously over the controls. A shudder ran through the car as the barge gently drifted into contact with the pier. The barge's engines roared as the pilot engaged them at full power to hold the craft in place. Simon gunned the cars accelerator, and the Nachtpanzer bumped up and over the lip of the pier and onto the concrete pad. The big car cut in a tight circle and then stopped. We were off the barge and onto the pier in a matter of seconds. I could dimly hear the barge's engines reverse as the craft pulled away into the night.

Saint Louis - Missouri

"We are truly in the shit now, boys," Simon whispered. He did a quick scan of the instrument panel and slowly moved the vehicle forward off the pier. It rolled bumpily over the cluttered pavement and into the city proper. The car's infra-red cameras provided a crude picture of the roadway before us. This information was presented on the heads-up display for the driver's position. It looked like an image from a video game. The blacktop still radiated heat, and the cars and other vehicles appeared as vague box-like blocks against the roadway and the shadowy buildings. Simon could literally see in the dark.

"Listen for any military chatter, Bishop," he directed. "And stay sharp, Stone; the Zeds are going to be all over us."

I slowly ran the radio scanner back and forth, checking for any military radio transmissions. I picked up some chatter from the patrol boat, there was nothing else.

I noticed a faint stench in the car. I coughed.

"That's just going to get worse for a while," Simon explained.

"You don't mean …" I began. "Wait, you mean that smell is coming from outside?" I asked incredulously.

"Yeap, that's the smell of Greater Saint Louis," Simon replied. "You smell the zombies outside the car."

"And if you think those bastards stink now," Stone laughed. "Just wait until you smell one up close."

I covered my nose with one hand and tried to breathe through my mouth. "Do you mean there are zombies out there right now?" I asked.

"What, you've never seen a Zed?" Stone laughed.

"No," I answered. "Why do you guys call them that?"

"It's an abbreviation; zombies are Zeds, Federals are Feds," he answered.

We moved forward, and Simon slowly guided the car back and forth, driving around abandoned vehicles and building debris in the roadway. The car's oversized tires occasionally bumped over some obstacle or trash. The crew was nervous, but it didn't seem that dangerous to me.

"What do the zombies look like?" I queried.

"Here, I'll show you, since this is your first time," Simon laughed grimly. He flipped a toggle on the overhead panel. Two of the car's forward running lights switched on, illuminating the roadway before us for a few yards. Dozens of zombies were milling about directly in front of the car. The light reflected eerily from their dead eyes. They turned and slowly approached us. Nothing I had imagined could have prepared me for the real thing. The Zeds were like my worst nightmares come hideously to life. The rotten, bloated, blackened flesh; the stained, broken teeth showing through their rotting lips and rictus grins, and the dead white, staring eyes.

I involuntarily moved away from the windshield, leaning back as far as I could into my seat. I had never seen a zombie before, and now that I had, I wished that I hadn't. They scared the living shit out of me. You couldn't have gotten me out of the car at that moment for love or money. If my daughter had been outside just then, screaming my name, pleading for help, I wasn't sure if I would have been able to leave the safety of the car to save her.

Simon goosed the car ahead, crushing three zombies beneath the Nachtpanzer's wheels. The rest were brushed aside. He quickly reached up and switched off the lights.

"They're all around us," I whispered. I was quite shaken. "Oh shit, you've been running over them the whole time."

"I told you before, there are more zombies per square foot here than anywhere else in the QZ," Simon replied evenly. "As long as we move slowly and don't make too much noise, we can push through."

"Don't they know we are here?" I asked tersely.

"Oh, they know we're here. Zeds are attracted to bright lights, noise, and vibrations, shit like that. They really love explosions. That's why I'm moving slow and dark, and avoiding hitting anything big or metallic," Simon explained. "Every one of those mother-fuckers behind us will follow us all the way to the other side of the city."

"Won't they just climb onto the car?" I asked.

"They'll try," Simon countered. "But there isn't anything for them to grab onto. The car's as slick as owl shit."

"So we just drive through?" I inquired.

"We will be okay as long as they don't get any thicker than this. But there is a certain point where there are too many zombies to push through. They bunch up so thick that the car can't move against them. They're like a solid wall of flesh," Simon answered, smacking his fist against his palm to illustrate the concept.

I shuddered at the thought.

"And the wheels get slick if you crush them constantly," Simon added. "You know. All the guts and goo."

I shrank into my seat and tried not to think about where I was. It didn't help much.

"Keep your ears open, Bishop, don't freeze up," Simon instructed me. "And watch the GPS; I may have to deviate from my planned route."

We left the docks behind us and slowly drove up Bank Street.

The roadway was partially blocked, and Simon had his hands full maneuvering the big car through. Hundreds of abandoned vehicles of all descriptions were parked where their previous owners had abandoned them. Many of the vehicles still contained the moldering corpses of the people who had died in them, and thousands of zombies filled the street.

Simon slowed the car and cut the wheels to align the Nachtpanzer with the front end of a smashed-up wreck in front of us. A burned-out city bus had crashed with a smaller SUV, and the pair totally blocked the road ahead. Once Simon had the cars aligned, he slowly rolled forward until Nachtpanzer's push bar hit the SUV's side. He gradually applied power until the mangled vehicle tore free from the wreckage. The Nachtpanzer pushed it down the street for several yards. Three of the wreck's tires were flat, and the shredded rubber separated from the rims as the SUV was pushed ahead. Sparks flew, and the protesting squeal of the metal rims on the pavement could be plainly heard from inside. Simon stopped the Nachtpanzer and then quickly maneuvered around the wreck. He accelerated for a moment to leave the gathering zombies behind.

"Great, we're getting a pretty good crowd," Simon pointed out. He flipped on the car's rear-view cameras. I could see a slowly moving mass filling the street behind us on Simon's screen.

"Can't we go any faster?" I asked nervously.

"No," Simon replied. "If I damage the car, or get us stuck, we're all dead meat. Triple A don't come down here no more, and believe me, you do not want to go outside right now."

"Relax!" Thumper growled from the rear. "You're harshing my ride, Bishop. Damn, Oksana was right, you are a pussy."

I tried to keep quiet.

"Here's our first turn," Simon grunted as he turned the wheel. "Tucker Boulevard."

The Nachtpanzer turned left onto the larger thoroughfare and Simon had to slow even more. The roadway was packed with wreckage and milling zombies, but Simon weaved his way tortuously through. A dim, but rhythmic thumping began on the car's outer armor.

"Fucking Zeds," Thumper growled.

We were moving slowly enough for the zombies to walk alongside and beat on the car.

"Is this normal?" I asked quietly.

"Nothing in Saint Louis is normal anymore," Simon responded as he scanned the car's gauges and heads-up display. "We only have to make another two miles and things should clear out."

"I was here a couple of times before the shit went down," Stone said. "There was a pretty good barbecue place right up the road from here."

I closed my eyes for a second, and tried to relax. I was thrown forward in my seat as the car suddenly decelerated.

"Fuck me running!" Simon growled as he slammed on the brakes. The car skidded to a halt. The thumping noise immediately intensified.

"Problem, Boss?" Stone asked. He grinned and threw the release for the mini-gun.

"Yeah," Simon responded. "A fucking water main or something gave way since the last time an aerial was taken. There's a bastard big hole in the road right in front of us. I almost drove right into it, and the fucking natives are getting restless."

"Shit," Thumper grunted.

"Stone, get topside and limber up the mini-gun," Simon calmly instructed. "Bishop, find our position on the map and backtrack me a way around. Take us back two blocks and then back around to Tucker. Got it?" he asked.

"Yeah," I replied. "I'm on it."

The car began to rock back and forth as the zombies piled up around us. They began to move the car forward, towards the gaping hole, their sheer weight and numbers gave them strength.

"Today, Bishop, while we are still fucking young," Simon urged.

I pulled up a roadmap on the GPS screen and quickly traced the route.

"Back to St. Charles on our right," I instructed. "Left on thirteenth, go two blocks, then left on Olive and back right on Tucker."

Stone reached up and opened the top hatch in the turret. A wave of nausea hit me as the stench of the dead filled the car's interior like a physical blow. I had never experienced anything remotely like it.

The smell was overpoweringly rotten and rich, and at the same time disgustingly, cloyingly sweet. It clung to me instantly like a foul, hideous perfume. Bile filled my throat. I gagged, and then threw up all over myself.

Stone climbed into the turret and pushed the 50 caliber gun up on its mount and out of the car, pointing it down and to the rear. He threw the arming bolt, leaned back into the firing seat and hunkered down behind it.

Simon applied power to the car's wheels, but instead of moving backwards, the Nachtpanzer was pushed forward, towards the yawning chasm before us. The zombies outside moaned for our blood. They pushed and heaved against the car.

"There's too many to back up! Clear 'em out!" Simon yelled.

Stone let out a rebel yell and pulled the trigger on the mini-gun. The brutal weapon's barrels spun, spitting a stream of lethal projectiles and bright red tracers into the zombies behind us. The rotting undead disintegrated under the murderous impact of the heavy 50 caliber bullets. Stone fired the gun in a tight arc into the street, sweeping it from side to side. A bloody lane to freedom, paved with mutilated body parts opened up behind us. The sound of the gun's electric motor was the whirring of giant deadly locusts, the rounds firing thousands of semi-simultaneous explosions, echoing around us inside the car.

Simon calmly watched the back-up camera's monitor, his hands poised over the overhead control panel and the wheel.

He slammed the accelerator pedal down and gunned the Nachtpanzer into reverse, climbing over the slippery, dismembered mass of human remains littering the road behind us. The big car jumped up and down as it crushed through the dismembered zombies, throwing me around and almost out of my seat. Stone continued to fire, but I could barely hear the roar of the gun over the ringing in my ears. With a final lurch, the car stopped, and then slowly slipped into forward motion again as Simon reversed direction, its wheels spinning wildly. Smoke rolled from the gore-slicked tires as the bloody debris burned away. Simon struggled against the controls as the car slewed right, and then shot ahead.

"We're clear!" Stone yelled as he slid back down into the car, pulling the still-smoking gun after him. The smell of burnt cordite immediately filled the car, displacing the odors of death and vomit. My eyes stung from the stench. I retched and coughed to clear my burning throat.

Stone slammed the hatch shut. He yanked the mini-gun's receiver open as Thumper tore into one of the ammo boxes. The men struggled to maintain their footing as they began to load fresh ammunition into the gun.

Simon turned the Nachtpanzer left, accelerated ahead, then slowed and turned left again. He spun the wheel to deftly avoid obstacles and made the last right. With a final bump and a thud, we were back onto Tucker Boulevard, the hole and most of the zombies behind us.

He looked over at me and laughed.

"You puked, but did you shit yourself?" he asked.

"I'm not sure," I shrugged as I checked my pants. "I don't think so."

"I guess Oksana was wrong," he chuckled.

Twenty minutes of slow maneuvering and we were free of old Saint Louis. The roadway became less crowded with wreckage, and then suddenly was almost clear. Simon opened the car's exterior vents to clear out the fouled air. He pushed the car up to forty miles per hour, slowing occasionally to veer around a wreck or other obstacle. Tucker Boulevard became State Highway 30. We followed it southwest into the night.

"Here," Stone suggested. He handed me a water bottle. I took off my shirt and rinsed it out before putting it back on. I diligently watched the radar screen, but nothing appeared.

The crew was quiet and the mood was tense. Simon had warned me that we were most likely to encounter an aerial patrol during the first forty miles or so. This leg was the most dangerous part of the trip. All I could do was ride along and pray we weren't acquired by the Fed's surveillance systems.

"Just how dangerous is this part of the trip?" I asked nervously. "I mean, the Feds won't be able to locate us, right? You told me that the car's invisible to them."

Simon shot me an annoyed look. "The Apache pilots have FLIR.

It's an advanced thermal imaging system. I know how it works, so I've done everything possible to counter their abilities. They could still spot us, especially if they surprise us while we are moving," he explained.

"How does FLIR work?" I inquired.

"Basically, it uses an advanced infrared camera system to measure differences in thermal gradients. Every material absorbs and diffuses heat at a different rate. A large object, say like a transport vehicle," Simon paused to wave his hand in a circle to indicate the car, "stands out like a neon sign against a different background material," he explained.

"But the Nachtpanzer is an electric car, and it's mostly plastic. I thought it didn't give off heat," I interrupted.

"Correct," Simon continued. "But as I was saying, the car is composed of a different material than the road, except for its coating."

I was confused. "Wait, you lost me."

"I thought you said this guy was supposed to be smart," Thumper interjected.

"The Nachtpanzer is coated with a thin layer of roll-on asphalt," Simon explained. "It gives the car roughly the same heat signature as the roadway. I can't hide the shape of the vehicle, so we made it as non-rectangular as possible. When we aren't moving, we tend to blend in, as long as we stay on the road."

"How in the hell did you think of that?" I queried.

"The Germans used to coat their tanks with concrete back in the day. It kept the Russians from sticking magnetic mines to them," he answered. "I just updated the concept."

I considered this for a moment. "What would we do if a chopper spotted us anyway?" I asked quietly.

"Don't even say that," Thumper growled. "It's bad luck."

"Sorry," I muttered, "I didn't know."

"If the Feds should spot us, our only option is to take them out first," Simon explained. "If the radar gives us a proximity warning, we've got about fifteen to twenty seconds before they can get a visual. We have to stop in a hurry. Then it's up to our gunner."

He pointed back to the surface-to-air missile beside the loader's door. "That's what that big bastard is for."

Stone grinned at me. "Don't worry, Bishop," he laughed. "I'm a crack shot with that there SAM missile. I never miss."

"No one misses with a SAM, you asshole," Thumper rumbled. "It's a self- guided surface-to-air missile." They both laughed quietly.

"Have you guys ever had to shoot down a chopper?" I inquired.

Stone grew serious for a second. "I did on a run a few years ago," he responded, "It was him or us. Those boys were just doing their job, and so was I. Nothing personal. I don't feel bad about it. They would have killed me if they could've."

"You're a real cold-blooded killer, Stone," Thumper laughed derisively.

Stone grinned at him. "Naw, just doing my thing," he replied. "Now Thumper here, he is one mean son of a bitch, Bishop. He has killed more Feds than anyone else I know. He loves killing 'em. Ain't that right, you old fucker?"

"Post-apocalyptic rules. I'll kill anyone that gets between me and what I want," Thumper responded. "The government's responsible for this whole fucked-up mess. If any dumb cock sucker is stupid enough to keep on working for the Feds after what they did, he deserves death."

I had never thought about it that way. I had always considered the guys who kept on enforcing the QZ as heroes, but I could appreciate Thumper's logic, twisted as it was.

"Nobody has anything on me when it comes to killing Zeds though," Stone bragged, "I've killed more than any man alive. I surely love shooting zombies."

"That's true," Simon broke in. "Stone will come along on a run just for fun, as long as he gets to man the mini-gun, and shoot Zeds. He doesn't even need the money anymore."

"Damn straight," Stone agreed. "I retired and opened my own bar years ago, but drinking ain't got nothing on shooting zombies. I like it better than sex."

"That's because you're a necrophiliac," Thumper stated.

"The rumors that I actually fuck zombies are grossly incorrect," Stone countered. "Everyone knows that I refuse to wear a condom, and unprotected sex with Zeds is just too damn dangerous. There is no telling what you might catch diddlin' around with those dirty mother-fuckers."

"All this talk about sex with zombies is making me hungry," Simon laughed. "Bring me up a sandwich and a water, Stone."

"Comin' up, Boss," he replied. Stone rummaged around through the cargo compartment and brought forward a pair of sandwiches and two bottles of water. He handed Simon one and offered me the other.

"No thanks," I said, waving the food away.

"More for me," Stone laughed, shoving the sandwich into his mouth.

"Old rule, Bishop, eat when you get the chance," Simon suggested.

"Maybe later, I don't have much of an appetite right now," I suggested.

The car rolled on through the Stygian darkness. No unseen attacker menaced us as we drove across the Missouri countryside. The landscape changed to rural as we moved away from the Saint Louis city limits. Fifteen minutes passed, then twenty. Simon slowed the car.

"We should be approaching the intersection with State Road 47," he informed me. "Check the GPS."

I looked at the monitor. Our icon arrow had reached the intersection. "We're there," I replied.

Simon carefully maneuvered the Nachtpanzer around the abandoned vehicles that lay scattered across the highway intersection. A few forlorn zombies approached us. We turned north onto 47, a two-lane rural highway and sped away. We had traveled only twelve miles before Simon slowed the car to a crawl and finally stopped at the crest of a small hill. The GPS display indicated that we were just about to reach the junction with Interstate 47. I asked Simon about it.

"That is correct," he agreed. "The problem is that the road may be blocked here."

"You knew about it?" I asked.

"Of course," Simon replied. "I planned the route. Aerial photographs showed a major pile-up here, but we may be able to get through. We won't know until we try."

Simon slowly moved forward. We rolled down the road towards the underpass and the highway onramps. Hundreds of wrecked vehicles of every description blocked the intersection as far as the car's cameras could see. Countless zombies wandered among them. We rolled up to the outlying wrecks and stopped. The underpass at the bottom of the hill was a logjam of trucks and cars. Simon slowly panned the cameras back and forth, looking for some path through to the other side.

"That looks pretty much impassable," he intoned.

Highway 47 was completely blocked directly before us. The onramp to the interstate was bumper-to-bumper cars, many abandoned, their doors still open, some obviously wrecked. Desiccated bodies lay scattered about like dried up leaves. The off ramp on this side of the underpass was the same. Desperate drivers had driven their vehicles the wrong way up the ramp, only to find the interstate impassable.

"Man, I hate to do this," Simon growled. He cut the car's wheels to the left and drove across a gas station's parking lot. Directly behind it stood a hay field. The Nachtpanzer rolled off the asphalt and onto the dirt.

"We are pretty well visible," he grated. "Everybody stay frosty."

Simon pushed the car up to thirty miles an hour. The big transport bumped along, throwing me around in my seat. We paralleled the road, traveling west through the field until the wrecks thinned out and we could cross. Simon slowed the car, and we turned to cross the highway. The Nachtpanzer bumped up over the median and onto the blacktop. Simon gunned the car towards the wrecks ahead of us to the east. He slowed slightly and veered off into a corn field on our left, skirting the wrecks across the roadway. Corn stalks slapped against the car's small windows until the field ended and we ran back into 47   on the north side of the intersection.

Simon turned the car back onto the asphalt, and quickly accelerated up to fifty miles per hour, steering around the occasional abandoned car until we had left the road block far behind.

The miles slipped by beneath us. Five minutes passed. Simon slowed the Nachtpanzer down to forty, and relaxed back into his seat. He let out an audible sigh of relief.

"The satellites may catch the damage we did to that corn field," he explained. "But at least we are back on the pavement."

We drove another twelve miles to the outskirts of the small town of Union. We would turn to the west towards Kansas City here on Highway 50.

Simon slowed the car as we approached the outskirts of town. We drove into and out of a pretty large crater in the road. The car swayed from left to right.

I looked askance at Simon.

"Shell craters," he responded. "I'm missing most of them."

As we drove into the town's center, Simon slowed the car more and more, until we were barely creeping forward. Finally, we stopped completely. Simon was staring fixedly at the heads-up display. I could only see a jumble of unidentifiable shapes.

"Fuck," Simon mumbled.

Stone and Thumper crept forward to look over our shoulders.

"We have to go outside and clear some of that shit," Simon said grimly.

"What is that?" I asked tentatively.

"A military checkpoint," Simon explained. "They strung wire across the roadway, from building to building." He pointed to a faint web of lines on the display. "They also set up gun emplacements." He pointed to a larger shape on the screen. "That's an Abrams tank; it looks like its hatches are open. It's just too tight to squeeze through. Let's make this really quick."

"Wait!" I urged. "Why don't we just go around?"

Simon spun around in his seat to face me. "Are you going to question every mother-fucking thing I do, Bishop? Because if you do, we will never get to Kansas City, I'll be too damn busy explaining everything to you!" he exclaimed angrily.

"Aren't there zombies out there?" I asked.

"Do you see this?" Simon asked. He tapped on the heads-up display. A set of six bar gauges, mostly red, each with a small section of green and amber, was illuminated under his finger. "These are the battery power level displays," he explained, "We are down to just above fifty-five percent power. If I drive around looking for an alternate route, we will run out of juice!" He accentuated the last six words. "If they went to the trouble to seal off this road, they will all be blocked."

"Just do what the man tells you to do and shut the fuck up," Thumper growled.

"Sorry," I mumbled.

"Stone, topside with the machinegun," Simon commanded. "Bishop, give Thumper a hand with the wire."

Stone pulled on a pair of night vision goggles and removed the Carr machine gun from the weapons rack. He opened the turret hatch and climbed out on top of the Nachtpanzer.

Thumper grabbed a large set of bolt cutters and hit the button that opened the side cargo door. The door slid smoothly outward and then back to the side. A blast of cold air filled the car's interior. I couldn't smell any zombies; the air was clean and crisp.

"Clear!" Stone yelled from above.

Thumper pushed me outside. He roughly guided me to the wire barricade. Simon switched on the car's blackout lights. The lights were low power and pointed down directly in front of the car. They gave us just enough light to see what we were doing.

"Pull the wire back out of the way as I cut it," Thumper directed. He bent down and began to cut the barbed wire. I nervously pulled it away. We worked as quickly as we could. The seconds ticked by.

"Zeds. Eleven o'clock!" Stone yelled. The smell of rotting human flesh rolled over me.

Thumper continued to hastily cut the wire.

"Shouldn't we get back in the car?" I stuttered.

"Keep on working!" Thumper snarled.

I jumped as Stone's gun went off. He fired the machinegun in short controlled bursts again and again.

I could hear the zombies approaching. Their rotting meat stench suddenly got much stronger. I pulled frantically at the wire to clear it away. The barbed wire tore my hands until they were bloody, but I didn't feel it. Thumper pushed down a sandbag gun emplacement. Suddenly, Stone's machine gun fired and the wire was yanked from my hands. I looked around wildly. A headless zombie had fallen and become entangled in the wire, its still-twitching body rolled into the light right at my feet.

"Get out of there!" Stone yelled. "They're all over you!"

"Go!" Thumper urged. He smashed the skull of an approaching Zed with the bolt cutters and pushed me ahead of him into the car.

Clawing, cadaverous hands grasped for us out of the darkness. Thumper leaded inside. He slammed the door button with his fist and turned to protect the still-open doorway. Dozens of zombies approached the slowly closing door. The machinegun roared and spat red tongues of flame at the Zeds. Their heads exploded one by one as Stone fired down into them, splattering the Nachtpanzer with rotting brains and blackened blood.

A lone zombie managed to get its rotting fingers on the closing cargo door, and it fought to keep the door open. Thumper calmly set the wire cutters on its bony wrist. With a grunt, he pushed the cutter's handles together, shearing off the entire hand. He kicked it outside just as the door clicked shut.

Stone dropped down into the cargo bay and pulled the hatch shut behind him. I climbed shakily back into my seat as Simon pushed through the checkpoint. The Nachtpanzer bumped over the gore-splattered sandbags and was clear. We rolled slowly through the streets of the dead town of Union.

"You did alright out there," Simon said. He looked over at my blood-stained hands.

"I cut them on the wire," I explained.

"Take care of that shit, an open wound can kill you out here," he ordered.

Stone brought me a first-aid kit. I spread antiseptic on the cuts and wrapped my lacerated hands with gauze and tape.

"Here," Stone offered, passing me a small flask of bourbon. I took a slug, grimaced, and passed it back. Stone grinned at me, and took a drink himself.

"Not too bad for a newbie," Stone observed.

"At least he didn't run," Thumper observed.

Stone tossed him the flask. Thumper drained the bourbon and tossed him back the empty container.

Simon slowed the car as we approached a main thoroughfare. I checked the GPS.

"This is 50," I stated.

Simon turned the Nachtpanzer left onto the state road. He accelerated the big car and swerved to avoid wrecks scattered along the way. A few minutes later, we rolled up to a destroyed military checkpoint. A burned-out Army armored personnel carrier sat abandoned on the sidewalk. The wire was cut and down. Someone else had done the job for us long ago. We slowly drove past the last few buildings and out of Union.

Highway 50 - Missouri

Highway 50 was surprisingly clear of wreckage and we made good time. There were a few abandoned vehicles still on the road, and a few more on the shoulder. I commented on this to Simon.

"Totally logical, Bishop," he explained. "The state roads are generally clear away from the towns. I guess most of the people in the rural areas just tended to hunker down at home when the shit hit the fan. But not the urban areas. Everyone tried to flee the cities. The interstates are a fucking nightmare, especially near the bigger cities. They're all parking lots. We learned real quick to stay off them."

"Just how long have you guys been doing this; raiding, I mean?" I queried.

"I started right after Z-day," Simon responded. "I knew Stone from before. We made some of the first runs together, back in the very beginning. I met Thumper later; he worked for me on a lot of different projects. He actually came out of retirement just for this run."

"The score was too fucking good to pass up," Thumper interjected. "After this, I can buy my own island and really retire in style."

I laughed at the idea.

"What's so fucking funny, Bishop?" Thumper asked.

"He's not kidding," Stone explained.

"Sorry, Thumper," I hastily replied. "I thought you were exaggerating."

"Nope," Thumper added. "My own island, private golf course, gourmet food and booze, imported whores, the works."

"Don't forget to send me your address, you old bastard," Stone suggested.

"I won't even remember your name," Thumper laughed.

No one spoke for a moment. I hadn't realized just how quiet the Nachtpanzer really was. The big car's wheels gave off a low hum, barely audible inside, that was it. The silence was disconcerting. I needed the sounds of conversation to deal with my fear.

"How did you guys come up with the idea to raid the QZ?" I asked, shaking my head in disbelief. "What did you do before all of this happened?"

No one answered me, but Stone laughed quietly.

Finally, Simon responded. "We're all ex-military, Bishop. I was an officer and a helicopter pilot before. Stone was a door gunner, of course. Thumper was an Army infantry sergeant. I resigned my commission after Z-day and attempted to rescue some of my family in Iowa. My bird was shot down by the Feds trying to fly back into Illinois. After they pulled that shit, I said fuck it, the gloves are off, and it's every man for himself. Hang on."

He paused to slow the Nachtpanzer as he maneuvered around a wrecked semi-trailer in the road. Once he was clear, he accelerated and continued, "At first, I was trying to rescue people inside, that went on for a while. But the Feds got more serious about the damn quarantine. They put up permanent barriers and their air surveillance got better. Hell, they even put up cameras on balloons, and started using drones. Once you got past the border, it wasn't much better. It got too dangerous inside the QZ to fuck around lightly, the virus spread like wildfire, and there were zombies everywhere you went. It took a little bit of action before we figured out how best to deal with them."

"Those were some wild and hairy days," Stone remarked. "We used to really play that shit fast and loose."

"What do you mean?" I asked.

Stone grinned at me. "You would have loved it, Bishop. Talk about shitting your pants. We used to sneak across the river and go in on foot. Then we would hot wire a four-wheel-drive truck and do a hit and run. Shoot our way through the zombies and take our chances. Back then, we would collect automatic weapons and ammo, jewelry, drugs and medicine, even expensive booze, anything we could sell on the black market. We would bribe a naval patrol to bring us back across the river. Man, I miss that shit!" he concluded.

"Yeah, well the Feds got wise to people moving around inside the QZ," Simon interjected. "They started up the helicopter patrols. Everything that moved inside the QZ was fair game, not just the zombies, and you couldn't drive regular cars anymore. I've always been one step ahead of the Feds; otherwise, I wouldn't still be here."

"So there were other raiders?" I inquired.

"Were, is the operative word," Simon explained. "I think most of them are dead now. I never really considered anyone else as competition, just someone else for the Feds to shoot at. No one is as slick as me, and no one ever will be."

"Shit man, Simon's a fucking legend in the underground," Stone explained, "Everyone knows the story."

"And I intend to stay that way," Simon replied. "Just a legend."

"There were a lot of raiders back in the beginning, Bishop," Stone began. "Hell, people started raiding into the QZ as soon as they figured out there was a black market for some of the shit just laying around out here. The Feds killed most of them before they got back to the real world, but just enough of them made it out to make it sound doable."

"Well, the Feds think they have that shit nailed down now," Simon added. "And we do everything we can to encourage that misconception."

I considered what they had just told me for a second. "If you guys have been going into the QZ this whole time, then you must know more about the virus than anybody else. How come you guys didn't catch it?"

Simon cleared his throat. "Bishop, you ask too many fucking questions. I feel like I'm riding with an eight year old."

"Come on," I pleaded. "What else are we going to do to pass the time?"

"Fuck," Simon relented. "Fine, I'll tell you what I think I know. As far as we can tell, the virus has mutated, or some such shit, and it isn't just floating around anymore. The only way you can catch it now is if you get bitten by a Zed, just like in the old zombie movies."

"How did you figure that one out?" I inquired.

"I didn't." he replied. "Doctor Cooper did. He was a scientist who stayed inside to work on a cure. He was broadcasting on a radio station out of Kansas for a while, at least until the Feds figured out where he was."

Stone made a jet engine noise, followed by an explosion. He pantomimed a plane dropping a bomb with his hands. "Your taxpayer dollars at work," he laughed.

"What did he say?" I asked eagerly.

"Before the Feds silenced him, he claimed that the virus wasn't contagious anymore, that you could only get it through contact with the zombies; that you had to be bitten. Of course, that didn't jive with our government's containment policy, so they shut his broadcast down real quick," Simon explained.

"Back when we first started, we always wore the full chem suits with the gas mask and everything. Man, what a pain in the ass those things were," Stone laughed.

"It's a lot easier to operate without them," Simon added.

"Tell him about the cure," Stone suggested.

"What cure?" I stammered.

Simon looked over at me. "Cooper claimed he had found a cure for the virus. He said all we had to do was dispose of the zombies and that things could go back to normal, more or less. He claimed the QZ wasn't necessary."

I was stunned. "Wait a minute. Why would the government shut him down? Wouldn't they want people to know?" I trailed off.

"Yeah," Simon replied to me. "You just answered your own question. Whoever came up with this whole cocked-up mess, the virus, the QZ, they're covering their ass. They're perpetuating the problem."

"No one would do that," I countered.

"Wake up, Bishop," Simon retorted. "The fuckers in charge condemned one-quarter of the country's population to a horrible death. They abandoned millions of people who didn't need to die. There are still survivors out there who could be rescued, just like your daughter. The QZ is being maintained to justify the decision to implement it in the first place. At this point, it's just a huge cover up. Someone pretty high up doesn't want to take responsibility for all those needless deaths."

"Why didn't you guys tell someone?" I asked.

"Who in the hell would we tell, Bishop? Huh?" Simon interjected. "Think about it for a second."

"You could have gone public," I countered. "I mean there are still newspapers, people need to know about this."

"The government censors all information regarding the QZ and the virus, you know that," Simon replied.

"You have a responsibility…" I began.

"Shut up, asshole!" Thumper yelled at me. "You bleeding heart, liberal, piece of shit!"

"What?" I stuttered.

"You're an idiot," Thumper laughed harshly. "We don't want them to shut down the QZ, you moron."

"What?" I repeated, "Why?"

"Job security, dickhead," he replied. "If they close down the QZ, we're unemployed. We've got a good thing going here. Why would we want to change it?"

I sank back in my seat, finally stunned to silence.

We rolled on in silence for a moment. Finally, Simon spoke again. "Look, Bishop, we're not the bad guys here."

"You could have ended all this," I replied quietly.

"No," he responded deliberately. "If any of us had said anything, anything at all, we would be just as dead as those fucking zombies walking around out there."

"It's wrong, Simon, and you know it," I stated flatly.

Simon responded thoughtfully, "Wait until you have your daughter back and then tell me about right and wrong. Decide to expose the government then, knowing that you'll die, that she won't have anyone to protect her, or that they'll kill her too. Tell me about responsibility then. What we are doing may be morally wrong, but we are just opportunists reacting to a really fucked up situation. We didn't create this mess, so don't be so fucking judgmental about what we're doing."

"You're not protecting anyone," I retorted.

"True," Simon responded. "What can I say? I'm a greedy bastard. Sue me."

I shook my head and frowned at him.

"Hey, if you don't want to ride with such a morally corrupt

bunch of thieving bastards, I can stop the car and let you out," he chuckled. Stone and Thumper laughed.

When I didn't respond, he added, "That's what I thought."

"I still think we have a responsibility to do something," I stated.

"That's your problem, Bishop," Simon concluded. "You think too much."

"Yeah, Bishop," Stone quipped. "You should really try recreational drugs. You might be tolerable if you were a little more mellow."

"I doubt it," Thumper jibed.

"You guys are all assholes," I said. "I don't ..."

"Proximity alert!" A mechanical voice loudly warned. "AH-68 Apache helicopter closing at three thousand yards." The short-range radar lit up, and its warning claxon sounded urgently. A steady blip appeared on the radar screen, directly east and closing very fast. I looked down at the screen in horror.

Simon locked the Nachtpanzer's brakes, full force. I was thrown forward in my seat.

Thumper launched himself against the bulkhead, striking the loading door's green control button as he fell hard on the cargo deck. Stone was through the still opening cargo door with the SAM before the car came to a complete stop. He hit the ground running and sprinted away from us into the darkness. Maybe five or six seconds had passed.

I could hear the flat beat of the helicopter's rotors approaching. The sound seemed unnaturally loud in the sudden stillness. I could only watch as the blip moved closer on the radar screen. I had never felt so helpless and exposed. My throat had gone suddenly bone dry, I desperately tried to swallow. Thumper stood slowly upright, blood running down his face from a cut in his forehead. He dabbed his fingers against the cut, grimaced and cursed.

I looked over at Simon. He sat with his hands poised over the Nachtpanzer's controls, perfectly calm and collected. He looked over at me and smiled.

Fifteen seconds had passed.

The helicopter's engines were a hurricane upon us. I closed my eyes and tried to pray.

A tiny red meteor leaped from the ground and exploded directly above us, almost simultaneously an impossibly brilliant flash lit up the darkness, filling the car with red light and noise. The afterimages were burned into my eyes. Suddenly, burning debris was falling from the sky all around us. With a horrendous metallic crash, the twisted fuselage of the Apache dropped onto the roadway, awash in flames. Blazing bits of twisted wreckage flew away from the wreck in all directions, and burning fuel spattered down from the sky.

Simon gingerly reversed the Nachtpanzer back to a safer distance and stopped.

Thumper stood up in the cargo doorway, silhouetted by the flames from the burning wreckage. He shouted Stone's name into the darkness.

As suddenly as he had disappeared, Stone was back. He clambered through the doorway, a grin on his face.

Thumper slammed the door's red button and collapsed to the floor.

Simon accelerated away from the wreckage, steering around the flaming debris. He pushed the Nachtpanzer up to its maximum speed, and fled the site of the attack. The whole combat had taken less than sixty seconds.

"That was a helicopter, an Apache," I stated in a shaking voice. "We're still alive."

"We got lucky," Simon replied.

My hands began to shake uncontrollably, and I realized I was crying. I raised my trembling hands to wipe away the tears. Simon pretended not to notice.

"That was intense," Stone stated.

Thumper broke out the first-aid kit and wiped an alcohol pad across the cut on his forehead. He grimaced and growled, "What the fuck was up with that? What were those bastards doing this far inside?"

"I don't know," Simon replied.

"Do you think they know we're here?" I asked.

"If the Feds were on to us, we would already be dead," Simon responded. "They would have sent a lot more than a single chopper." He paused to think for a few seconds. "Stone, do you think they spotted us? Did they have time to radio anything in?"

"No way, Boss," he stated. "I nailed that fucker the second he popped over the horizon! They never knew what hit 'em."

Simon considered this, "We've got some time before they figure out what happened, we'll just have to make it to the first resupply before we have any more trouble. That was our only SAM."

"I don't like this," Thumper stated flatly.

"What are we going to do?" I asked nervously.

"You ladies relax," Simon suggested sarcastically. "Everything's cool until I say otherwise. We're only about forty miles from Jefferson City. If we can make it to the airport we're golden."

He paused to look at the displays. "Just stay alert, I'm gonna' roll at max. It'll put a drain on the batteries, but we need to get the fuck on down the road."

Simon held the car at seventy miles an hour. He smoothly maneuvered around any obstacles in the road, only lightly touching the brakes, then accelerating again. From my seat, the heads-up display was a ghostly bent kaleidoscope of dim reds and yellows, populated with quickly approaching black blocks and lines.

Simon bent over the controls, his face a mask of intense concentration. I was grateful that I could see only darkness through the Nachtpanzer's small armored windows. I had to stop myself from constantly looking over at the battery power displays. I could see that the six bars were all in the red, but I had no idea how much power or time remained. I didn't dare ask Simon. The minutes and the miles ticked by. I pulled up the car's position on the GPS monitor. We were rapidly approaching Jefferson City. The green arrow icon representing the car was just outside the city's symbol on the map. Simon slowed the car as we passed more abandoned vehicles in the roadway. Their numbers increased as we passed the city limits. Finally, we slowed to a crawl as Simon maneuvered through the city's cluttered streets. I noticed a faint chemical smell, like someone had burned a Styrofoam cup inside the car.

"What is that smell?" I finally asked.

"Jefferson City burned completely to the ground sometime after they established the QZ," Simon answered.

"Damn," I whispered.

"A lot of the residential areas inside the QZ have burned," Simon added.

"I hadn't thought about that," I replied. I thought of Natalie. Fire was probably the least of her worries. I wanted to urge Simon to hurry, but I didn't. He had his hands full, and I knew we were doing the best we could.

We rolled through the blackened shell of the city, over the fire-warped asphalt.

"Did most of the zombies burn up when the city went?" I asked.

"Yeah, that's one of the good things about being in a burned-out area," Simon responded. "They're too slow to get out, and most of them burn. Of course, more of them wander in afterwards, but it thins 'em out a bit."

Simon turned the wheel, and we slowly rolled to a complete stop.

"What's wrong?" I queried. "The batteries aren't dead, are they?"

"Almost," Simon responded. "But that's not why I stopped." He powered down the car until only the auxiliary systems and the radar were still on. He turned around in his seat to face the crew. "We've reached the Missouri River Bridge. We have to cross to get to the first drop. There's too much shit on the approaches to get through, so we have to do a wreck-clearing op on each end to make room for the Nachtpanzer to get across."

"Damn it, Simon, you didn't say shit about this," Thumper complained.

"You can take the first watch, until one of us can't work the come-along anymore," Simon offered.

"Fuck me," Thumper growled. He grabbed the night vision goggles and the Carr machine gun from the rack.

"What's a come-along?" I asked.

"This is," Stone laughed, handing me an aluminum hand-cranked cable winch.

I examined the come-along. "How does it work?"

Thumper stuffed spare magazines into his jacket pockets. "You'll find out," he warned me. "That son of a bitch will flat wear you out. I hate those things!"

Simon climbed into the cargo bay. He put a hand on my shoulder. "Wait a minute," he instructed me. "Let your eyes adjust to the dark." We waited a minute inside the darkened car. "Ready?" he asked.

He hit the green cargo door button. The door slid out and back. The burnt plastic smell filled the car.

"Stay alert," Simon warned. "You won't be able to smell the Zeds out here."

I stepped outside the car. The blacktop crunched under my boots. It was very dark, I couldn't see shit. Thumper adjusted the night vision goggles on his head and looked around.

"What's the word, Thumper?" Simon inquired.

"All clear," he responded.

Simon led us forward. We wound through the charred, abandoned cars and trucks until we were in the clear on the bridge.

"Let's start with this one," Simon instructed, pointing to a crumpled sedan. The car had been crushed by a cargo truck. All of the vehicles were covered with a fine coat of black soot. Thumper climbed up onto the roof of a nearby pick-up. He scanned the area for zombies and gave us an all clear. Simon attached the come-along's hook to a bridge support while Stone played out the cable and hooked the other end to the car's rear bumper.

"Bishop, straighten out the wheels," Simon ordered.

I could see the desiccated remains of the previous owner still at the wheel through the windshield. I gingerly opened the door, and grabbed the corpse by its shirt. As I pulled the body out, it came to pieces until I was holding a rotting torso in a tattered shirt. I tossed it aside and reached inside to turn the wheel. My hands slipped on the slimy spots where the corpse had been gripping the steering wheel. I forced myself to turn it; then wiped the disgusting fluid from my hands on my jacket. As the car's wheels straightened, Simon pulled the come-along's handle quickly back and forth, resetting the release and pulling the winch through its short rotation smoothly. The winch clicked several times and the car jerked back a few precious inches with each pull. Four minutes work cleared the car from the lane. Simon and Stone quickly disconnected the winch.

Simon looked over the next wreck, a two-door hybrid sedan, only slightly melted. Amazingly, all of its tires were still inflated. He put the car in neutral and steered while Stone and I pushed the car back against the slight incline of the bridge. We quickly shoved the car back against the rail and returned to the pile-up. Thumper stood on the truck, scanning the bridge and the roadway, his gun at the ready. Simon and Stone set the come-along and repeated the operation on a luxury sedan with two flat tires. This time, Stone operated the winch. The muscles stood out on his arms as he strained against the weight of the big car. Half way through, he gave out and gasped, "Switch out somebody." Simon took over on the come-along, grunting and pulling against the handle until all the cable was rolled onto the spool and the car was resting against the guardrail.

The next three cars were still moveable. We pushed them back towards the center of the span. Even though the grade was slight, it was hard work, and my legs were screaming by the time we had removed the third car. I limped back to the wrecks after the other two. The closer we got to the entrance to the bridge, the more burned up the wrecks became, and the steeper the grade.

Simon looked over the next three choices. Only one car still had a tire holding air. He attached the come-along's hook to it, and played the cable back until he could attach the other end to the bridge's guardrail.

"Your turn, Bishop," he suggested. He showed me how to work the release, and reset the handle. I began to wrench the burned-out wreck aside. The car barely moved on its flattened tires. Ten pulls of the handle and I was done. Stone pushed me clear and began to crank the handle. After twenty-five pulls, Simon took over. We alternated until the wreck was astride the guard rail and clear. Stone slowly disconnected the winch and sat down for a moment. We all rested against the rail. I looked over at Stone and Simon and wondered if I was as dirty as they were. My hands were completely black.

"Man, I'm out of shape," I complained.

"I was going to say you were a pussy, but whatever," Stone laughed.

"First time running a come-along, Bishop?" Simon asked.

"Uh, yeah," I panted.

"Look at the bright side," he suggested. "There are only twenty more cars to go."

We reset the come-along and tortuously removed each burned-out hulk, one at a time, until we had cleared a path back to the Nachtpanzer. Thumper watched over us like an ugly, blasphemous guardian angel as we worked, but no zombies appeared. Finally, we were through. I collapsed back into the car. Simon powered up the Nachtpanzer and rolled us across the center span of the bridge to the other side. He coasted to a stop as he shut the power down again. A whole new section of abandoned cars stretched out before us, blocking the way through and off the bridge. At least this side of the approach hadn't burned. I wasn't sure I was up to another clearing op. My arms felt like limp noodles.

Stone broke out a round of bottled waters. We sat and drank them in silence.

Finally, Simon spoke. "Same drill as before. Stone, do you want to switch out with Thumper and stand guard?"

"No, I'll stick with you guys," Stone replied. "I'm exhausted. I don't want to fuck up and let someone get bit."

"Good call. Let's get to it," Simon said.

We painfully filed out of the car and approached the pile-up. Once again, Thumper climbed atop a wreck and stood guard. We mechanically approached the nearest car. It mercifully had four inflated tires. I noticed that the vehicles on this side seemed to be in much better shape. Most were simply abandoned, and none of them had burned. Some were wrecked, but none as badly as the cars we had cleared on the other side. I steered as we pushed the first wreck back onto the bridge.

"Maybe this won't be so bad," Stone suggested.

"We've got company!" Thumper yelled to us.

"How many?" Simon shouted back.

"Just a few coming onto the bridge," Thumper replied. "I got 'em."

"Keep working, but watch the cars," Simon ordered. "You had to say something, didn't you Stone?"

Thumper's gun went off repeatedly. He squeezed off five short bursts. I flinched each time he fired. We worked as quickly as we could. I completely forgot the fact that I had been exhausted before we started. We cleared seven cars before we had to break out the come-along. Some asshole had slammed into the cars in front of him, and now we had to deal with his shit driving while zombies were trying to kill us. His grinning cadaver still clutched the wheel of his smashed-up sports car. I hoped he had died slowly.

We strung out the come-along and attached it to the asshole's car. Stone pulled the cable tight. With a metallic groan and a lurch, the car came loose. Stone quickly worked to ratchet it aside. Thumper's machinegun went off again. Simon looked over the two remaining wrecks. He pointed to the car on the left, a smaller subcompact with a crumpled rear end. Its tires were still up.

"Come on," he urged. "We can move this one." He got behind it and began to push. I grabbed the wheel and turned it to maneuver our car around the one Stone was still moving.

At first, I didn't see it, and then I couldn't tell what it was. A zombie had crossed the bridge from the other side, behind us, and was limping towards Stone. He couldn't see the Zed coming. He was still working the come-along, his back to it. The thing was just a burned-up, blackened husk. Its face had completely burned away, or I wouldn't have seen it in the darkness. All I could see in the gloom was the teeth. The zombie's teeth clicked shut and open with every halting step. I had stopped pushing to stare at it.

"Stone!" I yelled. He looked up at me but kept on pulling the winch's handle.

"What the fuck, Bishop?" Simon yelled. "Push the bastard car!" He looked at me and then followed my gaze to Stone and the zombie.

"Thumper, Zed, six o'clock!" he screamed.

Thumper spun and fired just as the zombie bent down to bite Stone's neck. Its flame-blackened skull exploded into ragged shards of shattered bone and rotting grey matter. Stone threw his hands over his head and dropped to the pavement. He looked wildly up at us, and then scrambled away as the headless cadaver fell over onto the roadway beside him, one bony hand still grasping at his leg.

"Fuck!" he screamed as he kicked it away.

Thumper turned back and fired off another burst back onto the ramp. "It's getting pretty busy out here, Simon," he yelled.

Simon shook his head at me and walked over to help Stone up. "The next time you see a dentist, you better thank that motherfucker," he suggested.

"What the fuck for?" Stone asked, dusting himself off.

Simon pointed down at the headless corpse. "If that bastard

hadn't had his teeth whitened before he died, I never would have seen him," he laughed.

"Thanks," Stone said.

"Bishop spotted the Zed," Simon responded. "He didn't exactly go nuts trying to point it out, but he did save your ass."

Stone retrieved the come-along and walked over. He clapped me on the shoulder. "I owe you one, Bishop," he grinned.

"Sorry guys, I couldn't tell what it was at first," I offered.

"Forget it, it's over," Simon ordered. "Let's get back to work."

Thumper covered us as we moved the last few cars out of the way. The gunfire was attracting more and more zombies. By the time we were almost done, he was firing almost continuously as more and more zombies were drawn to the bridge. He had switched from full-auto to semi-automatic fire, squeezing off one shot at a time.

"Simon, I'm almost out of ammo!" he yelled as we moved the last wreck over to the rail.

Simon waved us back to the Nachtpanzer. Thumper slowly brought up the rear, firing behind him as more zombies stepped into the lane we had cleared.

We scrambled inside the car. Simon slid into the driver's seat and activated the electrical systems. Thumper paused beside the cargo door to fire one last shot. He ducked inside and hit the red button, closing the door. The Nachtpanzer rolled forward across the Missouri, bumping over the zombies on the bridge.

"Look at this shit," Thumper laughed, pulling the magazine from his gun. "I had two fucking rounds left."

Missouri River Bridge

We rolled north on Highway 54; it was only a few miles to the turn off for the airfield. The battery power display bars were gone, not even the red remained. Simon held the car at thirty miles per hour. I said a silent prayer that we would reach the airfield. I looked over at Simon. For the first time, he looked slightly worried.

"Come on, baby," he spoke quietly to the car, urging it to go just a little further. We rolled another mile down the road and then we were at the Jefferson City Municipal Airfield. Simon drove the

Nachtpanzer through the field's broken security gate without slowing and directly out onto the airfield.

"Stone, go topside, look for a strobe," Simon ordered. "Bishop, look for the strobe." He pointed outside the car's window. Stone opened the turret hatch and stood up on the seat. Our first resupply package should have been air-dropped directly onto the runway. A small strobe light had been attached to the package and would show its location, assuming everything had gone according to plan.

We circled the airfield. I could only see darkness through the window. Simon shut down the heads-up display and killed the gauge and indicator lights. The car's interior was plunged into complete darkness.

"There it is," Stone shouted. "Three o'clock, in the grass just off the runway."

Simon slowed the car to a coast and steered off the tarmac, following Stone's directions. Finally, I could see the weak pulse of the strobe light. A large military drop box sat just off the runway. It had rolled over onto its side, and the chute had draped across the strobe. We rolled to a stop directly beside the box.

"That was cutting it pretty fine," Simon laughed. He shut down the power. Stone dropped back into the cargo bay. "Stone, cover us while we switch out," Simon ordered. "Thumper, get that SAM broke out first."

Thumper hit the door's green button, but it was dead, so he pushed the cargo door open manually. Stone pulled the night vision goggles on and slammed a fresh magazine into the Carr machinegun. We all stepped outside and scanned the airfield. Stone moved a short distance away and looked around for any zombie activity.

"They've already spotted us," Stone warned. He lifted the Carr to his shoulder and squeezed off a short burst. "You guys had better work fast."

"What can I do?" I asked.

"Stay out of the way," Simon replied. "Help Stone look for zombies."

I stood by the Nachtpanzer and looked out into the gloom. Simon and Thumper cleared the chute away from the drop box. Thumper removed the strobe and shut it off. Simon cut the chute's cords and pulled it aside. "Let's sort this shit out," he grunted.

Thumper pulled the releases on the box's lid. The men worked quickly to pull the supplies out. Simon removed a large hard case from the equipment and set it atop the box. He opened it and removed the new SAM missile. After quickly checking it, he secured it in its rack inside the car. Simon leaped back to the box, the two men separated the replacement ammunition and other items from the fresh hydrogen batteries. Each battery was a flat black case, two feet wide by four feet long, with a built in handle on either end. Thumper and Simon laboriously moved them one at a time to the Nachtpanzer's rear.

Thumper ducked back inside the car. He knelt inside the cargo bay and pulled two recessed release handles in the cargo deck. Simon hit the car's rear armor with his fist. The edge of an access panel popped out. Simon yanked it down and open. Thumper helped him pull the expended batteries out of the power array. As they pulled each battery back, they paused to disconnect two electrical leads. They manhandled the six spent cells out and dumped them to the side.

I jumped as Stone fired the Carr. The machine gun spit red tracers across the airfield.

"Hurry up, you guys," Stone suggested.

Simon and Thumper struggled to load the fresh batteries into the car, pausing only long enough to reconnect the power leads to each one.

Stone walked in a tight circle around the car, pausing each few steps to fire off a short controlled burst into the darkness, then moving on. He loaded a fresh magazine into the gun. "We got incoming Zeds from every direction, Boss; I can only hold 'em for another minute or so!" He rattled off three short bursts and moved again.

Thumper and Simon heaved the last cell into the battery bay. Each man reconnected a power lead. Simon slammed the access panel shut and kicked it for good measure.

Thumper sprinted to the ammunition pile and began to throw 50 caliber ammo boxes through the open cargo door. Simon pushed me inside.

"Stone, Thumper, we're pulling out!" he shouted. He ducked

inside the car and slid into the driver's seat. The car's console lit up as he reenergized the electrical systems. The heads-up display sprang up, the power level display bars glowed green at full power. Simon engaged the drive wheels and depressed the accelerator. Thumper jumped into the cargo bay, an ammo box in each hand. Stone ran alongside, still firing the Carr. He jumped in, then stooped down and fired through the open door as Simon accelerated towards the gate. Thumper reached over him to hit the red button, closing the cargo door.

The Nachtpanzer sped out the broken gate and back onto the highway.

We rolled back down 54 and re-crossed the Missouri River. Simon turned onto Highway 50, and we left the scorched remains of Jefferson City behind us.

"We've got about three hours until dawn; we're really pushing it," Simon sighed. "I know you're not going to like it, but I think we should find a place to hole up for a while. We can't risk moving in daylight."

"But we could be in Kansas City by dawn," I countered.

"Yeah, but we still need to reach Lee's Summit and do the second battery change. I won't go into Kansas City without fresh batteries and a full load of ammo. There are going to be too many fucking zombies there to take that risk," Simon explained. "And you're assuming that we won't run into any trouble. That's not going to happen."

"What kind of trouble?" I asked pensively.

"I always trust my gut on these runs, Bishop, it's what keeps me alive," Simon continued. "Right now, my instincts are telling me to hunker down and lay low. I don't like that an Apache was this far inside, and I think the Feds are going to check it out pretty hard. They'll spot the wreckage, but they won't know exactly what happened. I want to be some place really secure right now, that's my gut feeling."

"You always go with your gut out here, Bishop," Stone chipped in. "It'll keep you alive."

I wasn't happy about stopping, but I couldn't help Natalie if we were dead.

"Okay," I relented.

Simon drove slowly west. I wasn't sure what he was looking for, but on the outskirts of the town of Avery, he came to a stop. A horrible crash had occurred here, and several cars were piled up around an overturned grain truck. The wreckage ran off the road on the right-hand side, into a stand of trees growing along the highway. Simon wedged the Nachtpanzer into the wreckage until he was partially under the canopy of the trees. He was careful to remain on the blacktop.

He shut almost everything down and stretched out in the seat.

"Bishop, I'm leaving the radio scanner on, you'll have to keep one ear open for any chatter. One of us will take over in a little while. Thumper, first watch," Simon said.

"Got it," Thumper replied. He sat back against the driver seat on the cargo deck. Stone drank bottled water and settled down in the cargo bay. Within minutes, he and Simon were asleep. I listened carefully to the scanner, but it didn't pick up anything near our location. All of the chatter was miles away, and came through dim and full of static. It grew very quiet inside the car. I realized that I was exhausted.

I stiffened as I heard a dull rapping on my side of the car.

"Thumper," I whispered.

"It's just a zombie," Thumper replied quietly. "Stay still."

The noise continued as the zombie worked its way down the side of the Nachtpanzer. Simon shifted in his seat.

"How long will it stay out there?" I asked.

"Fuck man, that thing will stay out there as long as we are here," Thumper laughed. "One time we got stuck in a huge pot hole, right in the middle of this little town called Warsaw I think. There must have been a thousand zombies outside the car, and we had to get outside to use the come-along if we were going to free the car. We shut everything down and tried to wait 'em out. We didn't make a fucking sound for three straight days, and they didn't leave. I guess they could smell us or something. Anyway, I just about went stir crazy. Finally, Simon said fuck it! We shot off everything we had and then went out guns blazing. Barely made it out. Those Zeds are patient mother fuckers."

That was the most Thumper had ever said to me. I pushed my

luck, "Thumper, I wanted …"

"Shut the fuck up, Bishop!" Thumper hissed. "The other two are trying to sleep."

I went back to listening to the scanner through a headset. I didn't hear anything unusual. Just about the time I couldn't keep my eyes open any longer, Simon poked me in the arm.

"I'll take over for a while, Bishop, just stretch out and go to sleep," he suggested.

Simon took the headset from me and cocked it on his head so that only one ear was covered. He opened a water bottle. I nodded to him; I was out as soon as I leaned back in the seat.

I woke up much later. I looked around; I couldn't remember where I was. There was a dim glow coming through the car's windows. I realized it was daylight outside. Simon was still wearing the headset; he seemed to be listening intently.

"How long did I sleep? What time is it?" I asked.

"It's six o'clock in the PM," he replied. "We'll roll out as soon as the sun sets, about another hour or so."

I yawned and stretched. I was ravenous. "Can I get a sandwich now?" I asked.

"Sure," Simon said. "Stone, get our boy Bishop some grub."

Stone rummaged around in a small locker in the cargo bay. He came forward with a pair of foil-wrapped sandwiches and a bottled water.

"Turkey and meatball, one each," he suggested, handing me the food and water.

"Thanks," I rejoined. I listened carefully as I ate. I could still hear a faint knocking noise. "Is our friend still out there?" I inquired.

"There are three of them now," Simon answered.

"They aren't very noisy," I retorted.

"Well between them, they only have two arms and one hand," Simon laughed. "We got lucky."

"Hey, Bishop," Stone began. "What do you call a zombie with one leg?"

"Come on, Stone," I shot back.

"Ilene, get it?" he laughed. "What do you call a zombie with no arms and no legs?"

"Matt," I answered. I had heard these jokes before.

"Nope," Stone replied. "Don't matter what you call him, he ain't comin." The gunner grinned from ear to ear. I couldn't help but laugh.

"Fuck, Stone, if I have to hear one more of your stupid jokes, I'm going to choke you out, I swear!" Thumper warned.

"Dude, you gotta' grow a sense of humor, relax, laugh every once in a while. I'm pretty sure you're gonna' stroke out before you get to retire," Stone laughed.

Thumper let out a long sigh and sadly shook his head, "Just cease with the bad jokes."

"Sure thing, big boy," Stone agreed with a grin.

"You two cool it," Simon interjected. "Let's just stay on task."

Thumper growled but relented.

"What do you guys normally do if you're stuck like this?" I asked.

"We don't normally get stuck, it's just in and out, like bad porn," Simon replied.

"I wish we had some porn," Stone said wistfully. "Why don't we put a DVR in this bastard?"

"Because you would do even less than you do now," Thumper answered.

"Hang on, be quiet!" Simon commanded. He had sat upright and put the headset over both ears. "I've got something," he whispered.

We all sat upright and held our breath. Simon listened intently. I noticed Stone stiffen, and then I dimly heard the noise too. A jet was passing overhead. I closed my eyes and waited, but nothing happened.

"I couldn't make out what he was up to," Simon said, cocking the earpiece up again. "But something weird is going on. That jet jockey reported that he was out of missiles. We're going to have to be extra careful the rest of the trip."

The minutes dragged by as the sun slowly set in the west. The windows gradually faded to black. Stone and Thumper argued about their preferred porn stars, each extolling their favorite actress' virtues over the others. I didn't join in, I didn't want their attention.

Finally, Simon handed me back the headset and energized the Nachtpanzer's systems. "Gentlemen, and Mr. Stone, we are rolling and underway," he intoned as he backed the car away from the wreckage. He pulled back onto 50 and accelerated towards Kansas City.

We had only covered about twenty miles when Simon began to curse. He brought the car to a violent stop and peered ahead at the heads-up display.

"What is it?" I asked.

"Those rotten mother fuckers," Simon rasped. "Pull up the GPS, Bishop. We have to go around."

"What is it, Boss?" Stone asked from the rear.

"Looks like the Feds are trying to throw up some obstacles for us," Simon replied. "They bombed the bridge over the river just ahead of us, pretty recently too or I wouldn't have caught it until we were in the drink. Some of the substructure is still burning. It showed up on the infrared."

"That's not good," Thumper suggested grimly.

"No, it's not," Simon agreed. "But I think they are just guessing someone is operating in this sector, so their blanketing the area, hoping to slow us down or stop us, hoping we'll fuck up and give them a shot. They don't know where we are yet."

"Maybe we should go to ground for a few days, until things blow over," Thumper suggested.

"We can't do that!" I countered.

"You're not crew," Thumper warned me. "You don't count for shit. Don't try to tell us what to do!"

"My daughter could die!" I added desperately.

"I'll make the decisions!" Simon cut in. "Both of you shut up." He stared us both down. "We roll and try to make it to make it to Lee's Summit. I know a place near there. If it is still hot that close to the KC, we'll drop off the radar for a while. Shit, if we come back without the scripts after all this trouble, Oksana will have a fucking cow. Bishop, I still need directions."

I nervously pulled up the GPS, and plotted an alternate route. "We just passed a road heading north. If we take it, there is a side road that leads to the Sedalia Airport. It has a bridge, unless they bombed it too," I explained.

"We won't know until we get there," Simon quipped. He spun the Nachtpanzer around and drove back the way we had come.

Simon turned onto the side road, and followed my directions. We were detouring about twelve miles out of our way to cross the river. Every extra mile was a drain on the batteries. I knew if the bridge was gone, we were in trouble. I crossed my fingers as we approached the river.

Simon slowed the car, and examined the heads-up display as we cautiously moved forward.

"It's there," he finally exclaimed.

We rolled across the Nadine River and headed west towards the airport.

Simon stared straight ahead, his eyes on the display. He lowered his voice and asked me quietly, "Is there any chance, any chance at all, that your friend Brad would sell you out?"

"No," I replied without thought.

"I've never had this much heat this far in," Simon stated flatly. "Something is up, and I don't like it at all. Someone may have talked. There is only one other explanation, and that's bad news for us too."

"What are you talking about?" I asked pensively.

"Survivalists; or you can call them rebels, even terrorists. Depends on whose side of the QZ you are on. I had heard rumors that survivors were banding together, forming independent military units, striking back at the Feds. There are tons of abandoned military assets lying around out here. I know for a fact that the government carried out preemptive strikes against all the nuclear missile silos inside the QZ. They also bombed all the airfields and communications equipment they could find."

"I knew the Feds were lying about survivors," I exclaimed.

"Yeah, well don't get so excited," Simon shot back. "They're bad news for us. Not only do they draw the Fed's attention, they're also blood-thirsty fuckers who'll shoot you on sight. They figure we're Feds, and they don't ask to make sure."

"How many can there be?" I asked.

"Who knows?" Simon replied. "Could be thousands of those fucks roaming around out there in the dark. Just one more thing to worry about."

We rolled past the airport without incident and turned south towards Sedalia. The GPS icon flashed on my screen as we approached the city. The highway led straight into the center of town, where it intersected with 50. Simon slowed the car as the roadway became more cluttered with abandoned vehicles.

"Something is up," Simon declared as we slowly proceeded. "Stone, get the 50 cal. up!" he ordered.

"What's wrong?" I asked.

"There aren't any zombies," he explained. "It's too fucking quiet here."

Stone opened the top hatch. He released the mini-gun and pushed it up into the gun turret.

Simon craned his head forward to stare at the display. He let the Nachtpanzer roll to a stop.

"I ain't believing this shit," he grunted. He flipped a switch on the control panel to illuminate the car's forward running lights. The low-power lights revealed a horror show.

The intersection with Highway 50 was completely filled with a mass of milling zombies. Thousands of the undead had converged on the center of the city. They filled the streets for blocks ahead of us, all pushing forward towards some unknown goal. Our lights attracted the Zeds closest to us. Dozens of them turned and began to shamble towards the car.

"Hold your fire," Simon said quietly. He killed the lights and put the car into reverse, backing away from the mass of undead.

I jumped as the scanner locked onto a radio signal. A frantic voice spoke into the headset, "Is someone out there? Please help us! We're inside the courthouse! Can you hear me?"

"Simon," I shouted. "There are survivors in there."

Simon snatched the headset and held it to his ear. We had backed several blocks away from the intersection. He brought the car to a stop.

"That's what they're after," Simon explained softly. "They must be the only survivors left in the entire town."

I turned on the CB radio and reached down to key the mic and respond. Simon slapped my hand away.

"Don't touch that microphone!" he hissed.

"What?" I responded.

Simon shook his head. "Damn it, Bishop, if you talk to those people, you will give away our position to the Feds. I don't want to hear their sob story anyway." He tossed the headset back to me. "We're not going to rescue them, don't even think about it."

"But there could be children trapped in there," I exclaimed.

"I don't care," Simon shot back. "Get this through that thick skull of yours, Bishop; we aren't the fucking good guys!"

"We could at least try to help them," I countered. I could still hear the voice pleading through the headset.

"Why don't we leave him here?" Thumper suggested. "Then he could help them all he wanted to."

Simon sighed loudly. "Every minute we spend not on mission, every risk we take, every round we fire off, that puts your kid, and all of us, in that much more danger. Is that what you want, Bishop? Do you want to risk your daughter's life trying to save people you've never even met?"

I hesitated. "I know you're right, it's just hard to turn your back on people begging for their lives..." I trailed off.

"Harden your heart, Bishop," Simon instructed me. "Get tough, or you'll never save your daughter."

Simon put the Nachtpanzer into gear. He turned away from the center of town, giving the zombies a wide berth. Stone lowered the mini-gun and closed the hatch. We rolled through the deserted streets until we had reached 50 again. Simon turned onto the highway and drove west, away from the doomed town of Sedalia. I listened to the pleas of the people we were abandoning until their voices faded away.

Sedalia - Missouri

The state highway was almost totally deserted and we made good time. Simon slowed the car as we reached Whiteman Air Force Base. The military had constructed a hardened road block at the turn off to the base, and a wedge of abandoned vehicles almost entirely blocked the road from side to side. A narrow lane was still open from where we had stopped through to the other side. Someone had used the road before us.

Simon considered the situation. He slowly threaded the Nachtpanzer through the slot in junkyard before us. We reached the far side with just a few scrapes and dings.

Simon accelerated to forty-five miles an hour, the highway lay open before us, and we had places to be.

I listened to the scanner carefully as Simon drove. I heard occasional chatter, all of it many miles away and faint with static. The radar was a silent green glow, no aggressor rose up to bar our passage. The miles flew by beneath the Nachtpanzer's oversized wheels. I glanced over at the power display bars. They had all gone over to amber and red, no green remained.

"How far to the Blackwater?" Simon asked me.

I pulled up our icon on the GPS map. "Just three miles or so," I replied.

"Awesome," Simon rejoined. "This will make or break us."

He slowed the car down to thirty, then to twenty miles per hour. Finally, we were creeping along the highway. The road climbed a small hill and then fell away towards the Blackwater River. Simon slowly rolled forward until the Nachtpanzer's wheels were at the approach to the bridge.

Broken concrete pillars stuck up from the swirling water below us, the bridge was gone.

All of us crowded forward to look at the GPS display. Simon grimly ran our options. Once again, we would be forced to detour miles away from Highway 50 to cross a river.

"The Nachtpanzer isn't going to make it to Lee's Summit," he concluded.

Thumper cursed, even Stone looked unhappy. I was crushed.

"What do we do?" I asked dejectedly.

"We'll drive the car until the batteries give out; we have to get as close to Lee's Summit as we possibly can. We can't move the car once the batteries go, so we'll have to hoof it to the resupply and bring the fresh batteries back to the car," he concluded.

"Fuck me," Thumper groaned.

"I figured you'd like that one," Simon laughed.

"Is that our only option?" I asked.

"Yeah," Simon replied.

"Fuck man, I love it!" Stone said excitedly. "And here I thought this trip was going to be boring."

Simon backtracked to the south and west on side roads until we found an intact bridge. We traveled another ten miles out of our way before we regained Highway 50. We were so close. Natalie was only about thirty miles away, but if the car was dead, all of our efforts would be in vain. Simon turned onto the highway, and once again, we were on our way. He turned off everything but the drive and the heads-up display to conserve energy. I glanced over at the power display bars; they were all thin red lines, barely visible against the black. I said a silent prayer that we would reach the airport, but we didn't.

We made another twenty-seven miles before the car finally gave up the ghost. Everything went dead suddenly, and the car's interior was plunged into complete darkness. Simon smoothly brought the Nachtpanzer to a stop on the shoulder.

He broke out a glow stick and activated it.

"End of the line," he said.

In the dim green glow, we geared up for the walk. Stone took down the Carr and an ammunition rucksack. He loaded the machinegun and checked the action. Finally, he pulled on the night vision goggles and adjusted them. Thumper heaved on the emergency supply pack and picked up the assault shotgun. He racked in a round.

Simon pulled a Scorpion sub-machine pistol and shoulder harness out from under the driver's seat. He slipped on the harness and secured several spare magazines into a belt pouch. He checked the magazine in his gun and slid it back into the holster.

"I didn't know you had that," I observed.

"That's okay, I didn't want you to," Simon responded.

"Don't I get a gun?" I asked.

"Sure," Simon answered. "Here you go." He pushed the SAM into my hands. "Carry that big bastard. Do not try to shoot it at any zombies."

"Great," I replied. I slung it over my shoulder.

Thumper manually pulled the cargo door open. We stepped out into the darkness. The air was cool and I could hear insects in the undergrowth. Thumper pushed the door closed until only a crack remained.

"Let's go ahead and remove the dead cells," Simon suggested. "We may be in a hurry on the trip back."

Thumper and Simon quickly removed the dead batteries, tossing them unceremoniously to the side one by one. Stone stood guard by the car while I watched the road.

Once they were done, we all stepped onto the roadway. Simon ordered Stone to lead the way.

"How far is it?" I asked.

"Three miles, more or less," Simon replied.

I groaned at the thought of walking that far.

"You're gonna' love the trip back," Simon added sadistically.

We started walking towards the airport. I looked back once, but the darkness had swallowed up the car. I hoped I would see it again. I had never considered that I might end up walking down a dark road in the middle of a zombie-infested wasteland. I tried to think about my daughter.

We walked along in silence. Stone took point; he walked a short distance ahead of us. Simon and I were together, and Thumper brought up the rear, a short distance behind us. We stayed on the asphalt; it gave us a clear field of vision, lessening the chances that we would blunder into any zombies. We left Highway 50 at the first side road traveling north. The closer we got to the airport, the thicker the Zeds would become. Simon had decided to bypass the town of Lee's Summit completely, traveling around it to the northeast. It would be suicide to try to walk through the urban areas. Of course, this added a full mile to our walk, but we had little choice.

Simon set a pretty brisk pace; I started having trouble keeping up. I never walked anywhere if I could help it.

"Come on, Bishop," Simon urged as I faltered. "We have to get there and get the batteries back well before dawn."

"How will we get the batteries back?" I asked. I picked up my pace a little.

"I'll figure out something, I always do," Simon countered.

We plodded on through the darkness. I did my best to match

Simon's pace. I tried to man up. I didn't bitch about the pain in my legs, or how tired I was. We began to pass abandoned cars, some in the roadway, more along the median and the roadsides. We encountered no zombies for the first two miles, but finally, our luck ran out. Stone rushed back to us and motioned us off the road. We huddled near a wrecked cargo van, and talked in whispers.

"There is a service station on the right-hand side. I counted five of them just ahead of us, could be more," Stone whispered. "We could probably sneak around if we went deep on the left."

"No good," Simon replied. "We have to come back this way. We need to clear everything between us and the airport."

"Are you sure there's just the five?" Thumper asked.

"I counted five," Stone answered. "Couldn't swear to it." He stood up and scanned the road ahead.

"Find me the tire tool," Thumper suggested, pointing to the cargo van.

"Five is pushing it," Simon rejoined.

"You guys lead them past me here. I'll get behind them and take 'em out one by one," Thumper explained. "Stone can cover me."

Simon considered it.

"Why can't we just shoot them?" I asked.

"Zombies are attracted to gunfire," Simon responded in a very annoyed whisper. "I keep forgetting how stupid you are, Bishop, damn. It could draw in hundreds of them."

Stone giggled quietly. "Why don't you just shoot them with the SAM, Bishop?"

I was not amused. "Why don't you guys have silencers on your guns or something?"

They stopped laughing. "That's my fault," Simon admitted. "We never leave the car; I didn't think we would need them. We are always trying to figure out ways to cut back on weight," he added remorsefully.

"I've always said we should have silencers," Thumper added.

"Silencers are for pussies!" Stone countered. He rummaged through the rear of the van and handed Thumper a steel tire tool. "Here you go, Thumper, show Bishop here how you got your nickname."

Thumper took the tire tool. He hefted it in his hand, checking its weight. He pulled out a bandana and covered his face, and finally removed a pair of clear safety glasses from his jacket pocket and put them on. He slid underneath the van's rear wheels.

"I'm ready," he whispered.

Stone stood to one side, the Carr at the ready. I stood behind Simon. He whistled loudly and shouted, "Come and get it, you ugly fuckers!"

The zombies staggered up the road, towards us. We slowly backed away, drawing them with us, past Thumper's position. Simon taunted them, keeping their attention, leading them along. They couldn't move very fast, we were in no danger. I didn't see any of the action, but suddenly, the closest zombie buckled, it was as if someone had cut its strings. It collapsed lifelessly forward, its skull crushed. Thumper was standing directly behind it. He cast aside the bloody tire tool and carefully removed his glasses and bandana. He shoved them into a pocket.

Stone scanned the road. When he was sure it was clear, he pulled a water bottle from his pack. He slowly poured it out over Thumper's hands to remove any blood splatter. Thumper shook his hands dry.

"Let's roll," Simon suggested. We resumed our walk.

We were now moving away from Lee's Summit into a more rural area. Empty fields stretched away from on all sides of the road. The airport was directly northwest of us. After we had covered about a mile, the road turned sharply away to the west. Simon led us off the asphalt and into a hayfield.

"We just need to keep walking roughly north and we'll hit the airport's perimeter fence," Simon said.

Stone led us forward. The hay was about knee high, it made me very nervous to walk across the field. I kept expecting a zombie to pop up at any moment. I jerked around at every noise.

"Settle down, Bishop," Simon finally rumbled.

"What if there's a zombie hiding out here?" I asked.

"They're not that smart," he countered.

"There could be a zombie with no legs crawling around out here," Thumper suggested. "I've seen a lot of those. We call 'em crawlers. They pull themselves along by their hands and arms.

Usually, their guts get ripped out by rocks and shit. They're nasty. They trip you up and crawl on top of you. It's some fucked up shit, I'll tell ya."

"He's just messing with me, right?" I asked Simon.

"No, that's true. I've seen some of those myself. They can be more dangerous than the walking ones. You don't see them until you are right on them," he explained.

"Fuck." I shuddered.

"But you're right, he is messing with you," Simon explained. "The odds of you stepping on a crawler out here are pretty slim, unless we find an unfortunate redneck."

"Hey, Bishop, I think I hear banjos," Thumper laughed evilly.

I kept on walking, but I was a little more careful about where I stepped. The ground was fairly even, but I occasionally stumbled. Stone led us onward through the field. He was an indistinct blob of darkness against a black backdrop that I strained my eyes to follow. There was no moon, and it was pitch dark. There were no more artificial lights in this part of the world, the power had been out for a long time. The stars seemed unnaturally bright without them. On the ground from horizon to horizon, all was darkness. Even so, I was amazed at how well I could actually see. I had never walked this far at night before.

We finally reached the airport's security fence. Stone turned and led us west along the perimeter. After fifteen minutes of walking, we stopped. Stone handed the night vision goggles to Simon; he used them to study the flight line. He quietly pointed out the strobe light to Thumper and me. It was several hundred yards away, beyond the fence.

We were directly opposite the control tower. The resupply pilot had dropped our package directly on the main runway, fairly close to the hangers and the tower.

"Damn, damn, double damn," Simon cursed.

"What is it?" I asked, not wanting to hear the answer.

"Zombies," Simon replied. "Lots and lots of them."

He handed the goggles off to Thumper. "Bad mojo, motherfucker," he cursed, scanning the goggles back and forth.

I couldn't see shit.

"What's the plan?" Stone asked.

Thumper finally handed the goggles to me. I held them to my face and blinked my eyes. Everything was a dim green glow, filled with large black shadowy shapes, and smaller blobs of blackness that wandered slowly back and forth beyond the fence. I realized they were the zombies. There were a lot of them. Stone took the goggles away from me.

"First, we cut away the fence here," Simon instructed. "Stone, you and Thumper go hard left a ways and start shooting; draw as many as you can away from the drop box. Bishop and I will get out the batteries. We need about five minutes, no more. Draw the Zeds as far west as you can, then ditch them and haul ass back to the fence here."

Thumper pulled out the wire cutters from the supply bag. He carefully cut away the fence while Simon held it to prevent any unwanted noise. Stone scanned the field, to make sure we were still unnoticed.

Thumper and Simon cautiously carried away the cut fence section, laying it in the tall grass behind us. We entered the airport. Simon pushed Stone and Thumper away. They disappeared into the darkness. He motioned for me to kneel down beside him. We waited.

I jumped as the shotgun went off. The blast was as loud as cannon fire in the stillness. It fired twice more and then the staccato shots of the Carr firing at full auto reached our ears. I could make out the tracers far away across the field.

"That's us," Simon whispered.

He held onto my jacket, leading me at a flat run across the tarmac. We reached the hangers and flattened out against a corrugated steel wall.

"What are we doing?" I gasped.

"We need a trailer," he whispered.

He led me quickly from hanger to hanger, with no luck. Finally, he turned and moved onto the runway. We stumbled into an electric cart and baggage train in the darkness.

Simon slid into driver's seat and tried to engage the cart. It lurched feebly forward and stalled. He jumped out and quickly worked to disconnect the rearmost trailer.

"Throw the luggage out!" he urged me. I worked feverishly to tumble the bags and suitcases out of the thin-walled cart. I could still hear gunfire, but each bag seemed to be unnaturally loud as they hit the tarmac. I tried to work quietly but quickly. Finally, Simon grabbed me and directed me to the rear.

"Push for all you're worth," he hissed in my ear.

He grabbed the cart's tongue and directed it across the field back towards the strobe light. I pushed as hard as I could. The small cart picked up speed. We crashed into the drop box, almost overturning the trailer.

"Get over here," Simon ordered me. He threw the latches on the drop box. I staggered over to help him.

"Grab the handle and lift," he instructed me. I seized the handle of the first battery and heaved it out of the box. The cell was incredibly heavy. My end sagged dangerously; I grunted with the effort. Simon pulled me across to the trailer, and we shoved the battery into the small cart's interior.

Simon grabbed me by my arm and pushed me back to the trailer. He held me upright and spat into my face, "Do this, Bishop! Don't think, just do it!"

We grabbed each battery and manhandled them across to the trailer, shoving them in two deep. My arms gave out completely; I moved the batteries with sheer adrenaline. Abruptly, I realized the gunfire had stopped, I wasn't sure how long ago. I knew the zombies were moving towards us through the darkness. As I heaved the last battery into the trailer, a terrible pain shot through my right shoulder, and I felt something rip. I had torn a ligament or worse; I couldn't move my arm.

Simon grabbed the trailer's tongue and pulled, guiding the cart towards the fence.

"Push!" he screamed. I threw my good shoulder into the trailer's frame and pushed with all my might. The cart rattled across the tarmac.

Suddenly, Stone and Thumper rushed out of the darkness and grabbed the trailer. We pushed it through the hole in the fence and bumped it away into the darkness.

The trip pushing that damn luggage cart across that hay field was the worst thing I had ever endured. The trailer was damn heavy, and it seemed to have a mind of its own. The front wheels kept dropping into holes we couldn't see. The trailer would come to a complete stop, and then it would take everything we had to get it rolling again. I kept banging my injured shoulder against it. Everyone was exhausted before we were even half way across.

The damn zombies from the airport followed us all the way across the field. Every time we stopped, Stone would have to fire back at the closest Zeds to keep them from catching up to us. For every one he shot, there were two further back. We left a trail of bodies across the field from the airport all the way back to the road.

Simon kept on pushing us, he just wouldn't let us quit. Finally, the trailer rolled over one final furrow and back onto the asphalt. We all let it roll to a stop by mutual consent. Stone lay in a prone position and fired back into the field behind us, killing each zombie that approached with a head shot until we had caught our breath. He shot through a thirty-round magazine before Simon decided we had rested long enough. The zombies were just going to keep on coming.

"On your feet, losers," he commanded. He grabbed the tongue and began to pull the trailer back down the road. I staggered against it and began to push. It was much easier to move on the asphalt. With Thumper's help, we could push the cart down the road without too much effort. Stone took up the rear, he stopped occasionally to fire back into the horde of undead that was following us along the road. I knew that he had to be almost out of ammo.

We pushed the trailer through the darkness as quickly as we could; Simon kept it on the pavement. Through a haze of exhaustion, I noticed we were passing abandoned cars along the median again. We had almost reached the service station.

Suddenly, the cart jerked to the left and rolled off the road. I bumped painfully into it and bounced off again.

"Zeds. Twelve o'clock!" Thumper screamed.

We had wandered into the midst of a large group of zombies moving towards us on the road, drawn by our gunfire. It was pure chaos, every man for himself.

Simon had dropped the trailer's tongue as soon as he realized what had happened. He snapped a glow stick and tossed it in the roadway, illuminating his targets. Before the zombies were upon him, he pulled his Scorpion and fired off short, controlled bursts into the undead around him at point-blank range. The small sub-machine pistol made a snarling, ripping noise with each squeeze of the trigger. I could see the gun's muzzle flash, and for a split second the distorted faces of the zombies as he shot them. He stalked calmly among the approaching undead, taking the fight to them one by one.

Thumper put his back to the trailer. He alternated shooting the twelve-gauge shotgun at the Zeds with savage butt strokes, dispatching anything that reached for him out of the darkness. He slammed in fresh shells between shots. A pile of broken, twitching, headless bodies grew in a gore-splattered semi-circle around him.

I didn't have a gun, so I squeezed under the trailer. I panicked for a moment as the SAM's shoulder strap hung on the trailer; I thought a zombie had me.

Stone knelt in the roadway at the rear of the trailer. He loaded his last full magazine into the Carr and switched to semi-automatic fire. By far most of the zombies were still behind us. They had followed us from the airport. They staggered up the road in quickly growing numbers; more were approaching every moment we remained stopped on the road in combat. Stone fired round after round into the approaching mob of undead. Each shot took a zombie through the brain. They fell one by one, but more came forward, walking over their own dead. The bolt locked back on the smoking machinegun, it was empty. Stone calmly loaded a partial magazine and released the bolt. He clambered onto the trailer and took careful aim.

"Bishop, get your ass up here!" he shouted.

"No way!" I screamed back over the constant gunfire.

"Give me the fucking SAM or we're all gonna' die!" he bellowed.

I pulled myself out from under the trailer. I pushed the SAM up towards him. A zombie grabbed me by my injured arm and snapped at my shoulder.

"Stone!" I screamed. "Help me!"

Stone took careful aim at a sedan wrecked two hundred feet

away. He squeezed off shot after shot into its gas tank. Zombie after zombie staggered past it.

"Come on, you motherfucker, blow!" he screamed.

Gas flowed from the perforated gas tank onto the blacktop. The zombies sloshed through it. Stone fired the Carr lower into the car's steel frame. A bullet sparked against the rear wheel's shock tower.

The sedan blew up. It rose on a curtain of fire, and crashed back onto the roadway, upside down and awash in flames. A handful of zombies were crushed or crippled by the explosion, but several zombies staggered through the flaming wreckage, and more came on behind them.

I struggled with the zombie who had me. She had been a teen-age girl in life, now pus ran from her rotting eye sockets, and her blackened teeth ripped at my sleeve. I pinned her against the trailer.

"Stone!" I screamed again. He finally looked over the edge. He pushed the Carr's barrel against her forehead and pulled the trigger. The Zed jerked violently as her brains blew out. Her grip on my jacket slowly loosened as she slid to the ground.

"The SAM, Bishop! Now!" he screamed.

I numbly pushed the missile up to him. He snatched it up and rose to a standing position. Stone locked the firing tube back and engaged the heat seeker. He pulled the trigger. The SAM flashed to the burning car and exploded almost instantly.

The heat-seeking ground-to-air missile evaporated everything around it in a two-hundred-foot diameter circle of fire and utter destruction.

I was thrown to the ground; everyone was. Stone was flung off the trailer like a rag doll. He landed hard on the blacktop, his jacket and hair smoldering. The trailer rolled towards him and stopped. Pieces of flaming asphalt and body parts rained down from the sky.

Simon limped towards me. "Get up and push, Bishop!" he shouted.

He and Thumper lifted Stone onto the trailer. He pointed towards the cart.

"Let's get the fuck out of here," he commanded.

I walked behind the trailer and started to push. We rolled around the scattered bodies that littered the roadway, away from the flames and back into the darkness.

I pushed against the trailer forever. I was numb. I wasn't thinking about Natalie anymore, I wasn't thinking about anything. I was just pushing, running on fumes and pure animal instinct.

"Bishop!" Simon yelled into my face. He shook me violently. "We're here, stop pushing the mother-fucking trailer!" I sank down to my knees and fell over into a fetal position. Everything hurt; my arm was a screaming mass of pain.

Simon and Thumper slowly loaded the fresh hydrogen cells into the battery bay. They reconnected the leads and slammed the access door shut.

Thumper painfully pulled the cargo door open. He and Simon carefully carried Stone inside and stretched him out upon the floor. I stumbled upright and crawled into the navigator's seat. Simon slid into the driver's seat and engaged the Nachtpanzer's electrical systems. The car's control panel lit up like a Christmas tree. Thumper slammed the red button on the cargo door's bulkhead. The door slid shut, sealing out the world outside. I sobbed in relief; tears ran freely down my face.

Simon looked over at me and shook his head. "Pussy," he laughed.

We moved back into the cargo bay to check on Stone. Thumper carefully peeled his burnt jacket away from his torso. The clothing and skin beneath was dirty but unharmed. Stone's face was red and blistered. His eyebrows and most of his hair had been burned away. Simon broke out the first-aid kit. He applied burn ointment to Stone's face and hands.

Stone stirred and opened his eyes. He struggled to sit upright, Simon helped him.

"Water," he croaked. Thumper brought him a bottle. He slowly sipped it.

"Does it hurt?" I asked him.

"What?" Stone replied.

"Oh, you'll know after a while," Simon replied. He handed him four painkillers. "Take these or you'll wish you were dead," he suggested.

Stone swallowed them. He looked up. "Did you guys see that

shit?" he whispered hoarsely. "That was the craziest shit I ever pulled."

"Yeah, you saved our asses, just like always," Simon responded. "Take it easy for a while, or you won't be able to pull gunner duty."

"Sure," Stone replied. He slid back against the navigator seat and closed his eyes. "I'll just stay here; wake me up if you need me..." he trailed off.

Simon climbed back into the driver's seat. He looked over the gauges and controls.

"We are at full batteries and ammo." He looked at the car's clock. "It's about two hours until dawn. We will rest here until just before sun-up and then we'll go into Kansas City."

He looked over at me. "We'll go get Natalie, and then we'll get the scripts."

Outside Kansas City- Missouri

I dozed off and on for a few minutes at a time; then Simon shook me fully awake.

"It's time," he said.

"Wake up, sleeping beauty," he instructed Thumper. The loader leaned down and shook Stone awake.

Stone sat upright, tears in his bloodshot eyes. "I need more painkillers," he groaned.

"Not yet," Simon replied. "I need you on the clock."

Stone struggled to his feet. Thumper handed him a cup of coffee, he also bought one forward for me.

Simon turned to look at us. "We're only about ten miles from the Kansas City Zoo; I'm going to time this so that we get there with a little light. We need to find Bishop's daughter and then get to safety fast, before the sun is fully up. We've got a really narrow window, so don't fuck it up."

He pulled the Nachtpanzer back onto the highway and accelerated towards town.

The highway quickly brought us into the outskirts of Raystown. I had brought Natalie here Christmas shopping when she was a little girl. Things had taken a drastic turn for the worse since then. The area looked like a battle zone. The streets were still crowded, but no one was shopping here anymore.

There were zombies here, substantially more than we had seen before. The streets were full of them. They were crushed against the Nachtpanzer's front armor like bugs on a car windshield. Simon held the car at thirty miles an hour, weaving dangerously around the multitude of abandoned vehicles littering the road.

"Something weird is going on here, Bishop," he complained. "I've never seen this many Zeds in one place. If I stop the car, we might not be able to get clear again."

Highway 53 was a disaster zone. Simon was hitting zombies faster than I could count. Their bodies thumped against the car like fat raindrops in a summer storm.

I looked down at the GPS map. We were only three miles from the zoo.

"Turn left on 63rd Street. We are almost there," I urged.

Simon turned the car onto the crowded roadway. We took the corner too fast and the Nachtpanzer slid across the blacktop, crushing a dozen zombies and clipping a wrecked car.

"Fuck," Simon spit through clenched teeth. He accelerated through a knot of zombies and then we were almost in the clear. For a moment, the rhythmic thumping abated. Simon took advantage of the situation. The Nachtpanzer sped down the almost-deserted street. We covered two miles before Simon began to slow the car.

"Why are you stopping?" I asked.

"Because of them," he answered.

The Nachtpanzer rolled to a complete stop. Directly before us, the roadway was entirely blocked. We had timed our arrival almost perfectly. The sun was just coming up over the buildings. It illuminated the horrific scene with a lurid, bloody red light. It was as if we had died and our souls were coming before the gates of Hell, to take our places at the end of the line.

"What the fuck?" Stone asked in awe.

The four-lane highway before us was completely filled with zombies, as far as we could see. They pushed against each other, a massive undead mob, all trying to reach the gates of the zoo. With growing horror, I realized why. They were all trying to reach my daughter. They were there to kill my little girl.

"Simon, we can't go in there," Thumper warned. "There's too many of those mother-fuckers, even for us!"

"For once, I have to agree," Stone whispered.

"Hang on," Simon growled. "We've gone too far to stop now."

He punched the accelerator down hard. The Nachtpanzer responded, lunging forward like a hungry animal. Simon punched the overhead rocker switches; three overlapping target cursors, two red and one orange, appeared on the heads-up display, locking onto the surging mass of zombies before us.

"Simon, what the fuck are you doing?" Thumper shouted.

With a metallic click, the forward mini-guns rolled out of their interior storage slots and dropped into their firing positions on either side of the car. Simultaneously, the missile rack popped up from the car's roofline.

"Oh shit!" Stone screamed. He scrambled to hold onto the gun seat. Thumper cursed and braced himself against the cargo doorway.

Simon rocked the car back and forth, picking off the outlying stragglers. The distance closed within seconds. The Nachtpanzer erupted in smoke and gunfire as Simon depressed both the firing buttons. The mini-guns spat a twin stream of destruction, shredding the tightly packed zombies into quivering, gory chunks. The nearest zombies were cut in half at the waist, their torsos literally disintegrated, leaving behind a hideous blanket of twitching, severed legs, arms, and heads, all coated in a mass of blackened, bloody gore.

With a screaming whoosh, the rockets deployed in rapid succession; slamming into the mass of Zeds at almost point-blank range. The Nachtpanzer rocked with each explosion, and huge smoking holes appeared in the zombie's ranks, as the high explosive rockets eviscerated the undead. Dripping chunks of rotted body parts and black blood rained down upon the car as it surged through the crowd. The roadway was a carpet of shredded, broken limbs, grey and green intestines and dismembered, shattered corpses.

"Hang on, you bastards!" Simon screamed.

The Nachtpanzer sped through the hole its guns created, only the car's forward momentum carried it through. The big car's wheels spun wildly until Simon eased off the accelerator, there was no traction. The car slid to a stop against the zoo's front gate, crushing the last few upright zombies and breaking the gates open with a horrific crash.

Simon mashed the accelerator down again. The car slid forward by inches until its blood-slicked wheels found the pavement. With a neck-breaking lurch, the gore-splattered car shot forward, through the gates and the Zeds, and into the zoo.

The still spinning empty mini-guns snapped back into the car, and the rocket launcher retracted.

Thousands of zombies poured through the broken gates behind us.

Simon drove the car along the zoo's walkways, the big vehicle barely fit between the animal cages to either side.

"Talk to me, Bishop," Simon demanded. "Where am I going?"

I had pulled up a map of the zoo on the car's computer screen. I used it as a guide.

"Left up ahead past the bird exhibit, then straight on to the Reptile House," I replied.

I was playing out my hunch; if I was wrong, Natalie would die.

"That's it!" I yelled joyously, pointing to the Reptile House. Simon brought the car to a stop as he turned it to face the direction we had come. He slid out of the driver's seat and slammed the cargo door button.

"Stone, man the 50. We'll have company in just a minute or so," he commanded. "Come on you two!" he yelled to Thumper and me.

Thumper grabbed the shotgun; Simon stepped out and threw the bolt on his Scorpion.

I stepped out of the car and approached the door to the Reptile House. I slowed on the steps and hesitantly reached out to grasp the door handle.

"Come on, Bishop!" Simon growled. "What are you waiting for?" he asked.

"What if I'm wrong?" I answered. "What if we're too late?"

"One more minute and we will be too late," he replied roughly. He shoved me aside and pushed the door open. Thumper covered him. The inside was clear, we ducked inside.

I quickly walked through the building, stopping short halfway through at the turtle display. At first, I didn't recognize her, and then when I did, I was sure that she was dead. My daughter lay on the floor next to a skinny kid in a wheelchair. Both of them were emaciated and filthy.

"Natalie!" I choked out in grief. I took two steps forward.

My daughter opened her eyes and slowly sat up. "Daddy?" she groaned.

I rushed to her and crushed her in my arms, and then I relaxed and rocked her back and forth.

"I knew you'd come," she whispered. "See Nicky, I told you so."

I looked over at the kid in the wheelchair. He was smiling, but there were tears in his eyes.

"Dad, that's my friend Nicky, he sent you the message," she explained.

I grasped his hand. "Thank you," I sobbed.

"Hate to break this up, but we've gotta' roll," Simon said, pulling me to my feet.

I helped Natalie walk slowly outside, the others followed.

Stone yelled down to us as we emerged from the building, "Hurry up, they're coming!"

"Get her in the car, Bishop!" Simon ordered.

"Wait, what about Nicky?" Natalie cried.

I turned to look at Simon in dread. "You can't leave him!" I implored.

Nicky painfully followed us out in his wheelchair, he stopped at the stairs.

"You know the deal, Bishop," Simon retorted. "You, your daughter, and the drugs. That is it, end of story. You'd better go back inside, kid."

Natalie struggled feebly in my arms. She reached out for her friend.

I stood my ground. "You bastards, you're not leaving a crippled kid here, I won't..."

Thumper's shotgun went off with a deafening roar. Nicky's head lolled over to one side, and he slowly crumpled forward, a shocked look on his blood-spattered face. I turned in horror to look at

Thumper as he racked in another shell and lowered the smoking gun. Natalie screamed and fainted in my arms.

"I wasn't going to leave the kid for the Zeds," Thumper stated defensively.

At that moment, I wasn't sure what to do. Simon pushed me and my daughter physically into the car. Thumper followed us and shut the cargo door.

I lay my daughter carefully on the floor and wrapped her in my jacket. I looked around at the crew in horror and confusion. I felt numb.

Simon slid into the driver's seat and engaged the car's controls.

Stone dropped back into the cargo compartment and shut the upper hatch as Simon pulled away. The Nachtpanzer accelerated into the wave of zombies coming down the path; it jostled and bounced as it crushed its way back through.

"Get back on station, Bishop!" Simon shouted. "We're not out of this yet!"

"I'm not leaving my daughter back here with this murderer," I shouted back.

"Fuck you, Bishop!" Thumper growled.

"What the Hell is going on?" Stone asked.

"Thumper shot a helpless kid in a wheelchair back there," I shouted.

"Dude, you shot a kid in a wheelchair?" Stone questioned. "That is harsh."

"Would you two rather that I'd left him for the Zeds?" he snarled at us. "I did the kid a favor. We weren't taking him out with us!"

Simon shouted back to me, "Damn it, Bishop, nobody is going to hurt your kid! You've got my word. I need you back up here, now!"

I hesitated for a few seconds, and then I moved forward and sat down in the Navigator's seat. "This is shit," I complained.

Simon crushed the last zombies between us and the gate. We turned back onto the main road and sped away from the horrors of the zoo. I looked back at my daughter, and then looked ahead. The sun was climbing into the sky.

"Time to hide," Simon declared.

We fled at high speed down 435. Simon drove at break-neck

velocity, swerving around wrecks and debris in the roadway. As we left the Kansas City Zoo behind, there were fewer zombies, but we were now more exposed to the Feds. I could tell that Simon was ill at ease; I too felt very vulnerable in broad daylight.

After a few minutes, Simon slowed the car and turned onto a side road leading into a residential area. He quickly found a house with an empty carport and pulled into the drive. The Nachtpanzer scraped against the carport's metal support posts as Simon wedged it into place. He sighed loudly and shut down the car's electrical systems.

Simon turned to look at me. "Are we going to have a problem, Bishop?" he asked pensively.

I looked back at my sleeping daughter and then replied carefully, "I know my kid, it was a mistake to kill her friend, not to mention a generally fucked up thing to do."

Simon raised his hand before Thumper could reply to my taunt. "It's done. Our deal isn't open to renegotiation. You knew the score before we came in here. You need to forget about that dead kid and focus on the one we did rescue, do you understand me? We still have half this trip to go, and if you keep stirring up shit, something bad will happen."

He paused to look back at Natalie. "Your kid is extremely malnourished, she needs medical attention. I suggest that you help us get the drugs so we can get the fuck back home as quickly as possible."

I didn't respond; I simply nodded. I was in a bad situation, and I knew it. I didn't know what these guys would do once I took them to the scripts. I also realized that Simon was correct. These bloodthirsty bastards were my only option, and I needed to get Natalie out of the QZ quickly.

"We have to stay put for the rest of the day," Simon explained. "I want Stone to check Natalie out and hook her up to an IV. We can give her some nutrients and a mild sedative." He looked directly into my eyes. "She needs to rest, we all do."

I nodded my acquiescence. Stone rummaged through a storage locker. He removed a medical kit and produced a syringe.

I slid into the cargo bay and stood protectively over my daughter.

"Relax," Simon spoke softly. "Stone is an EMT; he's got plenty of combat experience."

Stone knelt down beside Natalie. He gently turned her arm over and slowly inserted the needle. She groaned softly but didn't awaken. He hung a small saline bag from the bulkhead and inserted an IV into Natalie's arm. Once he finished, he tucked her back under my jacket. "Sit down for a while, asshole," he suggested.

I sat down on the cargo deck. Stone laid Natalie's head in my lap.

"She's a tough kid," he said respectfully. "You sure she's yours?"

"Yeah, she's mine," I laughed.

"Everybody rack out for a few," Simon ordered. "I'll take the first watch."

I stroked my daughter's filthy hair. I closed my eyes. I was exhausted, but for the first time in a long time, I was happy. We were safe for the moment, and I had my daughter back.

Off Highway 435

Thumper kicked me awake much later. I had slept through the entire day.

"Simon needs you up front," he grunted.

I gently shifted Natalie's head off my leg and painfully moved forward to the navigator's seat. Simon had energized the car's systems. He had the scanner's headset half-cocked over one ear.

"It's almost dark," Simon said. "I need to know where we are going."

I yawned and replied, "Can I at least get some coffee?"

"Thumper," Simon ordered. The loader growled but quickly brought me a cup of strong black coffee.

I pulled up the GPS system and punched in the address. We were only seven miles away.

"Follow 71 south," I muttered. "The warehouse is in Overland Park."

I had played my hand, and thrown in my last ace. I waited for the crew to shoot me, or worse.

I flinched as Simon handed me the headset.

"Stay sharp," he instructed me. "We had some chatter while you were asleep."

He activated the drive system and pulled the Nachtpanzer out from under the carport, and back onto the roadway. He maneuvered back through the subdivision and left onto Highway 71. We accelerated and drove south.

I followed our icon on the map. "Turn right onto Bannister Road, it's the next exit," I said.

Simon followed the exit and drove onto Bannister. The road was crowded with wrecks and abandoned vehicles. Zombies wandered the road in great profusion. Simon slowed the Nachtpanzer, and we immediately began to hit them as they moved to intercept us.

"This ain't gonna' be no picnic," Simon growled. "If these bastard Zeds are this thick at the target, we are going to have ourselves a serious problem."

He maneuvered the big car back and forth, avoiding the worst of the wreckage blocking our passage. The car bumped up and down as we crushed the zombies in our path.

"Talk to me, Bishop," Simon grunted.

"Turn left on Bunsen Way," I instructed him. "We're entering Overland Park."

Simon turned the car onto Bunsen. The zombies were just as numerous on the smaller side road. We entered an industrial park; large commercial buildings flanked us on either side.

"Wheeler's Pharmaceutical warehouse is the fifth building on your right," I droned in dread.

Simon turned the Nachtpanzer into the warehouse's parking lot.

"Stone, get the mini-gun up," Simon yelled back to the cargo bay. "Thumper, be ready!"

Stone released the mini-gun and opened the turret hatch. He pushed the gun up and climbed into the gunner's seat. Thumper slung the shotgun over his shoulder and stood by at the cargo door.

The pharmaceutical building was huge. Abandoned cars filled the parking lot. We drove around them to the building's rear loading docks. A few semi-trucks and trailers were still parked there. Dozens of zombies wandered the immediate area. They began to converge on us immediately as Simon slowed the car. Simon rolled along parallel to the loading docks

"Which door is it, Bishop?" he asked tersely.

"I can't see anything!" I responded in a panic. The building was just a huge black rectangle in the darkness. Simon hit the Nachtpanzer's forward running lights, illuminating the building.

I quickly counted the large loading bay doors.

"That one, the third one down," I answered.

Simon cut the car in a tight semi-circle, stopping with the car's cargo door directly adjacent to the building's loading bay door. Thumper hit the green button as the Nachtpanzer ground to a halt. The car's cargo door slid open.

"Go!" Simon yelled. He killed the running lights.

The mini-gun went off with a whirling roar. Red tracers flashed over the car's roof line as Stone swept the parking lot, cutting down the approaching zombies.

I followed Thumper outside. He stepped up onto the loading platform, and pulled me up behind him. He pulled out his flashlight and played it over the door's exterior. He raised the shotgun and fired four rounds into the steel shutter cargo bay door, blowing out the locks. With a grunt, he heaved the door slowly up. I rushed forward to help him. We gradually forced the dead weight of the heavy door upwards until it locked open.

Thumper swung his light over the bay's interior, the shotgun at the ready. No zombies were in sight, only pallets of shrink-wrapped cardboard boxes. He moved quickly forward and checked the boxes' shipping labels.

Outside, the mini-gun continued to fire in short controlled bursts.

Thumper stopped suddenly. He turned to me, a twisted smile on his ugly face. I involuntarily stepped back in fear.

"Bingo!" he laughed. The loader tore into the packages like a kid at Christmas. He ripped a box from the pallet and tore it open. He thrust his hand inside the box and pulled out a foil envelope of pills. He quickly scanned the label and then ripped the envelope open. He shook a hand full of the white tablets into his palm, and swallowed one.

Simon yelled to us from the car, "Hurry the fuck up!"

Finally satisfied, Thumper began to pull the smaller boxes loose and throw them through the door.

"Help me, Bishop!" he laughed.

I began to throw the boxes towards the Nachtpanzer's cargo door. Simon stood in the doorway. He quickly pushed the boxes into the cargo bay.

The mini-gun stopped firing. "I'm out! Reload!" Stone screamed from the turret. Simon cursed loudly. He ripped open an ammo case and handed the end of an ammo belt to the screaming gunner. Stone jammed the belt into the mini-gun's receiver and opened fire again.

"They're getting pretty thick out here!" he yelled down into the cargo bay, "The gun's bringing in every damn Zed for blocks! Hurry, I'm fucking serious, you guys!"

"Wrap it up, Thumper!" Simon screamed.

"No fucking way!" the loader yelled back. "We're not full yet!"

"Damn it, Thumper, it's too hot here, Stone can't hold the Zeds off us much longer. I'm pulling out! Button this shit up, now!" Simon bellowed. He climbed back into the driver's seat and engaged the car's drive. He moved the car a few feet forward to show he was serious.

"Fucking pussies," Thumper growled. He pushed dozens of boxes ahead of him through the doorway.

I threw one final box inside and yelled to him, "Come on!"

Thumper strode forward to the car. He smashed the shotgun against my temple. I saw stars and collapsed to the ground. He grabbed Natalie by her arm and roughly pulled her outside the car. He dumped her next to me, and kicked me in the ribs as I tried to rise to all fours.

"Come on!" Simon yelled again, unaware of my predicament.

Thumper smashed in the last few boxes and squeezed inside the car. He hit the door closure button.

I tried to sit upright and reach out for the cargo door. It closed just beyond my fingertips, sealing us outside. I beat feebly on the door's armor.

Simon looked back in annoyance, "Damn it you two…"

Thumper pushed the shotgun's barrel into his shoulder. "Drive!" he ordered.

"Where's Bishop?" Simon asked.

"I dumped him and his fucking precious daughter," Thumper responded with a snarl. "They were taking up valuable cargo space."

The loader slid cautiously into the navigator's seat, still

maintaining pressure with the gun barrel. "Let's go."

"I don't think so," Simon snarled back.

The mini-gun went suddenly silent. "Ammo!" Stone screamed.

"You've gone soft," Thumper growled. He forcefully jabbed the gun barrel into Simon's shoulder. "Drive or I'm gonna' blow your damn head off!"

"I'm out! Ammo now!" Stone screamed in a rising panic. He thrust his hand down into the cargo bay for an ammunition belt. The zombies surrounding the car staggered forward, climbing onto the butchered bodies heaped in piles around the immobile vehicle. They scaled the car from three sides, pulling the struggling gunner out of the turret. Stone desperately hooked his foot into the gunner's seat. The zombies inexorably pulled him outward. Cadaverous hands ripped his clothing and skin away. Blackened teeth sank into the meat of his arms and legs, clutching hands ripped open his abdomen and eviscerated his organs. Stone's screams rose to an anguished howl as his foot slipped loose. Dozens of tugging hands reached out, dragging him down into a mass of gnashing teeth and grasping claws. His screams ceased as the zombies tore him to bloody pieces.

Simon sat immobile. "You just killed Stone," he grated.

"You're next," Thumper warned, his finger tightening on the trigger. "It's a two-way split now, Simon. Play it smart, I don't need it all."

"Alright!" Simon relented. He crushed the Nachtpanzer's accelerator down. The big car lurched up and over the heaped corpses before it, and slammed back down.

Thumper was thrown forward in the seat, against the control panel. Simon elbowed the shotgun back as it went off. Three pellets ripped through his upper back and shoulder, the rest tore away the top of the driver's seat. Simon grunted in pain. He leaned forward, his hand darting under the steering column.

Thumper pushed himself upright and racked the shotgun's pump, chambering a fresh round. He looked down in shock as Simon drove the knife into his chest, just below his left nipple. Blood gushed over the knife's handle and down his shirt.

Simon pushed the gun barrel away, behind him, as Thumper feebly struggled to shoot him again. His nerveless finger slipped from the trigger. Finally, he coughed up bright blood and his head sank down.

Simon drove the Nachtpanzer across the parking lot and into the darkness.

I could hear Stone's screams, and I knew if I didn't move fast, Natalie and I were next. My head was splitting, and I couldn't beat back a wave of nausea. Desperately, I banged on the car's cargo door and yelled as loud as I could. Nothing good happened. I did draw the attention of the zombies at either end of the car. Their black shadows began to move around the Nachtpanzer towards me. I quickly stopped screaming and tried to rouse Natalie, but whatever they had given to her earlier was still working. At least I knew she wouldn't suffer once the zombies reached us.

I pulled her inside the warehouse; it was all I could think of. In cold terror, I watched as the Nachtpanzer pulled away. Just beyond the car, the Zeds were finishing up what was left of Stone. I almost panicked as a few stragglers shambled forward towards the open doorway. Frantically, I dragged my daughter deeper into the loading bay and looked around for a weapon of some sort. I tripped over the bottom steps of a metal stairwell that rose to a catwalk above the bay. Fear gave me the strength to heave my daughter's limp body over my shoulder and stagger up the steps. Alerted by the sound of my movement, the zombies followed me into the warehouse.

I climbed to the top and gently lowered Natalie to the catwalk. My straining eyes couldn't see very far into the darkness, but by the sounds on the stairs, I knew that the zombies were following me. Their groans and horrible stench preceded them as they stumbled up the steps below. I threw my hands over my eyes as suddenly the bay was flooded with light.

Simon turned the Nachtpanzer in a tight circle. He flipped all the car's forward lights on. A few zombies were still scraping over the last bits of his former gunner, but most had turned and were streaming into the warehouse bay. He could see that Bishop was trapped on a stairwell through one of the warehouse windows; the Zeds were almost upon him.

Simon flipped through each toggle on the weapon's master control panel. Each came up as a flashing red icon on the heads-up display, indicating an out of ammunition status, until he activated the antipersonnel mines. Simon grinned and mashed the accelerator down hard.

The Nachtpanzer crashed through the bay door, taking out four feet of the left wall and dozens of zombies with an earsplitting crash.

Simon lurched forward with the impact; then he recovered and triggered the mines.

From each side of the Nachtpanzer, hundreds of marble-sized, hardened plastic balls were fired outward by small high explosive shaped charges mounted on the car's outer armor. All of the zombies inside the bay and in the doorway were shredded by the projectiles. They were hurled back and thrown down by the blast, their bones broken and skulls crushed. Everything surrounding the car was utterly perforated and destroyed. The projectiles missed Simon and Natalie by a foot, as Simon had guessed they would.

Simon reached back and hit the cargo door's green button. The door slowly slid open.

"Are you coming or not?" he shouted.

Slipping on the gore-covered stairs; I painfully carried Natalie back down the steps and pushed her into the car. I slammed the red button as Simon reversed the car back through the shattered warehouse wall. Relief flooded through me as I watched the cargo door slide shut.

As I moved forward, I noticed Thumper's corpse, and all the blood splattered throughout the car's cockpit. With alarm, I realized that Simon has been shot, much of the blood was his.

"You're shot," I stated.

"No shit," Simon replied. "But at least I'm not stabbed," he laughed, nodding towards Thumper.

I sank down against the seat. "What now?" I asked.

"I won't last much longer," Simon replied. "So I have to get us somewhere the survivors might be, it's our only chance."

We fled back the way we had come down Bannister Road, to the east. I padded Simon's ragged wounds with a pair of bandages, but the bleeding wouldn't stop. He struggled to stay alert and conscious as he piloted the car through the ruins around us. Several times we bounced off a wreck as Simon reacted slowly, but he refused to stop the car. He was fading by inches as his life blood seeped away. The Nachtpanzer was battered and bloody, but it held on its way. We rejoined Highway 50 just above Lee's Summit and turned to the south.

Simon began to fade in and out; I had to watch him closely.

"How much further is this place?" I asked in concern. I was afraid Simon would black out completely, leaving us stranded and him dead.

"Pull up the GPS," he gasped finally as we cleared the town to the east and turned south on a side road again.

"What am I looking for?" I asked.

"There is a wildlife area just ahead," he moaned deliriously.

I pulled up the map. Sure enough, there was a fishing and wildlife preserve just a mile away. I helped Simon guide the car until we reached a wooded area near a large lake. He parked the Nachtpanzer and painfully shut down the car's electrical systems, until only the radios were left.

He pointed his bloody fingers at the CB radio. "Channel eight. Use it," he gasped. His head lolled to the side and he slumped forward in his seat. There was blood everywhere.

I turned the channel dial to eight and keyed the mic. "Is anyone there?" I spoke. "We are survivors located at the wildlife preserve just outside Lee's Summit. We need assistance. Please respond." I tried the channel twice more, then I shut it down. I was afraid the Feds would trace the signal to us. It was all I could do.

I moved things around inside and pulled Thumper's corpse to the cargo door. If there were zombies outside, I hoped they would be busy with his body long enough to close the door again. I hit the green button and rolled him out, pushing the red button before the door even opened half way. It stopped and reversed to close.

I felt for a pulse in Simon's neck. I wasn't sure if I felt it or not. He still felt slightly warm, but he was completely unresponsive. I was afraid that he was dead.

It took several minutes to rouse Natalie; she finally woke up and looked around in confusion.

"Where are we, Dad?" she asked.

"I don't know," I responded with a sigh.

We sat and held each other. At least we would die together.

I stiffened as I heard a rapping noise on the car's outer armor. It slowly moved around the hull and then sounded on the cargo door.

I looked at Natalie and held my finger to my lips, "Zombies," I whispered.

"If you're alive in there, come out with your hands up," a voice dimly penetrated through the car's armor.

"Don't shoot!" I yelled back. "We're raiders, not Feds! We've got injured people in here!"

"Just come out, now!" the voice ordered.

"Natalie, wait inside for me until I talk to them," I whispered. "I'm going to make a deal."

I threw the driver's hatch open and climbed up onto the seat. "Hold your fire! I'm coming out!" I yelled. "I've got good news for you guys!"

Mannings - Kansas

"Will you just get the damn door open?" French asked for the tenth time.

Tech Sergeant Ed Smith looked up from the dangling control panel in his hand, and cursed back, "French, I swear, I'm gonna' break my boot off in your ass, if you ask me one more time about this mother-fucking door."

French looked around the access gantry nervously, his riot shotgun clutched tightly in his sweaty hands. The small propane lantern near the door hissed and sputtered, casting dancing shadows down the tunnels that converged on their position. "Can you open it or not?"

Sergeant Smith slowly stood, and rubbed the small of his back. He cast aside the wire pliers he was holding and cursed. "Let's just blow the fucker. Give me the dynamite."

Neither man had wanted to risk blowing the door. Even though the access tunnel was reinforced concrete, set into the bedrock deep under the Kansas soil, it was damn risky. Too much explosive could seal the tunnel permanently, and Smith and French wanted what was waiting on the other side, badly. They had already gone through Hell to get this far, and they wouldn't leave without the fifty mega-ton warhead waiting for them in the launch bay beyond the door.

So Smith lit the fuse, and the pair fled down the tunnel, back the way they had come.

A teeth-rattling explosion shook the tunnel, and dust drifted down in the lantern's light. French cursed, and silently prayed the tunnel wouldn't collapse and bury them both. Finally, the noise faded away, and the men stood. Smith held the lantern out before him, and they slowly made their way back towards the door. The smell of smoke filled the stale air of the tunnel. Before they had covered twenty feet, brown, brackish water rushed through the passageway, covering their boots, and flowing on.

"What the fuck?" French growled.

"Ground water," Smith posited.

"Do you think it's hot?" French asked fearfully.

"Probably," Smith growled back. "Come on, let's get this over with."

The two men moved slowly forward, sloshing through the stagnant, fouled water. A horrible reek of decomposition overrode the smoke smell as they progressed through the passage.

"What is that stench?" French gagged. "My fucking eyes are burning."

Sergeant Smith's eyes were watering too, but he attributed it to the smoke. "Don't know," he choked back. "If it was Zeds, I think we'd know it by now. Come on." They progressed slowly forward, and as they went, the water became deeper, moving up their legs. By the time they regained the access gantry, the brackish water was up to their waists. The lantern's light revealed the shattered doorway. The metal door had held, but the concrete casing had split, and brown water now poured from a two-foot-wide crack down the door's left hand side.

"Where is that water coming from?" French asked.

Smith didn't answer; he just waded forward, and thrust the lantern through the hole. He could see that the crack opened into a flooded tunnel on the far side, and just at the limit of the light, the passage terminated in the launch bay. Smith pushed through the crack, fighting to wiggle through against the flowing water. "Come on, we're there."

French didn't want to go through, but he didn't want to wait in the darkness behind them alone, either. He fought his way through, the sides of the crack catching his ample belly and ass. The water drenched him as he pushed through to the far side. If it was possible, the stench was even stronger there. Sergeant Smith was already wading forward. French could see the side of the Minute Man Missile gleaming coldly in the dim light, just at the end of the tunnel. As he progressed, the water rose until it was just below his armpits. He held his shotgun and tool bag above his head and slogged forward, cursing. His pants snagged on something below the water, and he almost tripped and went down. He jerked his leg free, but after another step, his leg snagged again.

"Damn it, Smith, hold up!" French bellowed. He jerked his leg back, and then icy terror gripped him as he felt clammy fingers brush across his back. Something gripped his ankle, and he went under before he could scream. Darkness flooded over him, and the foul, oily water filled his mouth as he fought to break loose. He dropped his gun and struggled to pry the cold, dead fingers from his ankle. In pure panic, he kicked and jerked at his attacker, and suddenly he was free. French broke the surface of the water, choking and screaming for help, but now the tunnel was as black as a tomb. Sergeant Smith and the lantern were gone. French backpedaled away, screaming Smith's name. Panic overwhelmed him until he backed into the cold slimy stone of the concrete wall. He stood coughing out the foul water for a few seconds before he remembered his lighter.

French desperately rifled his jacket's pockets, until his fingers closed around his lighter. He blew on it, and shook it, before spinning the wheel with his thumb. Feeble red sparks burst forth in the absolute darkness for the briefest of seconds. French turned the lighter over and shook it. He blew on it to clear it again. Finally, he tried it. The lighter flared to life, burning brightly for a full two seconds in the flooded tunnel.

The rotting, bloated green heads of a dozen zombies were illuminated, half submerged in the swirling black water. They turned their dead white eyes towards the light.

French screamed and dropped the lighter.

Lake Jacomo - Missouri

It took some fast talking to get the rebels not to kill me. They were dead set on wasting me, but I really didn't want to get shot after all I'd been through. I peeked over the top of the hatch, and quickly jerked my head back inside. Two men in full chem suits were hiding in the trees a few yards from me; I could see the business ends of their rifles. One of them kept screaming for me to come out, but I wasn't convinced that was in my best interest.

"Listen, guys," I began. "You really don't want to shoot me."

"Come the fuck out of there!" one of them screamed back.

I hunkered down on the seat and hoped they didn't have any grenades. Natalie was creeping forward; I waved her back. "Who's in charge out there?" I yelled in reply.

It was quiet for a few seconds, then a man's muffled voice answered, "I am."

"What's your name?" I shouted. When he didn't answer, I just kept going. "My name is Robin Bishop, and I've got my daughter in here with me. She's just a kid. The guy who drives this car is in here too. His name is Simon; he's hurt bad. I think he's dying. He brought us here, to try to find you guys. We need your help." I could hear the men outside talking in low tones, but they weren't talking to me. "Just promise me, you'll hear me out before you shoot me!" I yelled through the open hatch.

"Fuck you, Fed!" someone shouted.

"I'm not a Fed!" I cursed back. "Simon is a raider. He brought me inside the zone to save my daughter. She's been in here since the beginning. She's a survivor like you guys!" I added in a moment of desperation. "I swear it." It was silent for a moment.

"Come out," the man who had identified himself as their leader commanded. "Everyone stand the fuck down!" he added. "Come on out. We won't fire."

I poked my head up and slowly climbed out through the hatch. I clambered down and stood with my hands as far over my head as I could reach. One of the men came forward to meet me; the others covered me with their rifles.

"Who the fuck are you?" he asked.

"I'm Robin Bishop. I'm a computer programmer. I came here to save my daughter, just like I told you."

"Why aren't you wearing chem gear?" the man rumbled.

"Watch him!" one of his men shouted. "He's probably got the shit."

"The virus isn't airborne anymore," I quickly explained.

"Bullshit," the man growled.

"I've been inside the QZ for several days now," I said, slowly lowering my hands. "I've been in close proximity to zombies. I'm not sick. I swear it."

Their leader looked me over closely, he seemed indecisive.

"The man inside the car, the one who's hurt, he can explain everything to you. If you could help him," I added.

"Tell you what, Bishop. We're going to go for a walk. All of us. If what you are telling me is the truth, then you'll live. If not..." He trailed off.

I carefully brought Natalie out of the car. She didn't seem to be afraid of the rebels, and they treated us both a little more kindly once they saw how ragged and starved she looked. The leader asked her a few questions, but finally seemed satisfied that she was a survivor. His men fashioned a stretcher for Simon. They raided the Nachtpanzer, taking all the weaponry and ammo short of the mini-guns. Their leader looked the car over, he seemed most interested in it, and my story of how Simon used it to raid the QZ and return to the real world. Finally, he pulled off his gas mask, and took a deep breath of fresh air. His bearded face was dirty and haggard. He sighed and told me his name. "I'm John."

Our small column wound quietly through the woods. We walked for about an hour and finally emerged on the shore of a large lake. Three of John's men pulled covered flat boats out from where they had been hidden in the tree-line, and dragged them down to the water. We climbed aboard the small boats and were paddled across the still water to a heavily forested island, near the lake's center. The rebels took great pains to be quiet. Once we reached the shore, the boats were quickly unloaded and hidden again. More men came out of the trees to meet us. John lead us through the woods until we emerged in a small campsite, covered with camouflage netting and interwoven branches. I noticed berms of mounded earth, with heavy plastic covered doors scattered through the trees around the campsite. Simon was carried inside one.

John sat down heavily on a tree stump. He pulled off his muddy boots and struggled to remove his clinging rubber chem suit.

One of his men protested, but John cursed him down. "If they're wrong, and I turn, shoot me."

"It's safe," I assured him.

"I don't care anymore," the burly leader spat. "I'll take my chances. I hate these stinking things." He stood and stretched.

His men seemed torn. Some argued against removing their protective gear, others happily came out of their suits. People rushed around the camp, spreading the news of our capture.

A woman came out of one of the shelters, and approached us. She gently took Natalie's hand, and coaxed her, "Come with me, you must be starving." My daughter looked askance at me. I shrugged my shoulders and told her to go ahead. Our only chance lay with these people.

John sat back down, and pointed to a beat up camp stool nearby. "Sit down, Bishop, I want to hear all about you."

I spilled my guts about everything. What had happened to me, the rescue, the shit we had seen inside the QZ, the stuff Simon had told me and what was happening in the outside world. People crowded around me and hung on every word. John interrupted me occasionally to ask a question, but mostly he just listened. They hadn't had news from outside the QZ since before Z-day. Once I finished, the camp erupted into total chaos. People shouted questions over each other, or argued loudly about what they should do next. Finally, John bellowed everyone down, and I could hear again.

The rebel leader gave me a ragged smile. "You sure know how to stir things up, Bishop."

Once John was finished grilling me, they took me to see Simon.

Inside the small shelter a rude, but clean clinic had been set up. Simon was stretched out on a cot, hooked up to a blood transfusion bag and an IV. The camp's doctor assured me that although he had almost bled to death, Simon would live. I left him there to rest, and had John take me to find my daughter.

We walked across the campsite to another clearing where a crude bathhouse had been set up, with a cistern and a wood fired boiler. Natalie ran to hug me as we walked forward. I almost didn't recognize her; she was clean, and was wearing a pair of military BDU pants and a too-large sweatshirt. I fought back tears as I realized how skinny she was. We just stood and hugged each other.

"Thank you, John," I finally choked out.

"Sure," he replied.

A day later, Simon was up and asking for me. He and John had hit it off pretty quick. Simon had convinced the rebel leader to take me back to the Nachtpanzer in order to use the radio. I was pretty sure that Brad would be looking for us; we were overdue at the extraction point. Simon was worried that Oksana would do something desperate, and he wanted to get a message to her.

I reluctantly agreed to go back to the car. I figured I owed Simon that much. John and two of his men took me back just before dusk. We moved carefully through the woods, keeping a close watch for any sign of Zeds.

"Are there zombies way out here?" I asked.

"Not so much," John answered. He held his finger to his lips for silence, and we moved on. Finally, we reached the car. It was just as we had left it. I had jammed a stick between the driver's hatch and the frame so that we could get back inside. John and I climbed up, and shimmed down through the hatch into the interior. Simon had given me the code to activate the Nachtpanzer's electrical systems. I slid behind the wheel and punched in the access code. The car sprang to life, and the heads-up display activated. I moved across to the navigator's position.

"This is one hell of a rig," John whistled. He had settled into the driver's seat, and was examining the display.

"Yeah," I replied. "Don't touch any of the controls. Some of them are for weapons." I explained Simon's security precautions.

I powered up the radio, and slowly scanned the military frequencies. A few weak signals came through, but not anything I was looking for. John and I settled in to wait. Eventually, I leaned back into the seat and dozed off a little. A voice came in through the headset, jerking me back to consciousness, and I looked around in confusion. I wasn't sure how much time had passed. I keyed the mic three times, and listened. The voice came again.

"Supply Three to Bishop One. Do you copy?"

I keyed the mic. "This is Bishop One." I thought for a moment, and continued in my crude code. "Primary mission accomplished. We have wounded, and are stationary, these coordinates."

"Copy that," the voice replied. "Be advised, you will have a package delivery at dusk tomorrow. Supply Three, out."

"What did he mean?" John asked me.

I groaned as I shut off the equipment. "Nothing good. Simon's girlfriend is coming."

Black Springs - Arkansas

Big Jim Stark brought the mules he was leading to a stop, slid his lever action 30-30 out of its scabbard, and dismounted. He cursed Twitch, his lead mule, for a nervous son-of-a-bitch. The mule had his ears laid back, and was showing his teeth. The bastard was mean and contrary all the time, but Jim was certain that Twitch wasn't just being difficult. The pack mule could smell a zombie from a mile away. Twitch had been acting nervous for the last half hour, and Big Jim was pretty sure there were some Zeds around, pretty damn close. Patrick and Greg walked up to see why Jim had stopped. Both of them had their rifles up and ready.

"What's the problem?" Greg asked.

Big Jim scanned the scraggly pines and scrub nettle on the hillside around them. They had purposely stayed off the roads, and were only traveling cross country or on the occasional fire road or hiking trail. They were in the back woods, in some really thick shit. Jim knew for a fact that there wasn't a town within twenty miles of them, at least nothing on his road map. Still, Twitch was never wrong.

Big Jim spit tobacco juice on the rocky trail under his muddy boots and cursed, "There's some fucking Zeds a following us or I'm a pecker-head."

"Where?" Patrick asked, looking around wildly.

"Don't rightly know," Big Jim growled back. At that exact moment, Twitch bucked like he'd been shot in the ass, ripping his lead out of Big Jim's hand, and knocking him aside. Twitch took off down the trail at a dead run, the other four pack mules braying hot on his trail. Then the men's saddle horses panicked and bolted too. Before Jim could regain his feet, a half-dozen zombies clambered out of the thick brush around them. Patrick cut loose with his AR-15 on full auto, cutting three Zeds in half and damn near shooting his way around to Jim. Big Jim cursed, but he calmly raised his rifle and fired, working the lever action to chamber a round, and fired again, dispatching two approaching zombies with clean head shots. He looked around for another target, but the only moving Zed was tangled up with Greg. The zombie had hit him from behind, and the pair were rolling around on the rocks.

"Lift his head!" Jim yelled over his gun barrel. Before he could take the shot, Patrick fired his AR, stitching both his target and his friend with hollow-point rounds. The mostly decapitated zombie pitched forward over its stone dead victim, who had been shot through the left eye. Black and bright red blood pooled on the stones under the bodies.

Big Jim slowly stood, shaking his head at the mess. "Nice shootin', Annie Oakley," he spat. "You done shot Greg, you dumb fucker."

"It was an accident," Patrick replied numbly, as he lowered his still smoking gun.

"Well, he's done dead now, and we ain't got time to bury him." Big Jim drawled. "Let's get them fucking mules!"

Big Jim and Patrick followed the trail the fleeing mules had left. Jim figured they wouldn't run far, but he was wrong. It took the rest of the day to catch up to their pack animals. He was a little nervous about running into more Zeds, but he was more nervous about finding the mules.

He and Patrick struggled up a steep part of the trail and crested a rocky hilltop. He drew up short and threw out an arm to stop Patrick. Both men drew in a sharp breath. The mules and horses were calmly munching grass in the valley below them, but Twitch had slipped his pack straps and shook off his cargo just over the top of the hill. A pair of ten megaton nuclear warheads lay on the rocks, their cases dented and battered, only a few feet away.

Patrick swallowed hard and looked at Big Jim. "Do you think they'll go off?"

"Nope," Big Jim answered. "We'd be a' singing psalms upstairs if they were gonna' blow." He calmly walked over to look down at the warheads and spit on the rocks beneath them. "Let's get Twitch up here and load these bastards back up. We got a deadline to meet."

Lake Jacomo - Missouri

I heard the plane's engines long before I could possibly see it. The skies were grey and overcast, with low cloud cover and a light breeze. The temperature was hovering around forty degrees, and it had been threatening to rain all evening. The conditions were just right; it was the perfect day for what we were attempting.

"Do you see anything yet?" John asked. The rebel leader stood a few feet away from me, slowly scanning the sky with a pair of heavy military-grade binoculars. Two of his men flanked us, rifles at the ready, watchful for any zombie activity.

"Not yet," I answered. The aircraft's engines grew steadily louder, but I still couldn't see it. I had learned quickly that sounds carried further inside the QZ.

"He's right over us," John warned.

I twisted to my right, and shaded my eyes with my hand, looking for any sign of a parachute.

"There, three o'clock!" John pointed to the sky.

An olive drab chute drifted slowly down from the clouds, and began to waft away from us. Its passenger adjusted the descent, and gently touched down a quarter mile away in the tall grass.

"Let's go," John commanded.

We walked quickly across the field, our guards flanking us to either side. Oksana had removed her harness and rolled her chute up in it. She dropped it into the grass and strode towards us.

John whistled softly through his teeth. "She is way hotter than you said," he commented.

"John, this is…" I began.

Oksana's combat boot slammed into my head. I saw stars and flew sideways into the grass. The lithe bitch continued her spinning side kick and landed gracefully beside me. She knelt forcefully atop me, crushing my testicles with her left knee. Before I could react, she drew a combat knife from her boot top and thrust the blade against my throat.

John racked the slide of his 45 and released it. We both turned our heads to look at him. I could barely see him through the tears in my eyes.

"That's enough!" the burly rebel barked. "If you kill Bishop, I will shoot you!"

Oksana tensed, and then she withdrew the blade and stepped away from me.

I turned over into the fetal position and tried not to puke. Waves of pain forced a tortured groan from me. I rocked back and forth, gasping for breath.

"I told you I would kill you if anything happened to Simon," Oksana growled.

"He's okay," I moaned. I rolled over and painfully sat upright.

John continued to cover Oksana with his pistol. "Simon is with my people," he assured her. "Our medic has him stabilized. He lost a lot of blood, but he'll be fine. If Bishop hadn't gotten him to us, he would have died."

Oksana scowled at me, and then she slipped her knife back into its sheath.

I shakily stood upright, and slowly took two steps back away from her. Through clenched teeth, I grated, "John, this is Oksana, Simon's girlfriend. Oksana, this is John, the leader of the Kansas City rebel militia." I pointed to each of them in turn.

John slowly lowered his pistol, and holstered it. "Pleasure to meet you Oksana, I've heard a lot about you," he said firmly.

Oksana gave him a curt nod. "Take me to him."

John led us back to the rebel camp. I knew better than to strike up a conversation with Oksana; all it would probably get me was another boot to the balls, so I limped along in silence. I noticed that John was splitting his attention between Oksana's ass, and laughing quietly at my discomfort. I wasn't too happy with the situation.

Once we reached the camp, John took Oksana directly to Simon. She threw herself roughly on the wounded driver, and laughed in relief, tears running down her face. I had to face the fact that she was slightly human after all. Simon bitched her out for coming, but he was obviously glad to see her. We stepped outside and left them alone for a while. I looked around for Natalie. She had made friends with a pair of the teenagers in the camp. I spotted her near a campfire, where they were skinning out a deer.

John looked at me, mischief in his eyes. "I take it you and Oksana don't get along?"

"Understatement," I replied.

"What happened?" John asked.

"Nothing," I answered. "She's just a total bitch. You'll see."

John just shook his head and walked away.

I tried to get some rest while I could. John had set aside a warm place for me and Natalie in his hut. I took advantage of it, sleeping through most of the next day. The aroma of roasting meat rousted me out for dinner. I was starving, so I followed the smell outside to the blazing campfire. Simon, Oksana, and Natalie were standing there, eating smoking hunks of roasted venison, pulled from spits. Natalie walked over and hugged me. Simon looked up at us; his face was drawn, but he looked hale enough.

"Good work, Bishop." He grinned.

"You're welcome," I replied. I assumed that was as close to a thanks as I was likely to get out of him. I didn't mind. He had saved our lives, so I had been happy to return the favor. Besides, we were still a long way from being in the clear, and he was the only one who could drive the car.

Natalie let me go and walked around the fire pit to stand next to Oksana. They shared a piece of meat, laughing and joking like old friends. I started to say something, and then I shut my mouth. Simon shook his head slowly and smiled.

Oksana looked across the fire, and grinned wickedly. "Natalie is one tough kid. I'm pretty sure your wife fucked around on you, Bishop," she laughed.

I bristled when Natalie laughed too, but Simon interceded. "Easy, Oksana."

"I'm just saying," the bitch laughed.

I tried not to let her get to me, and failed miserably.

"Are you up to getting us out of here?" I asked Simon.

"Sure, I can drive, but it's not going to be that clean and easy," he explained. "We can't just roll out of here."

"Why not?" I inquired testily.

"For one, we are now indebted to these people for saving our asses," Simon retorted. "And since you were kind enough to tell them everything, you can probably guess that the situation has altered somewhat."

"Oh," I mumbled.

"Dumb-ass," Oksana added.

"Dad was just trying to save Simon," Natalie interjected in my defense.

"Well, the cat's out of the bag now," Simon sighed. "So we'll just have to work out some kind of deal with John."

"Where is he anyway?" I asked.

"I would imagine they're having a discussion about what to do with us," Simon explained.

"Could we just slip out? While they're busy," I said softly.

"Don't be so stupid," Oksana hissed. "There are men watching us right now. We'd have to fight our way out."

"Really, Dad," Natalie scolded.

"I just want you safe," I shot back.

"No," Simon stated. "I always pay my debts. We work something out."

I looked around the fire. It was three to one and dangerous too, so I let it drop.

We had finished eating and were passing around a pint of bourbon that Oksana produced from her coat, when John walked up to the fire. He got straight to the point. "Everyone here is for trying to escape the QZ," he stated. "If you'll help us."

Simon didn't hesitate with his answer. "I owe you my life; we'll get you out. All of you."

"How many survivors are there?" I asked.

"There are forty-two people here," John replied.

"That's too many to take out at once," Oksana observed.

John looked from Oksana to Simon, and back again. "I won't leave anyone inside," the rebel leader stated grimly.

"It's cool," Simon interrupted. "We'll figure out a way to do it."

"I never considered it before," John spoke. "I thought it was too dangerous. But if the virus isn't a threat anymore, and we just have to deal with the zombies and the Feds…"

"It will still be incredibly dangerous," Simon interjected. "But if we can recover all of the scripts from the warehouse, I think we can buy our way out."

Oksana opened her mouth to object, but Simon stopped her with a subtle hand gesture. I noticed it, but I wasn't sure if John had.

"Are those painkillers worth that much?" John asked.

"Yeah," Simon assured him. "The pharmaceutical companies jacked up everything after Z-day. The government gets a fat cut, of course. That made black market drugs extremely valuable. Extremely," he emphasized.

"But that's a full semi-truck shipment back there," I countered. "Even if we can get it out, how do we move it all back to the east coast?"

"I don't know yet," Simon admitted. "But I love a challenge."

"There's one more small problem," John interjected.

We all looked up. I didn't like where this was going.

"And that is?" Simon inquired.

"There isn't going to be any east coast left to move it to."

New Madrid - Missouri

Colonel Ethan T. Greene looked up from his map table as his second-in-command, Master Sergeant Cole Yates, entered his tent. Yates didn't come to attention; he simply threw his battered boonie hat on the table and flopped down in the folding chair opposite Col. Greene. The men were friends, and had been through too much together to follow old formalities. They had survived inside the QZ, but their families hadn't. Greene had lost a wife and two small sons to the zombies, and Yates a daughter, and granddaughter; shot trying to run the barricades.

"Any luck?" Greene asked.

"Not yet," Yates answered, then coughed horribly for a moment. He wiped specks of blood on his filthy pants leg.

"This isn't what I was hoping to hear," the colonel grumbled.

"I'll go back out at first light," the sergeant offered. "They're not technically late, yet."

"No, I'll send out Phillips and some of the other men. You look like shit. I need you here to recheck the detonators, anyway," Greene said flatly.

"They're fine," Yates argued.

"Yeah, but you're not," the colonel countered. "I don't want you rigging a detonator to a nuclear warhead in your condition. You need to rest. I'm still not sure this will even work."

"If I do it, it'll work," Yates growled. "Don't worry about me. I'll live long enough to get the job done." He coughed into his hand again. "We both got a pretty good dose. How are you feeling?"

"I'm fine," Greene lied.

Yates uttered a harsh laugh. "Yeah, right. Sure you are." He paused thoughtfully for a few seconds. "If we don't get the last few warheads in here, will what we've already rigged be enough to set off the fault-line?"

"I'm not sure," Greene admitted, with a shrug of his shoulders. "This is all guess work. As is stands, we have seven of the one-megaton tactical artillery shells, and three of the bigger, missile warheads. If they all go off at the same time, centered here, I don't see how the fault-line can't go. But, just to be sure, I'd like to have the other warheads in the mix. Some of them might fail to explode. I'm counting on the first detonation to start a chain reaction." He tapped his scabbed finger on the map, at the exact epicenter of the earthquake he hoped to create. Greene looked up from the map and smiled. "And then all hell will be loosed, and those fuckers in Washington will pay for their sins."

Lake Jacomo - Missouri

I stepped around the fire until I could reach Natalie. "What do you mean?" I asked fearfully.

"There are former military personnel within the QZ, who hate the Federal Government so much that they are acting to destroy what's left of the country. At least Washington, and the east coast," John explained.

"How is that even possible?" Natalie asked.

"Nukes, centered on the New Madrid fault line," John expounded.

"Were you planning on telling us about this?" I finally stuttered out.

"Trust is a hard commodity to find these days," John stated sadly. "And I hadn't decided to trust you, until now."

"This certainly changes things," Simon grunted.

"Were you part of this plan?" Oksana asked with a degree of admiration.

"Sort of," John admitted. "Some of us assisted with the plan. We helped with transport. Most of us want revenge, and all of us want the barricades to come down. The Feds have no right to keep us inside here. We're not prisoners; we're not sick."

"What kind of transport?" Simon interrupted.

"The warheads were moved by mules, and on horseback," John elucidated.

Simon whistled softly, and shook his head in amazement. "Man, that's just crazy."

"Yeah, but it worked, as far as I know," John countered.

"When is this all supposed to happen?" I asked in alarm.

John shrugged his shoulders, "I don't know. For all I know, it could have already gone down. We don't have any means of communicating with the guys who moved the nukes through here."

"I think we would know if something like that happened," I observed.

"Awesome," Simon groaned. "As if we didn't already have enough on our plates."

"Who cares if they destroy Washington?" Oksana laughed. "They deserve it."

Simon looked at her in annoyance. "You're not thinking this

through. A nuclear detonation centered on the New Madrid fault line could trigger an immense series of earthquakes. It wouldn't just break the barricades, it could cause major geological damage. The Great Lakes could drain into the Mississippi River basin. Chicago could be destroyed," Simon finished.

"The plan was just to breach the barricades, and release the zombies from the QZ," John explained. "That way, the Feds would have to deal with the problem, instead of isolating themselves from it."

Everyone was silent for a moment as the idea sank in.

Simon paced back and forth, thinking quickly. He turned to John, and grabbed his arm. "Are you willing to help me stop this?"

"Why should I?" the rebel leader retorted.

"If this happens, millions more will die. My home will be destroyed," Simon growled. "There won't be anyplace left for you and your people to escape to. It could destroy everything that's left. Is that what you want?"

John hesitated. "You don't know what we've been through," he cursed.

"All that can end," Simon offered. "We can change it. But I need your help. You may not have had anything to lose, but now you do."

The rebel leader made his decision quickly. "Alright," John relented. "What do we do?"

"We re-outfit the car. We get the drugs, and we stop the nukes." Simon grinned. "And then we all have drinks at my place."

It took a long time to get everything organized, a lot longer than I liked. John had his hands full getting everyone ready to leave. His men went out in small groups to gather the things we would need. The rebel leader did see to it that Simon's Scorpion was returned, along with its ammunition. Simon painfully pulled its harness over his bandaged shoulder. Oksana had brought in a custom Dragunov sniper rifle equipped with a night scope, and a matching pair of Makarov pistols. With her hair in a ponytail, in her black leathers, she looked like a killer angel. The bitch was scary.

I didn't have a weapon, but I felt like I definitely needed one. I asked around until one of John's men found a battered 1911 Army .45 for me, and a half-full box of ammo. The pistol's slide was so loose I was afraid it might not fire, but it beat a blank. Natalie didn't ask for a gun, and I didn't want her to have one anyway.

As darkness fell, the camp was like a kicked over ant hill. People moved about, lugging food and gear to the boats, and transferring them to the shore. Finally, John came to collect us. He had a 30.06 hunting rifle slung over his shoulder.

"I've done everything I can think of," he grunted. "My people are all moving out. Let's go."

He led us down to the boats, and we were ferried across. John spoke to a couple of his men, and then he led us on into the woods. We made our way back to the car without incident. Several of the rebels were still there, unloading the bundles of painkillers we had taken from the warehouse, taping them into bundles, and loading them onto pack animals. A good twenty horses were tethered in the tree-line near the Nachtpanzer.

Simon slid into the driver's seat, and energized the car. John and I helped move the last of the drugs out of the cargo bay. Once it was empty, we all climbed inside. John waved to his men as Oksana hit the button, closing the cargo door.

I started to climb into the navigator's seat, but Oksana grabbed me by my collar and pulled me into the cargo bay. "That's my seat," she growled.

Simon let out a long sigh. "Oksana, you'll have to man the mini-gun. In the turret," he added.

"I'm the fucking navigator," she snarled.

"Damn it, woman. Bishop can't shoot for shit. You're the only one besides me who can handle the mini-gun," Simon complained.

"Fuck that. There's no ammo for the mother-fucker!" Oksana shouted.

"We are going straight back to the last drop crate, you contrary bitch. Shut your pie-hole and let Bishop sit down!" Simon grated. "Use the time to show John and Natalie the loader's station."

Oksana grumbled, but she moved aside to let me slide into the nav seat. I could tell she really just wanted to shoot me in the back of the head and dump my body outside.

Simon engaged the drive, and the Nachtpanzer bumped across the gravel lot and back onto the pavement. I let out a long sigh. I felt much safer inside the car, than out.

I looked over at Simon. I could tell by the grin on his face that he was very happy to be back behind the wheel. It was where he belonged.

"Listen up, people," he spoke up. "It's only a few miles back to the airport. The car's weapons systems are all completely empty. We are down to hand weapons only. On the bright side, we have almost full battery power, so we're mobile, and good to roll. The airport is crawling with Zeds, so we're going to do a snatch and run. I want to grab all the crap in the cargo box and then get the hell gone. Got it?"

"What do you want me to do?" John asked.

Simon turned the car onto the highway, and smoothly accelerated up to forty-five miles an hour. "I'll pull the car's cargo door right up next to the drop box. Oksana will go topside with the Dragunov. John, you and Bishop hop out as soon as we stop and throw everything in the drop box into the cargo bay. Don't pay any attention to what is going on outside. Oksana will cover you. Just move cargo, quickly. Natalie, I need you to man the open-close button. As soon as I tell you, you slam that button. Got it?" he asked.

"Yeah, I got it," Natalie answered eagerly.

"Good," Simon replied. "Because we'll be there in just a minute."

I was a little nervous about Natalie manning the door, but at least she was staying inside the car. Simon turned off the highway at the airport, and slowed to nose the Nachtpanzer through the snarled wreckage surrounding the terminal. He pushed his way through to an open gate and rolled out onto the tarmac. The Nachtpanzer's blackout lights came on, illuminating the ground around the car. I knew zombies were already moving towards us.

"Showtime," Simon warned.

Oksana threw open the turret hatch and climbed up to stand on the seat. She wrapped the Dragunov's strap around her arm and brought it to her shoulder. The bloodthirsty bitch opened fire before the car even slowed, rattling through a magazine, and smacking another home into the receiver. Natalie hit the door button, and it cycled fully open as the car came to a smooth stop beside the drop box.

"Go!" Simon shouted. He jerked his head back around to the heads-up display.

John and I leaped through the open cargo door. The road-kill stench of the Zeds immediately filled my nostrils. I slipped, and almost went down. I had stepped into the rotten abdominal cavity of a headless zombie, stretched out face-down on the blacktop, just outside the car. I grimaced and pulled my boot free. The Dragunov roared repeatedly above my head. John pushed past me with two boxes of ammunition, as I stumbled forward to the drop box. I snatched out the SAM, and turned to fling it inside the cargo bay. Natalie was hastily pulling the ammunition boxes inside. John passed me again, flinging the heavy boxes through the open door, two at a time. I grabbed up the lighter stuff, and tossed it inside the car as fast as I could. As I turned, I heard Natalie scream; she was pointing past the box into the night. I jerked around to look behind me.

A crawler had slipped past Oksana in the darkness and pulled itself onto the drop box. As John staggered away from the box with an ammo crate, the half-zombie flung itself on him, and they went down together, rolling across the tarmac. All hell broke loose, and everyone was screaming at once. Oksana's rifle went silent, and I heard her cry, "I can't see him!" I snatched out my .45 and took three steps into the dark, toward the sound of the struggle. Oksana still wasn't firing; I hoped she wouldn't take my head off, accidentally. "John!" I shouted.

"Here," he grunted back from the darkness. "Get it off me!" I could dimly see two heads in the gloom, so I aimed at the one that I thought wasn't talking and pulled the trigger. The big .45 bucked in my hand, and then John was pushing past me, wiping black goo off his shirt. "I'll thank you later," he yelled.

We tossed in the last few boxes of ammo and jumped in after them. Oksana's rifle went off on full auto, spraying the darkness behind us. Simon yelled out, "Close the door!" and slammed down the accelerator. Natalie beat at the button, and screamed again as dozens of grasping skeletal hands filled the closing cargo doorframe.

The car accelerated away from the slower pursuing Zeds, and the door cycled shut, sealing out the undead.

"Wow," John laughed, pulling off his gore covered shirt. "Do you guys always cut it that close?"

I struggled to shove my shaking pistol back into its holster. "Yeah, I'm afraid so."

As Simon drove away from Lee's Summit, Oksana sorted through the ammunition and reloaded the main mini-gun. She pushed it back into position on its cradle and shouted forward to Simon, "The main gun's hot!"

Simon took us a short distance away from the airport, and then once he was sure we were clear of any zombies, he slowed the car to a stop alongside the highway. He asked Natalie to come forward to the driver's position. He slid out, and had Natalie sit at the wheel, pointing to the heads-up display. "Do you see this boundary?" he asked, indicating a green line on the edge of the display.

"Yes," Natalie answered.

"I want you to watch it for me," Simon instructed her. "If a zombie gets close to the car, the boundary marker will flash red. If that happens, I need you to yell immediately, okay?"

"Sure," Natalie replied. "Could you teach me to drive this thing?"

Simon ruffled her hair. "When we get out of here, I'll teach you to drive the panzer. No problem."

"Cool," Natalie squealed.

Simon dimmed the interior lights. He hit the activation switches for the side-mounted mini-guns and the missile rack to open them, and then he moved to the rear. We waited for our eyes to adjust, and after warning us, he hit the button, opening the cargo door. Cool night air flooded the interior. Oksana had sorted the ammunition, and she began to move it outside, into position.

"Can we help?" John asked.

"Yeah," Simon replied. "You go to the front, and Bishop, you go to the rear. Watch for Zeds. More important, listen for Zeds."

"Alright," I agreed. We all moved outside. Simon reloaded the forward mini-guns, first removing the empty ammo boxes and then threading a fresh belt of ammunition into the gun's receiver. He shoved a full box of ammo into the gun's ammunition tray and moved on to the other one. Oksana moved around the exterior of the car, removing the spent backing plate of each anti-personnel mine, and clipping a new one into place. She worked quickly, and was done before Simon could reload both guns.

I nervously paced back and forth, the .45 in my sweaty hand. Being in the dark with zombies made me feel extremely vulnerable. I strained my ears and eyes into the surrounding darkness, and jumped at every little sound.

Oksana pulled the missile crate to the driver's side of the Nachtpanzer and opened it. Simon used the open gun mount to pull himself up onto the car's roof. Oksana carefully handed him the short-range missiles, one at a time. Simon gingerly lined each rocket up in its respective slot, and carefully pushed it back until it locked into position. Once he was done, he swung back down, and gracefully dropped to the blacktop. He slid back into the car, and took back the driver's seat from Natalie.

Oksana herded us back inside, and hit the close button with her fist. The cargo door cycled shut. The whole operation might have taken five or six minutes, although it had seemed much longer to me. I was just glad to be back inside a fully armed car.

Simon checked the display to be sure all the weapons systems were hot and loaded, and then he looked back. "Let's go score some drugs."

Simon had me pull up the GPS maps, and I directed him back onto Bannister Road. We followed it straight west, back into Overland Park. Simon told us his plan as he maneuvered the Nachtpanzer through the wrecks that littered the roadway.

"I don't want to use the car's weapons systems unless we absolutely have to," he explained. "I have a feeling that this shit is going to just keep getting worse as this trip goes on. This is the easy part."

"Great," I complained.

"This place has a big parking lot and loading bays," Simon expounded to Oksana. "There are going to be a lot of Zeds wandering around. I'll pull in, and stop. Oksana, you go topside with the sniper rifle. We'll kill as many as we can with small arms fire. At least we can scrounge around to replace the ammo for our rifles."

"I don't like the idea of being out of ammunition," Oksana grumbled.

"We'll get more," Simon assured her.

"Alright," she agreed. "I could use some target practice."

We rolled into Overland Park and went straight to the industrial parks. The bastard zombies were thick. Simon began to hit them with the car. We turned into the lot for the pharmaceutical warehouse and circled around the building. Simon swerved the Nachtpanzer back and forth, crushing the zombies within range. Oksana opened the turret hatch and stepped up onto the seat. She brought the Dragunov up, but waited to fire. I knew she wanted every round to count.

The zombies closed in from all sides, drawn by the movement of the car. Oksana switched her rifle's fire selector to single shot and began to snipe them. She methodically squeezed the trigger, taking each Zed through the head with a well-placed shot, and then turning a little to her right, and acquiring another target. I counted her shots. The rifle went off every few seconds until she had fired through an entire ten-round magazine. Simon slowly rolled across the lot as she reloaded, so that the zombies couldn't gather too close to the car. As the Nachtpanzer rolled to a smooth stop, Oksana opened fire again, turning in a slow circle in the turret, until she had fired off another magazine. Simon rolled forward through the ring of head-shot corpses surrounding the car.

We continued this for some time, firing and moving. I stopped counting shots after three hundred. Oksana reloaded her rifle and shouted to Simon, "I'm on my last mag." She turned in the turret, and fired until the bolt locked back in the big gun's smoking receiver. Simon pulled a short distance away, and stopped the car.

"I'm still getting a proximity warning," he shouted back. "How many Zeds do you think are still out there?"

Oksana looked through her rifle's scope, slowly turning to scan the corpse strewn parking lot for movement. "Not as many as there were before," she grimly laughed. "Maybe a few dozen, scattered here and there. The gunfire is drawing in some stragglers. Doesn't matter, I'm out."

"Use mine," John suggested. He slid his 30.06 through the turret hatch, and traded her guns.

"I won't be as accurate without the night vision scope," she said. "But, it'll have to do." She turned in the turret, firing the rifle, and working the bolt to chamber a fresh round. I heard her curse occasionally as she missed a kill shot, but two out of three dropped a Zed. She fired through most of John's ammo before she stopped and slid back into the cargo bay. She closed the hatch, and moved forward to the cockpit.

"I think I got them all," she suggested.

Simon watched the heads-up display for a moment. "There's nothing on the proximity display," he announced. "Let's get the drugs."

We rolled through the corpses piled up beside the open loading bay door, and came to a stop. This time, the cargo door faced away from the building. Simon posted Natalie to watch the heads-up display. He grabbed a pair of small flashlights and the night vision goggles and opened the door. We all stepped out into the darkness.

"Here's the plan," Simon said. "Oksana, you watch the perimeter for Zeds. John, you and Bishop carry the scripts out."

"What about you?" I asked.

"You'll see," Simon replied." Just do what I tell you. There's not much time."

Simon handed Oksana the goggles, and she moved away from the car a short distance, scanning the lot for movement. We carefully entered the warehouse, and looked around. The bay was as we had left it. Rotting corpses and ripped up packing materials lay scattered about.

Simon walked outside and ducked back into the Nachtpanzer. He broke into the emergency supply kit and brought out a flare gun. The driver walked a short distance away and shot it into the night sky. The bright green flare slowly sank back to earth on its small parachute.

"Be ready," Simon warned. "That could bring in something we don't want.

Fifteen minutes later, we heard scattered gunshots that got steadily closer. Finally, a voice shouted at us from far off in the distance, telling us not to shoot. Simon yelled them in. John's men began to emerge from the darkness, leading dozens of horses on rope leads. They dismounted, and began to quickly load the boxes we had brought out of the warehouse. Oksana moved beyond them, and began to shoot at the zombies that had followed them in.

We all worked quickly. More of John's people came in, bringing more pack horses and mules. Within thirty minutes, we had cleared out the loading bay, and all of the scripts were loaded and ready to go. John wished his people luck, and they rode off into the darkness. I guessed they must have brought in over a hundred pack animals.

"Where did all those horses come from?" I asked.

"This is the country, boy," John retorted. "There are more horses than people now."

"I just stole John's idea to move the drugs," Simon pointed out. "That part's done, but we've still got some serious shit to do. Let's mount up."

We drove away into the Missouri night.

Simon had me plot the route to the south. We picked up the 435 Bypass, and followed it around to Highway 71. We had burned up an awful lot of the night getting the Nachtpanzer rearmed and securing the painkillers. We also had a very long way to go if we were going to try to stop the rebels at New Madrid. The highway was crowded with abandoned vehicles, and knots of wrecks. Simon had his hands full for a while, but finally, we left the city behind and the roadway gradually cleared. Simon and I discussed our options as he drove south.

"I know for a fact that Springfield is about the limit of our range on these batteries," Simon declared. "We won't make it there before sunrise, so we'll have to find someplace to lay low, and set up another supply drop, or this will be one short trip."

"A C-140 will be over the KC at six in the morning," Oksana interrupted us. "I set up over-flights to maintain contact with Bishop's friend Brad, before they dropped me off. We should be able to make radio contact with him, if we're not out of range."

"I knew there was a good reason I kept you around." Simon smiled at her. "We'll go a little further, and look for a place to hide."

Simon drove south until 71 merged with State Highway 7, and

turned to the southeast. He found a burned-out gas station and nudged the Nachtpanzer under the fire-blackened pump awning. I yawned, and stretched out in the seat for about five seconds before Oksana grabbed me by my bad arm, and forced me back into the cargo bay. She slid into the nav seat and fired up the short-range radar and the radios.

I moved back and sat down on the hard cargo deck next to my daughter.

"Dad, what did you do to Oksana?" Natalie asked me quietly.

"Nothing," I answered.

"Then why does she hate you so much?" Natalie pressed.

"I don't know," I replied.

"There has to be a reason," Natalie insisted.

"Look," I retorted. "I didn't do anything to her. She just didn't like me when we met. I think she's psycho. She's just a very mean person."

"No, she's not," my daughter argued. "I like her. I'd like to be just like her."

"Don't say that," I growled. "I don't want you around her. She's a bad influence."

"I'm not a little kid anymore, Dad," Natalie spat back. "You can't tell me what to do."

"I'm still your father," I reminded her.

"Things have changed," Natalie responded sadly.

She was certainly right about that.

Eventually, I fell asleep. I didn't remember where I was when I woke up. Oksana was speaking quietly into the radio mic. She had found the C-140 pilot, and they spoke briefly before she broke contact. I moved forward, carefully stepping over my sleeping daughter.

Simon looked back at me. "We've got two drops set up," he explained. "The first is at Springfield Regional. It's west of the city. We might just make it if we're lucky."

"Cool," I replied.

"Go back to sleep, Bishop," Simon suggested. "It's almost daylight outside. We can't roll for another seven or eight hours."

I climbed back into the cargo bay, and stretched out beside my daughter. I was so beat I didn't feel how hard the floor was. I closed my eyes, and I was out.

When I woke up later, the car was moving. I slid to the back and used the Nachtpanzer's toilet. It was just a sliding plate that exposed a bent tube that exited outside the bottom of the car. I hunted around until I found a bottle of water and drank it. There wasn't really much to eat. No sandwiches on this trip, just some deer jerky. I grabbed some and slid back forward to the cockpit.

"Where are we?" I asked.

"Coming up on the Montrose Wildlife Refuge," Simon finally answered. "I'm trying to avoid any road that crosses a bridge."

"How's that going?" I asked with a yawn.

"The Lakes of the Ozarks are between us and Springfield," Oksana growled at me.

"Just asking," I offered. I slid back to the cargo bay.

John looked up at me with a grin. "Still charming the ladies, I see," he laughed.

"Shut up," I laughed back.

I slid down to the floor opposite him. "What did you do before Z-Day?"

John grew more serious. "I was deputy sheriff."

"Is that how you ended up being the leader of your group?" I inquired.

"Suppose so," he answered. "Nobody else was stepping up, so I did."

"Family?" I pushed.

"Divorced, no kids," he replied.

"Did your ex make it?"

"Man, I hope not," he grinned. "What about you, Bishop? Running around with raiders. Crossing into the QZ? That's pretty ballsy for a computer programmer."

"I did it for her," I responded, nodding towards Natalie.

"Gotcha," John agreed. "Don't worry. We'll get her outta' here."

"Yeah," I replied. I left unspoken, the 'or die trying' part.

We rolled on for maybe another twenty minutes or so before Simon slowed the car, and then stopped completely.

We all crowded forward, and I asked, "What's up?"

"We found a bridge," Simon replied.

"That's good, right?" I said.

"Not necessarily," Simon quipped back. "It crosses a canal that's not on our maps."

We had driven deep into the wildlife refuge, and were pretty far off the main drag.

"I'm going out to look at it before we cross," Simon declared. "Everybody stay frosty."

"I'm coming," Oksana added. They grabbed the NVGs and a flashlight, and cycled the cargo door open. The nocturnal sounds of a swamp filled the car, along with a faintly rotten smell and moist, cooler air. John stepped just outside with his rifle.

I watched Simon and Oksana walk the short span of bridge from end to end, and then return. Simon played his light over the bridge's support spans, and then flipped off the light. They walked back to the car.

"It might be safer if everybody walked across first, and then I drive the car over," Simon said.

"What's wrong with the bridge?" I asked.

"It's really old and rotten, like your Mom's pussy," Oksana snapped at me, then she added. "Sorry, Natalie, no offense to your granny." My daughter giggled.

"Whatever," I finally muttered.

We climbed out of the car and walked across the bridge. I felt really exposed, but at least Oksana and John were with us. I pulled my .45 out; its weight was reassuring in my hand.

Oksana watched the Nachtpanzer through the NVGs, giving Simon hand signals to line up the car's oversized wheels with the bridge's narrow span of timbers. Simon slowly pulled the vehicle forward onto the bridge. The old timbers began to creak and groan alarmingly.

"It's not going to hold," I warned.

"Shut up, Bishop," Oksana hissed. "It's gonna' hold."

The bridge made an alarming snapping noise, and I knew it was going to collapse. We'd be stuck in the middle of nowhere at night, on foot, with two hundred miles of zombies between us and the boundary, where they'd shoot us on sight. I closed my eyes and prayed.

The Nachtpanzer rolled across the rickety bridge and stopped on the other side next to me.

"Get in," Simon laughed.

We rolled for a few miles more on the unmarked road, and then it dumped us out on Highway 54. Oksana used the GPS to plot our route over to Highway 13, where we turned to the south again. The road seemed fairly clear, and Simon brought the car up to almost fifty miles an hour, weaving around the occasional abandoned car along the shoulder. Things were going too smoothly, and I began to get a bad feeling. I said so.

"Damn it, Bishop, don't wish bad things on us," Simon warned.

"I can't help it," I replied. "We're on Highway 13."

"Thirteen is my lucky number," Simon shot back.

"Go sit in the back!" Oksana demanded. "Before I kick your ass. Again."

"Shit," Simon exclaimed. He brought the Nachtpanzer to a smoothly controlled stop in the middle of the road. He was staring straight ahead at the heads-up display. I couldn't make anything out. It was just a jumble of black blocks and dim shapes.

"Simon?" Oksana asked.

"It's an overpass," Simon explained. "It collapsed directly onto the highway. There's no way around it."

"Don't say another word, Bishop," Oksana ordered me. "You're bad luck."

"Find me a way around," Simon demanded.

Oksana pulled up the GPS, and began to back-track our route.

"Back two miles. There's a side road, on the right going back. It will take us over to Highway 83 and 83 parallels 13, going south."

Simon threw the car into reverse. He backed up slowly until he could turn, and then drove back the way we had come until he reached the side road. The Nachtpanzer sped down the road, and two miles later, we turned south again onto Highway 83. It was clear.

We blew through the small town of Bolivia without slowing down. Simon crushed the zombies who stumbled into the path of the oncoming car. Five miles down the road, we merged with Highway

13 again.

"Twenty miles to the airport," Oksana reported in a tense voice.

I crept forward to look over Simon's shoulder at the battery power level displays. They were all slim red lines, almost nonexistent. I noticed that Oksana was giving me a dirty look, so I moved back to the rear. I slid down to the floor and said another silent prayer.

Very slowly, the minutes and the miles ticked by. I kept on waiting for the batteries to give out, but they didn't.

"We're here," Simon reported. I could hear the relief in his voice. He drove the Nachtpanzer through the service gates on the backside of the airport and we rolled out onto the flight line. Oksana spotted the box, and Simon pulled the car up alongside it. Natalie hit the door button, and the cargo door cycled open.

"I didn't see any Zeds coming in," Simon said as he slid out the door. "You guys cover us for five minutes, and we'll have the batteries switched out."

Oksana moved with him, and they opened the battery access compartment. Working quickly, they pulled and dumped the spent batteries, one by one.

John strode out on the tarmac a short distance away, and looked around with the NVGs. I went ahead and started on the drop box. I couldn't move the batteries by myself, but I started to transfer the ammo crates, and grabbed the SAM.

Simon and Oksana moved past me, grabbing the first battery and hauling it back to the open tray. "Good work," Simon grunted. I got most of the ammo out by the time they came back for the fourth battery.

We were almost done when John rushed back to the rear of the car and grabbed Simon. "Zeds, incoming!" he warned.

"How many?" Simon hissed.

"A lot. Hundreds maybe."

"Oksana. The mini-gun. Quick!" Simon urged. He grabbed John. "Help me with the batteries."

Oksana pushed past me into the cargo bay. She threw open the turret hatch and pushed the mini-gun into position. "Bishop, Natalie, open those ammo crates!" she screamed, pointing to the spare ammunition containers. She climbed up into the gunner's seat and slid down behind the mini-gun's sights.

Simon and John struggled to finish replacing the batteries. They shoved the fifth cell into the tray, and Simon jammed the leads on, before running back to the box for the last battery.

The stench of rot and death washed over us. Oksana screamed like a gut-shot panther and depressed the mini-gun's trigger. The weapon's electric motor droned, and the bullets erupted in a blur of destruction. Bright red tracer rounds illuminated the hordes of shambling undead that had surrounded the car. The gun's rounds walked back and forth just over Simon and John's heads, blasting the grasping cadavers that reached out blackened claws into gory, eviscerated chunks. Zombies staggered forward out of the darkness and disintegrated into black puffs of rotted flesh.

Simon and John staggered away with the last battery, towards the rear of the car.

The mini-gun's barrels ran dry. "Ammo!" screamed Oksana. Natalie thrust the end of an ammunition belt into Oksana's grasping hand. The gunner thrust it into the red-hot receiver, and slammed it shut, but the gun hadn't fired in fifteen long seconds. I pulled my pistol and stepped through the open cargo door. Zombies were streaming around the drop box toward the open door. I fired off my magazine at point-blank range, aiming for the Zed's rotting eyes.

Oksana stood up in the seat and pushed the mini-gun down to its maximum declivity. "Get out of there!" she screamed, squeezing the trigger. The mini-gun howled at full auto, spraying the rounds back and forth just beyond the car's rear armor.

Zombies were streaming in from every direction. I slammed a fresh magazine into my pistol and fired it dry, just stopping the Zeds from reaching the open door.

"Oksana!" I screamed.

John and Simon leaped through the door just ahead of more zombies; the driver slammed the close button as he slid into the front seat. John turned and began to kick and punch the cadavers as they entered the car. It was pure chaos. Natalie and Oksana were both screaming, and my gun roared, as I fired at anything moving that wasn't alive.

Only the fact that so many zombies were jammed into the closing door frame saved us. Simon fired off the forward anti-personnel mines, and pushed the car into the blast lane. We accelerated away from the battle, bouncing up and down over the shredded corpses that surrounded the car. The cargo door cycled shut, but three Zeds had managed to grab John's clothing. They almost pulled him out before their rotten arms were pinched in the closing door. As Simon sped away, the cadavers were wrenched along until their rotten limbs ripped free, and they dropped behind us, skidding across the pavement.

I helped John loosen the grasping claws, and then sank down to the cargo deck. It was impossible to tell over the stench of cordite smoke and decomposed flesh, but I was pretty sure I had shit my pants.

Simon looked back over his shoulder. "Is everyone alright?" he asked. I grunted, and John gave him a grim laugh. Oksana slid past me and plopped down in the navigator's seat.

"One more battery change like that…" I trailed off.

"Yeah, that was pretty hairy," John agreed. He opened the cargo door and kicked the severed limbs into the void. John stared out into the rushing darkness before hitting the close button again.

"You guys need to get out more," Oksana laughed.

Simon weaved his way down the service road around the airport, and turned onto a side road that led east. We were very close to Springfield, and abandoned cars and trucks jammed the roadway. The Nachtpanzer slowed to squeeze between wrecked cars, accelerated down a short stretch of clear road, and decelerated to force its way through again.

The driver was tense; he peered intently ahead at the display. The car scraped past a wrecked truck, slowly accelerated, and then we were in the clear again. Simon let out a sigh of relief.

No one spoke for a few minutes. I was just happy to still be alive, but the whole trip had taken an unexpected turn that I wasn't thrilled about. I wanted to get my daughter and myself out of the QZ. I considered talking to Simon, but I knew Oksana would give me grief, so I bit my lip and stayed quiet. It was like I was married again.

We drove east, away from Springfield for several minutes, and I had just started to relax when I heard Simon curse. He and Oksana began to argue. I risked a punch in the face and moved forward.

"What is it?" I asked.

Simon pointed to a flashing red light on the control display. "The batteries are overheating," he explained.

"Why would they do that?" I muttered, perplexed.

"Bishop, I'm going to ..." Oksana began.

Simon cut her off, "They have a right to know." He stared at Oksana until she leaned back into the seat, and then he continued. "The primary coolant pump has failed. The batteries generate a lot of heat. They are liquid cooled. One of the quick disconnects must have come loose after the last battery change out. I had to do that shit in a hurry. Anyway, we lost coolant and the pump burned up. End of story."

"But what does that mean?" I pushed.

"The batteries will lose their charge much quicker. They may even burn up. The wiring harness could catch fire, even the entire car. We definitely won't make the next drop point," Simon concluded.

"Can you fix it?" John inquired grimly.

"Maybe," Simon answered. "The pump isn't anything special. It's just an electric fluid pump. I could jury-rig a spare into the system, if we can find one that's fairly close to the original. Any car parts store should have one."

"Can we keep going, without the pump?" I asked fearfully.

"Nope," Simon replied. He pulled the Nachtpanzer off the roadway and parked it beneath some broadleaved trees. "We're going to have to hoof it."

"Brad could drop us a spare pump," I countered.

"No time, Bishop," Simon retorted. "We are still in Springfield. There's got to be a parts store or car dealership within a few miles of us. We get the pump ourselves."

"Shit," I groaned.

"You can stay here in the car," Simon offered. "Probably safer, anyway."

Simon and Oksana moved to the rear and readied their gear. I considered my options. It was safer to stay in the car, but if they didn't come back, we'd be stuck. There was safety in numbers, but I would be putting Natalie in harm's way.

John looked at me. "I'm going," he declared.

"I want to go," Natalie spoke up. "They may need our help. I'm not staying here alone."

That decided it. "Hang on, you guys," I growled. "We're coming too."

Simon waited a moment, then he hit the button. The cargo door cycled open, and we all stepped out into the waiting darkness. The door snapped shut behind me, making me jump. I reached out to squeeze Natalie's hand, then I let her go.

"Everybody stay close, and stay quiet," Simon hissed. "Let's go."

We walked down the abandoned roadway, using the scattered wrecks for cover. Simon led us east. It was a fifty-fifty shot to find a parts store; we could have driven past one in the darkness. Theoretically, the further we moved away from Springfield, the fewer zombies there would be. The road was a major artery, and we filed past darkened storefronts and empty parking lots. Then I caught the unmistakable scent of rotting human flesh, and Simon brought us to a sudden halt. I ducked down behind a wrecked sedan as a pair of Zeds noisily staggered by us. I clamped my free hand over my pistol's barrel to keep it from shaking; the slide was loose enough to rattle.

The zombies finally passed us by, and Simon led us forward again. I didn't know how he planned on finding the right store in the darkness. I couldn't read any of the signs; they were just indistinct square blobs on poles. It was all I could do to move slowly along without constantly bumping into the others. We walked for a good twenty minutes, staying in cover, moving from wreck to wreck, before Simon brought us to a halt.

Everyone huddled up, and Simon talked in a whisper. "There's a car dealership here, right across the lot." All I could see were rows of indistinct blobs, stretching into the gloom beside the roadway. "I'll lead us in. Nobody shoot unless I do!" he hissed. He ducked down, and we loped across the pavement to the first row of cars. Simon slowly led us forward, down the lane of parked automobiles. I tried to stay low, but it was hard on my legs. Oksana helped me by roughly pushing my head down and whispering, "Stay down, asshole." We stopped at the end of the row. I could see Simon peering forward with the NVGs. He whispered back to us in a barely audible voice, "I count six Zeds between us and the showroom door."

"I'll take it," Oksana whispered.

"No," Simon hissed.

"I'll be right back," she urged. She pushed past me, back the way we had come.

"Damn it," Simon cursed. He peered ahead and then back into the darkness.

I jumped as Oksana suddenly reappeared. She pushed past me again, and knelt beside Simon. "I saw this on the way in," she murmured. She held an eight-foot length of heavy chain in her hands. I heard it rattle as she turned it in her hands, showing it to Simon. "You spot for me," she urged.

"Alright," he reluctantly agreed.

Oksana wrapped the end of the chain around her left arm, across her shoulders, and down into her right hand. She stepped out from cover, and began to whip three feet of the heavy chain in a vicious circle, over her head and slightly to the side. The Zeds heard the noise, and began to moan. They staggered towards her out of the darkness.

Simon spotted for her with the NVGs, quietly calling out the zombie's positions as they stepped forward. "First Zed, two o'clock," he warned.

Oksana adjusted the chain's trajectory slightly to her right and snapped it forward. The rusty steel links smashed into the drooling zombie's temple and its cranium exploded, splattering the pavement with rotting brains and shattered bone fragments. The destroyed cadaver pitched lifelessly to its knees, and slowly toppled over. Oksana brought the chain's momentum back up to speed just as Simon called out, "Ten o'clock, and three!"

Oksana spun the chain in a tight figure eight before her, smashing the zombie on her left, and then snapping the bloody chain to her right, catching the second Zed directly between the eyes with a bone-crushing crunch. The zombies fell back and over.

I flinched involuntarily at the sickening sound.

Simon called the remaining three as they approached their destruction, one at a time. Oksana spun the chain in a whirling blur overhead, nearly decapitating the last zombie to step forward. She laughed grimly as the Zed fell, and let the gore splattered chain wind down.

"That bitch is crazy," I muttered.

Natalie stood and walked forward to stand beside Oksana. "That was awesome!" she whispered in awe. "Could you teach me to fight like that?"

"Sure," Oksana replied pleasantly. "Every girl should learn to fight."

"Later, ladies," Simon urged. Oksana gently dropped the gory chain atop one of her victims.

Simon led us around the headless cadavers. He opened the door and checked the lobby, before leading us inside the showroom.

We moved through the deserted building into the back, where the parts room was located. Simon handed off the NVGs to Oksana, and produced a small flashlight. He searched through the parts bins until he found the water pumps.

I waited nervously while he discarded pump after pump. Finally, he selected one, and slowly turned it over in his hands, examining it closely. "This will do," he remarked. "Come on." He snapped off the light and reclaimed the goggles. "Same as before, follow my lead." We left the building and made our way across the lot, back to the street.

Simon led us slowly back the way we had come, stopping twice to avoid wandering zombies. Finally, we reached the Nachtpanzer. I gratefully collapsed back inside, and sat against the far wall, shaking and laughing with release. Natalie hugged me; she seemed to be handling the whole zombie apocalypse better than I was.

Oksana stood watch with the NVGs while Simon opened the battery compartment and went to work on the burnt out coolant pump. I kept expecting the zombies to find us in the darkness, but twenty minutes later, the new pump was in place and working. Simon rechecked all the cooling line connections, and then buttoned the car's armor up. We all stepped back inside and John closed the cargo door.

Simon slid into the driver's seat and reenergized the electrical system. He watched the gauges for a moment, and then, satisfied that his repair would hold, engaged the car's drive and pulled back onto the road. I let out a long sigh of relief as we finally resumed our travel to the east. Simon circled far around Springfield, finally turning to the south. He stuck to the side roads, always traveling to the east and south, and gradually we left the city behind us. Oksana conferred with him, and she directed him onto State Highway 14.

I sat down next to Natalie and tried to relax. It was harder traveling in the cargo bay. The accommodations were Spartan, to say the least, and you felt every bump. There was nothing much to do, but ride along and hang on. At least in the navigator's seat, I had something to keep me occupied. Natalie looked bored, but kids always looked like that. John had slid down against the far side of the cargo bay, and was sitting with his eyes closed.

I hadn't had much time to talk to my daughter, but now I did.

"Natalie," I began. "I'm sorry I wasn't there for you and your mother."

"It's not your fault, Dad," she replied sadly.

We were both quiet for a moment.

"Your mom was a good person," I offered.

Natalie grunted. "She was weak. When everything fell apart, and we were starving, she couldn't take it. She left us, and just wandered away to die. She killed herself."

"Don't say that," I responded sternly.

"It's the truth," Natalie stated.

I didn't know how to respond.

"A lot of people committed suicide," John interjected. "It was just too much for them. We've been insulated from anything really bad, for so long."

I considered his words. He was right. I was weak, out of shape, soft. I wasn't physically or mentally prepared to handle this kind of stress. I couldn't adjust or cope. The zombies terrified me. The virus frightened me. Everything in the QZ scared the shit out of me. Now that I had Natalie back, I wanted out.

"Nothing like this has ever happened to Americans," John continued. "We were so lucky, and we just took it all for granted. So lucky…" he trailed off.

"There's still a life out there," Simon said loudly. "Cheer up, assholes! You're riding with the baddest mother-fucker this side of the Mississippi. I'll have you eating apple pie and sipping martinis in twenty-four hours' time. Drinks, my place, remember?"

Despite Simon's assurances, I was far from happy, or relaxed. We had a long way to go. Everyone rode along in silence for a while.

Highway 14 led away from Springfield into the rural countryside. There were very few cars on the road, and Simon easily held the Nachtpanzer at fifty miles an hour. We sped through the darkness into the east.

A little over an hour's travel brought us to the edge of the Mark Twain Nation Forest. Everything was going smoothly, then I heard Oksana curse, and she snatched off the headset. She and Simon began talking quietly. They seemed to be arguing over some part of the route. Finally, Simon asked John to come up and talk to them.

"We're moving into the forestry. Did you have any contact with the rebels in this area?" Simon asked.

"No," John replied. "We were pretty well on our own. Every once in a while someone would wander through, but we didn't make contact if we didn't have to."

"I'm picking up some local chatter on the radio," Oksana explained. "Something is going on here. I've got a really strong local signal, and there's at least three other bands going. The rebels wouldn't break radio silence if they didn't have to. It could bring the Feds down on us."

"What are they saying?" I interrupted.

"Nothing I can understand," Oksana shot back. "They're using some kind of stupid code, and it's just short bursts."

"If they're using the radio in the clear, it means the nukes are going to be detonated soon," John said flatly. "They may even be trying to draw the Feds into this area, away from the real threat."

"That's not going to work out well for us," Simon growled. "Our best bet is to just get clear, the quicker the better."

Simon pushed the Nachtpanzer up to speed. The state road was clear of vehicles, and the big car flew down the tree lined road.

Simon gripped the wheel, his eyes locked to the heads-up display. "Please tell me there's no more water between us and the Mississippi."

Oksana looked askance at him. "Do you want me to check?"

"Yeah," the driver answered. "I do."

Oksana pulled up the GPS map, and studied the screen. "We are coming up on the White River; it's going to have a bridge. I thought you had the route locked down," she growled.

Simon replied sullenly, "I wasn't planning on being this far south, bitch."

"You two sound just like an old married couple," I joked from the rear.

"Fuck you, Bishop," Oksana grumbled.

Simon slowed the car gradually as Oksana guided him onto the approach to the bridge. Finally, the Nachtpanzer was creeping forward, and Simon flipped on the blackout lights. The first hundred feet or so of the bridge was fine, but then the dim lights revealed gaping holes in the decking, some big enough to drop through into the darkness below. Simon stopped the car with a loud sigh and covered his eyes with one hand.

No one spoke for a moment, then I couldn't stand it any longer. "What now?" I asked quietly.

Oksana turned to stare daggers at me. "We can go back to 95, and then north or south. Either way will lead us to another bridge if we turn east again."

"We don't have time." Simon slid out of the driver's seat and hit the button to open the cargo door. "Everybody out."

"What are you doing?" Oksana asked.

"I'm driving across," Simon answered.

We bailed out, and stood on the bridge while Simon and Oksana argued.

"I hope there aren't any Zeds around," John suggested grimly. He looked back the way we had come.

Oksana walked back to address us. "Follow the car."

Simon slowly drove the Nachtpanzer across the bridge, steering around abandoned cars and the bigger holes, and straddling the smaller ones. Oksana ground guided him, shouting instructions through the open cargo door. I watched tensely. We were almost across when Simon stopped the car. A bomb had ripped away a ten-foot-wide section of decking, and a mass of burned wrecks blocked the lane beside it. Oksana stood beside the door and conferred with Simon, then she walked back to us.

"Stay clear," she warned.

Simon reversed the Nachtpanzer slowly back, midway across the bridge, and then nudged the vehicle's nose up behind a wrecked box truck. Oksana climbed up into the cab, and stood in the open door. She pulled against the steering wheel as Simon began to push the truck slowly forward.

"Is she doing what I think she is?" John asked.

"I told you that bitch was crazy," I replied.

Simon pushed the truck forward, and Oksana drove the wreck directly into the gaping hole. At the last second, she dove to the side, and rolled across the pavement. The box truck dropped into the hole with a loud crash and a shower of sparks. The truck jammed against the broken concrete and rebar, one wheel spinning, hanging over open space.

Oksana stood and walked forward to examine her handiwork. "I don't know," she shouted to Simon.

The Nachtpanzer shot forward, dropping onto the truck and driving it deeper into the hole. The armored vehicle bounced and nose-dived onto the pavement as it cleared the broken edge of the decking, leaving chunks of gouged-out plastic armor behind. Simon slowed, and the car came to a stop at the far end of the bridge.

"Come on," Oksana urged, waving us across.

We walked to the far side and climbed back inside. Oksana hit the close button, and the door cycled shut.

Simon grinned at us; he hadn't even broken a sweat. "Now we're having some serious fun," he joked. "I haven't done anything that dangerous in quite a while."

I didn't bother to tell him I thought he was nuts. I just collapsed against the bulkhead in the cargo bay and wished I was the fuck back home.

Simon brought the Nachtpanzer up to speed, and we flew down the state road. The roadway was rural, and almost clear. Thirty minutes brought us to the intersection with Highway 160, and the town of West Plains. Simon slowed the car as we approached the outskirts of town. Oksana guided him with the GPS, and we pulled off the road into a small parking lot.

"Why are we stopping?" I asked.

"We need small arms ammo, and Jim's Guns is where we're going to get it," Simon replied. He shut down the car's lights and moved to the rear. "John, come with me." He handed the NVG's and the Carr 223 to Oksana, and readied his machine-pistol. "Cover us from top side, we're just going to do a snatch and grab."

Oksana grumbled, but she threw open the turret hatch and climbed up into the seat. The smell of rotten flesh came to us immediately. Oksana began to fire, turning in the turret until she had fired off an entire magazine. She slapped in a fresh mag, and threw the rifle's bolt. "You're clear to the door."

Simon hit the open button and the cargo door cycled wide. Head shot Zeds lay scattered across the pavement between the car and the building's front door. Simon and John rushed to the door, and disappeared inside. I knelt in the cargo door's frame, my .45 in hand. A Zed wandered around the building from the right, but before I could react, Oksana fired, blowing its rotten brains onto the cinder block wall behind it.

"Come on," I urged. I knew it had only been a minute, but the time seemed to stretch into infinity. Oksana fired through another magazine as Zeds began to emerge from the darkness at both ends of the car. The Carr's green laser illuminated their rotten heads briefly just before each one exploded. Twitching cadavers lined the lot to either side, and more stumbled forward, climbing over their own, drawn by the gunfire.

Finally, Simon and John emerged from the store. Simon calmly walked forward, firing a short burst from his Scorpion to either side. John rushed across to the car, and pushed two ammo bags inside, before leaping in. Simon pushed past me and hit the button. I rattled off my pistol's ammo at the zombies approaching the car as the door cycled shut. Oksana climbed down and grabbed an ammo bag. She rummaged inside until she found the ammunition for her Dragunov. The psycho bitch reminded me of a kid with candy.

"Rumanian? Is that all you could find?" she complained.

"I was kind of in a hurry," Simon retorted. He energized the car and pulled back onto the highway. "Less bitching, more reloading," he suggested.

John handed out the liberated ammunition; he had even grabbed two boxes of .45 bullets for my pistol.

Simon kept the car on the outskirts of West Plains. It was a good sized town, and wrecked cars and wandering zombies filled the streets. Ten minutes of driving brought us around the town and back out onto Highway 160 to the east. The roadway began to clear as we left civilization behind us.

Oksana sat cross-legged on the cargo bay floor. Natalie watched her deftly reload the Dragunov's magazines. John knelt down beside me, and whispered conspiratorially, "I grabbed this for Natalie, but I thought you should be the one to give it to her." He handed me a small, square gun. "It's a nine millimeter Mac-10, the semi-automatic model."

I looked up at him, and slowly took the gun.

"I don't know about this," I suggested. "I'm not sure I want Natalie to have a gun."

"Trust me, it's better to have a gun and not need it, than to need a gun and not have it," John elucidated. "You're making a mistake."

"What have you got?" Oksana asked, interrupting us.

"Great, thanks, John," I groaned.

"A Mac-10," he answered, handing the gun off to her.

Oksana took the gun. She pulled the bolt, and peered into the receiver. "American junk," she said disdainfully before handing it back.

"Can I see it?" Natalie asked.

"Sure," John answered. He pulled the gun's magazine, locked the bolt back, and handed Natalie the gun. "Always make sure the gun is empty before you give it to someone," he cautioned.

Natalie held the gun in her hand. "Could you teach me to shoot, Oksana?" she asked.

"Of course," the woman answered.

John looked at me.

I sighed heavily. I didn't want my little girl toting around a pistol, but considering the circumstances, I was probably failing as a father to not give her the gun.

Oksana divined our intentions. "The gun is for Natalie?" she asked.

I shook my head. "Yeah."

Natalie squealed with delight, "It's for me?"

"Only if John shows you how to handle it," I warned.

"I will show her," Oksana demanded.

I frowned, but relented. "Sure." I didn't like Oksana, but if there was one thing that she was good for, it was shooting things with guns. The bitch was awesome with a rifle.

Oksana sat with Natalie, and explained how to load the Mac-10. She then taught her how to break the pistol down and clean it. Natalie spent the rest of the ride working with the gun. Since Oksana was busy in the rear, I moved forward and slid into the navigator's seat.

"What's the plan?" I asked Simon.

"We run east to the next battery change. It's not that far," he explained.

"After that?" I pushed.

"Fuck man, I don't know," he laughed. "I'm making this shit up as I go along."

We traveled east through the night, and finally, luck was with us. The last battery drop had been set up at an intersection along the road we were traveling. We approached the junction of State Road 19 slowly. The road was clear. Oksana climbed up into the turret and looked for the strobe. The drop box had landed in the tall grass alongside the highway, but luckily she spotted it as we passed. Simon backed the Nachtpanzer into position, and we bailed out. John and I watched for Zeds while Simon and Oksana switched out the batteries and the spent weaponry. We loaded all the spare mini-gun ammo and rockets into the cargo bay, and took the SAM too. No wandering zombies came to attack us, only the crickets disturbed the quiet of the night.

"That was too easy," I grumbled.

"It'll get real hairy again before this is all over," Simon predicted. "Just wait."

We climbed back into the car and drove to the east.

Simon held the car to forty-five miles an hour, and we made good progress. We avoided the towns as much as possible, and Highway 160 played out before us like a long dark ribbon. Finally, we came to its end, where it joined with State Road 67 coming north out of Arkansas. Simon brought the Nachtpanzer to a halt in the middle of the road.

The driver stared ahead at the blackness of the heads-up display.

"I've been thinking this over, and there's only one way we can find the resistance, and the nukes," he declared.

"And that is?" I inquired.

"We have to contact the Feds," Simon answered. "Their satellites can see the nukes, they just don't know that they are supposed to be looking for them."

"If we contact them, they'll send the choppers," Oksana warned. "We are inside their range. It's suicide."

"Maybe," Simon agreed. "It depends on whether they believe us or not."

"Even if they do believe us, as soon as the bombs are neutralized, they'll zap us," Oksana declared. "We're on their shoot list. You know I'm right. They'll never let us go, no matter what we do!"

"But if we operate with that knowledge, it gives us an edge," Simon argued. "We use the Feds, but we play that there are no friendlies."

Oksana shook her head. "We won't make it."

"Do you have any other ideas?" Simon asked bluntly.

"How will the Feds be able to see the nukes?" I asked.

"The nukes have major safety protocols in place," Simon answered. "Each warhead should have a GPS tracker attached. Even if the guys who moved them knew that, the satellites should still be able to get a fix by analyzing their radioactive signature."

"The warheads are shielded," I pointed out. "They shouldn't give off a signature."

"Normally," Simon agreed. "But the Feds bombed every location with a weapons system capable of reaching outside the zone. They did preemptive strikes to deny any military assets inside from retaliating. Especially the nuclear assets. But they didn't figure on anyone digging the warheads out and moving them by mule. I guarantee you at least one of those warheads was compromised. They're tough, but not indestructible. At least one warhead is leaking, leaving a trail that will lead us to all of them."

"No one would transport a damaged warhead," I pointed out. "That's suicide."

"These guys would," Simon retorted. "They just want payback. They got nothing else to lose."

"Is that our only option?" John asked quietly.

"If the bombs go off now, we're dead anyway," Simon replied. "The closer we get..."

We were all quiet for a half a moment.

"Give 'em a call, babe," Simon suggested.

Oksana switched on the radio.

CIA Operations - The Pentagon

CIA Deputy Director Schissler placed her call directly through to SAC-NORAD. Her voice trembled slightly, "Do you believe this report to be accurate, General Roberts?"

"I wouldn't have, normally," the general replied evenly. "But given the current circumstances, I'm afraid I do believe it to be true."

"I thought the first call I got from you was as bad as it could ever possibly get," Schissler groaned. "Have you verified that the nukes are at New Madrid?"

"Satellite readings confirm that a high-grade radiation trail leads to that location. It's faint, but it does exist, and that confirms the report. We can't verify that more than one warhead is at that location, but one is bad enough ..." He trailed off. "We have to take the report seriously, especially since it originated from inside the QZ."

"Damn it!" Schissler cursed. "I knew that eventually the survivors would strike back, but I never imagined anything like this."

"It was pretty ingenious," the general agreed.

"I wouldn't be so proud of those men, general. They're traitors."

"They're U.S. soldiers, officers," Roberts retorted. "We gave them a damn good reason to hate us. We abandoned them."

"Spilled milk, general," Schissler growled. "What options do I present to the President?"

"Nukes are out," General Roberts laughed grimly. "Conventional air strikes, guided missiles maybe. Anyone we send in won't ever come back out, even if they stop the detonation."

"I see," the deputy director considered.

"There is one more option," the general spoke. "The asset inside wants to assist us."

"What?" Schissler asked.

"He's a raider, named Simon," Roberts answered.

Schissler jerked to attention. "Did you say Simon?"

"Yes," the general replied. "He called the report in. He wants the location, says he can stop the detonation. All he'll get from me is an air-to-ground missile up his ass."

"General, you are to assist the raiders in any way possible. Do you understand me?" Schissler demanded.

"That's outside SOP!" Roberts retorted.

"Fuck your SOP!" Schissler shouted into the phone. "Assist the raiders, and ready air strikes, immediately!"

"I can't do both," the general argued.

"Yes, you can," Schissler said coldly. "Two birds with one stone."

County Road CC - Missouri

Simon peered intently ahead at the heads-up display. He had the car held at forty miles an hour, and had been driving due east ever since they had contacted the Feds on the radio. Everyone was dead quiet, waiting for the hammer to fall. Static hissed through the radio's speakers. I jumped when a voice spoke.

"Unidentified raider, this is border control, Easy Sector. Do you copy?"

Oksana hesitated, then she keyed the mic. She was giving the Feds their position, and she knew it. "I copy, go ahead."

"You are cleared to proceed to target. Target's coordinates being sent now."

Oksana gripped the screen, waiting for the missile that would kill them all, but the radar remained clear. The GPS screen flashed, and Oksana looked up.

"Got it."

"Guide me in," Simon snarled.

Whitman Air Force Base - Missouri

Steve Marshall pulled the tab on his last road flare and tossed it onto the runway. The flare sputtered to life, joining the others already burning down either side of the tarmac. Sporadic gunfire rang out as the occasional Zed wandered into the cleared area.

Steve waited patiently, hoping against all hope that this wasn't all just some stupid dream. Faintly at first, and then growing louder as it approached, a C-130 cargo plane flew in from the east. The plane circled the runway, and then slowly settled into position. Steve jumped up and down, and then screamed for joy as the plane's wheels touched down. He pulled his train of skittish horses forward onto the runway, and led them towards the slowly taxiing plane.

New Madrid - Missouri

Colonel Greene walked along the bank of the Mississippi River, idly kicking stones and drinking old scotch straight from the bottle. Faintly, far off in the distance, he could see the lights of some unidentified town far off on the eastern horizon. That town wasn't far away, and yet, it was worlds away. Everyone there was safe and warm in their beds. No zombies stalked their streets, no one would shoot them if they tried to leave. For those people, the apocalypse hadn't come: yet. But it would. Greene looked down at the wristwatch he had worn for the last twenty years, the watch his dead wife had given him. It counted down the seconds until sunrise, the seconds until the second apocalypse.

He turned and walked back into the camp, past the perimeter guards he had deployed along the riverbank. Beyond them were gun emplacements, and covered firing pits. A ring of SAM missiles, anti-tank defenses, and heavy machine guns defended the camp on all sides. Every man available was on site, manning a gun or missile. At the camp's center was ground zero, a camouflaged sandbag bunker that housed all the nuclear warheads.

Greene stepped inside. Master Sergeant Yates stood and saluted. He was pale and thin. Even in the predawn gloom, Colonel Greene could see that the man was dying.

"At ease," Greene commanded.

Yates eased himself back down into a folding chair beside the master control board. A rat's nest of wires ran from the board into the open warhead casings that formed a loose circle around it.

"You going to live long enough to detonate these things?" Greene asked gruffly.

"Hell yeah," Yates answered. "I'm almost done."

"Well, if you don't mind, I'll sit here with you for a bit." He passed the bottle.

New Madrid - Missouri

Simon eased the Nachtpanzer forward until he was just below the crest of the hill. The Mississippi River and the resistance camp were just over the rise. He knew the rebels weren't expecting an attack from the west on the ground, only Zeds would come from the woods in that direction. At least he hoped they had believed that, otherwise he'd be dead in a few minutes. John had loped off to the east with a pair of SAMs, and the assault shotgun. Simon was giving him a few minutes to get into position. Oksana had moved off into the trees to the west with the Dragunov sniper rifle, and she would need a minute to crawl forward.

"Time to go," Simon warned.

Natalie hugged the driver fiercely, and stepped outside the car. I looked at Simon, and turned away.

"Hey asshole, if I don't make it out of here and you do, make damn sure you tell everyone what a fucking hero I was," Simon laughed.

"Sure thing," I said slowly. "Thanks Simon, for, you know…" I trailed off.

"Just make sure you get her home," Simon agreed.

I hit the close button, and the cargo door cycled shut, sealing us outside.

"Come on, kiddo," I said huskily. I grabbed Natalie's hand, and we ran.

Simon switched on all the Nachtpanzer's weapons systems. The rocket cursor filled the heads-up display, superimposed over the mini-gun's crosshairs. His hands tightened on the steering triggers, and adrenaline flooded his veins. Simon depressed the accelerator. The Nachtpanzer leaped over the hill and rolled down the other side to the edge of the camp. There was no noise until Simon depressed the gun triggers. The mini-guns howled crimson death, eviscerating the outer defensive positions as Simon slewed the twin 30 caliber guns back and forth. Machine-gun fire raked the car's front armor, and the windshield cracked as a survivor fired almost point blank at the car.

Simon turned hard and ran his attacker down; the Nachtpanzer crushed the gunner into a crimson ruin. The car's front tire sank into the hole, and the Nachtpanzer stopped.

It was as if someone had kicked over an anthill. The soldiers on the far side reacted quickly. An anti-tank missile screamed across the camp and tore into the Nachtpanzer's left side. The heavy round was designed to combat tank armor, and passed through the lighter plastic-ceramic mesh before detonating on the far side. Still, the car was rocked back, and engulfed in flames. Machine-gun fire raked the Nachtpanzer from all sides.

Without warning, three Apache attack helicopters popped over the horizon from the east and attacked the camp with salvos of air-to-ground missiles. Gun emplacements and sandbagged foxholes were instantly reduced to smoking black holes. Still, the defenders weren't done. A single SAM streaked from the ground to impact a helicopter directly overhead. The Apache broke into two flaming pieces and dropped directly onto the SAM position beneath it. The surviving choppers turned their mini-guns on the site in retaliation, blasting anything that still moved.

Colonel Greene looked over the sand bags as his defenses crumpled around him.

"Detonate it now," he ordered.

"They're not all online," Yates replied.

"Do it!"

The Nachtpanzer was shattered and burning, but still had some fight left in her. Smoke and the acrid stench of burning plastic filled the cockpit, but Simon concentrated his attention on the heads-up display. Only one position on the display had not fired during the combat, the sandbagged position at the camp's center. Simon swiveled the rocket cursor over the position and depressed the thumb button. The rack emptied as all twelve short-range missiles screeched into the target. The camp's center exploded in a daisy-chained crimson fireball.

The Apaches turned and locked onto the burning car below them. Before they could fire, a lone figure stood and shouldered a surface-to-air missile. The SAM streaked from the edge of camp and hit the lead Apache dead center. The chopper detonated in a cherry-red cloud of flaming fuel and high explosives. Burning JP-4 and debris rained from the sky. John cast aside the empty SAM launcher and raised the second one to his shoulder. The surviving chopper spun like an angry wasp and shredded the missile's point of origin with mini-gun fire. A continuous salvo of missiles blasted the entire hillside into tattered pits, as the ship's gunner fired the rocket rack dry.

Simon climbed into the burning turret and swiveled the 50 caliber mini-gun up towards the hovering helicopter directly overhead. Machine-gun rounds were still panging off the car's armor all around him. He depressed the trigger and walked the tracer rounds down from the chopper's center out onto its tail. The ship's armor deflected the rounds until they reached the tail boom. The tail rotor disintegrated in a screaming hurricane of mechanical destruction, and the stricken helicopter turned on its side and slammed into the hillside. The explosion lit the camp in a wash of red light and noise.

Oksana walked the Dragunov's night-scope over the camp's perimeter, picking off anyone foolish enough to give her a target. As the first chopper exploded, it gave a few seconds of light to pick out a target. She pressed her eye to the sight and fired off the sniper rifle's magazine, killing a machine gun crew. She slammed in a fresh magazine as the last chopper crashed and exploded. She could find no other targets. The Nachtpanzer was engulfed in flames. Simon bailed out through the turret, and dropped to the ground. She covered him with the rifle until he reached the hill behind her.

Oksana stood and ran back the way she had come.

Albuquerque - New Mexico

It was two hours until dawn, and all was quiet on the west bank of the Rio Grande. Lieutenant Bob Roberts yawned, and leaned back against the slit trench wall. He stared out beyond the stacked sandbags and the sights of his machinegun. The abandoned buildings of Old Albuquerque were barely visible just beyond the swirling black waters of the river. No one had tried to cross in a long time, and Roberts was pretty sure that there was no one left alive over there anymore. Not that there weren't any zombies. Albuquerque had those by the thousands, but they couldn't cross the river.

Roberts wished something would happen to break the monotony of his watch. He yawned again, and tried to stay awake. A brilliant flash of light illuminated the sky to the north, and a few seconds, later a tremor moved through the ground. The sand bags shifted, and one fell into the trench. Roberts jerked upright, and strained to see anything in the darkness. He fumbled around in the trench until he found his radio, and turned up the volume. A jumble of static filled the air, and then a voice came through, broken, but audible.

"Be advised, all units in Whiskey and X-ray, we have a nuclear detonation north of your locations. Go to MOPP-4 immediately. Repeat MOPP-4." The voice faded under the hiss of the static.

Roberts broke out in a cold sweat. As he fumbled with his gas mask bag, a warm wind rushed over his position. He hurriedly pulled his suit on, and jammed the gas mask down over his head. Roberts didn't notice that the Rio Grande was dropping until the swirling red mushroom cloud rose over the northern horizon, illuminating the skyline. By that time, Roberts stopped staring at the cloud; the river was dry, and hundreds of Zeds were stumbling across the muddy riverbed towards him.

The exact same scenario was playing out over two hundred miles south at Las Cruces and El Paso.

Saint Louis - Missouri

At exactly 7:00 AM Eastern, a ten megaton nuclear warhead detonated on Two Branch Island, just northwest of the ruins of metropolitan Saint Louis. In a flash, the ground detonation vaporized a one square mile area and millions of gallons of water, creating a quarter mile deep crater. The course of the Mississippi River was instantly changed as the boiling water rushed into the crater, and spilled out to carve a new channel on the southern side. The mighty arc of the river that circled Saint Louis to the east ran dry in moments, and the ruins of Saint Louis now stood on the eastern side of the QZ, inside the population zone.

Drawn by the growing mushroom cloud that stood on the northern horizon like a beckoning finger, the one million plus Zeds that still populated the city began to move north and east, across the muddy riverbed and out into population.

New Madrid - Missouri

I stood on the edge of the Mississippi River, looking across to the far side. Off to the north, a tremendous explosion had lit up the dawn sky. Natalie and I stood holding hands, waiting for whatever would come. I spun, my pistol in hand, as Simon and Oksana emerged from the trees behind us.

"Easy," Simon suggested. "It's us."

I lowered my gun, and Oksana did the same.

"What's going on?" I asked fearfully.

"It looks like the nukes here weren't the only ones," Simon explained. He held out the radio from the car's survival pack. "The QZ's been breached on both sides with tactical nukes. The Zeds are out. The quarantine is broken."

"That can't be good," I whispered.

"It's good for us," Oksana countered. "We should be able to cross the river once it gets dark. The Feds will be very busy."

"But what about radiation?" I insisted.

"We're south of ground zero, and the winds will carry the fallout east," Simon assured me. "If we can get back into Kentucky, I can arrange transport for us to Chicago."

"What about the car?" I asked. "Aren't you out of a job now?"

"Simon says, I'm retired."

EPILOGUE

The trees flashed by on either side of the gravel road, and the air was cold. I shivered and pressed as far back against the truck's rusted cab as I could, trying not to complain. Natalie was asleep beside me, and we were alive. More importantly, we were leaving the QZ behind.

Simon sat nearby, picking mud out of the soles of his combat boot with a knife. Oksana's back was to us; she sat crossways over the tailgate, her rifle across her knees.

"Cold?" Simon inquired.

"Obviously," I grumbled back.

"But you're not bitching about it," Simon observed. "Maybe this trip toughened you up a little."

I shrugged.

"What will you do now?" the raider asked.

"I don't know," I answered. "I guess I'm kind of unemployed."

"Not to mention a felon," Simon laughed.

I groaned back, "Didn't really have much of a choice." I stretched out my dirty hand and gently brushed the hair back from Natalie's face.

"You did okay out there. I'm short a couple of crew, and you're pretty handy with computers," Simon offered.

"I thought you said you were retiring. Are you actually offering me a job?" I whispered.

"I'm too young to retire. What else would I do?" the raider replied. "More importantly, what are you going to do? The Feds are going to be looking for you. You might as well go all in."

"What about Oksana?" I asked, nodding towards her.

"She likes your kid," Simon observed. "That's probably enough to keep her from actually killing you."

I closed my eyes. My future was uncertain, but so was everyone else's now. Things had changed too much, and there was no turning back. My old life was gone. I would have to find some chance for Natalie, and if that meant more risk for myself, that was a chance I was willing to take.

"I'm in…"

The End

The Weaponry of More Bullets Than Zombies

The weapons depicted in this book are for the most part generic clones of very common weapon types (12 Gauge Assault Shotgun), or completely fabricated by the author (Carr 223 Machinegun). The heavy weapons are based on actual military weaponry (50 and 30 Caliber Mini-gun, SAM, and Short Range Rockets.) Their listed capabilities are a close estimate based on the actual weapon's real characteristics.

The exception to these is the Scorpion Sub-machinegun. First manufactured in 1961 in Czechoslovakia, the Scorpion is one of the smallest sub-machineguns ever built. With its wire stock folded it is only 10.6 inches long and weighs less than 3 lbs. empty. Its larger capacity magazine of twenty rounds of .32 ACP ammunition can be fired in less than two seconds with a single pull of the trigger. The weapon is extremely well balanced and designed, and can be fired like a pistol quite easily. Of course, it is a short range weapon, but it can be fired accurately to approximately 500 feet if fired from the shoulder with the wire stock extended. It was later manufactured in a variety of heavier calibers.

Caseless ammunition actually exists, but has not come into common usage. The round has no jacket. The chemical propellant is molded into the shape of the round, and attached directly behind the actual bullet or projectile. Once fired, the propellant burns away, leaving no shell casing to be ejected. This saves on weight and space occupied by the round. More caseless ammunition can be packed into a magazine than conventional rounds. Caseless ammunition can also be designed in other than round shapes. Square casings are possible.

Plastic projectiles are also real, but are usually limited to practice shooting, as they are less lethal than their metallic counterparts. This is not to say they are non-lethal. During World War Two, the Germans utilized many non-standard projectile materials as they suffered material shortages, including even wooden bullets.

Scorpion Sub-machinegun, Model 61

Specifications:
Caliber: 32 ACP
Weight: 2.87 lb. (1.30 kg)
Length: 20.4 in (517mm) Stock extended, 10.6 in Stock folded
Barrel Length: 4.5 in (115mm)
Magazine Capacity: 10 or 20 Round magazine
Action: Blowback

Capabilities:
Maximum range: 450 ft. (150m)
Rate of Fire: 850rds/min

Carr 223 Machinegun

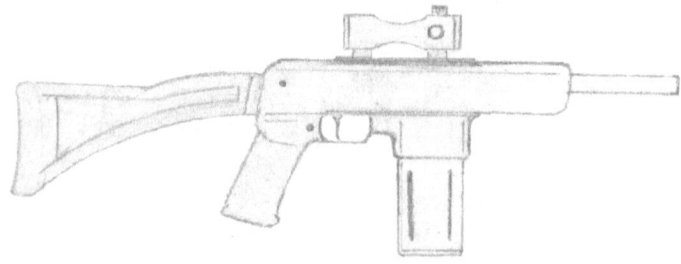

Specifications:
Caliber: 223mm Caseless Ammunition
Weight: 7.5lb (3.5kg)
Length: 31in (785mm)
Barrel Length: 20in (508mm)
Magazine Capacity: 40 round magazine
Action: Gas operated

Capabilities:
Maximum Range: 980ft (300m)
Rate of Fire: 750 rds. /min

12 Gauge Assault Shotgun

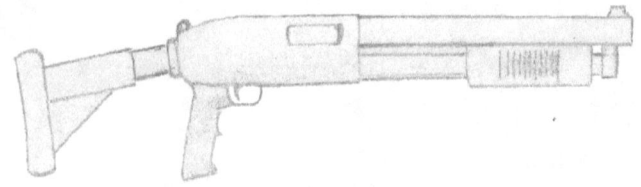

Specifications:
Caliber: 12 Gauge Shotgun (OO Buckshot)
Weight: 5lbs (2.3kg)
Length: 40in
Barrel Length: 18in
Magazine Capacity: 8 rounds
Action: Pump

Capacities:
Maximum Range: 150 ft. (50m)

50 and 30 Caliber Mini-Guns

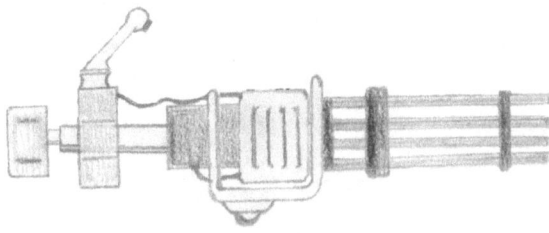

Specifications:
Caliber: 50 or 30 Caliber Specialty Caseless Polymer Ammunition
Weight: 85lb
Length: (801mm)
Barrel Length :(558mm)
Magazine Capacity: Belt feed
Action: Electric driven rotary

Capabilities:
Muzzle Velocity: 2800f/s (850 m/s)
Maximum Range: 3280ft (1000m)
Rate of Fire: 2000-6000 rds./min

SAM Surface to Air Missile

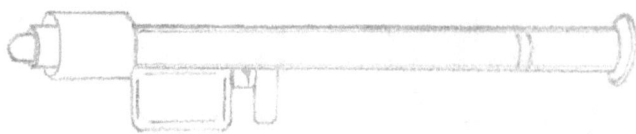

Specifications:

Weight: 33lbs (15kg)
Length: 5ft (1.5m)
Magazine Capacity: Single shot, heat-seeking missile
Action: Rocket engine

Capabilities:
Maximum Range: 3 miles (4.8 km)

Short Range High Explosive Rockets

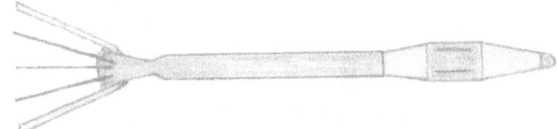

Specifications:
Caliber: 60mm High Explosive Warhead
Weight: (2.5kg)
Length: 35in
Magazine Capacity: Rack of twelve
Action: Solid fuel rocket engine

Capabilities:
Maximum Range: 600 ft. (200m)

Dragunov Sniper Rifle

Specifications:
Caliber: 7.62x54mm
Weight: 9.5lbs (4.3kg)
Length: 45in.
Magazine Capacity: 10 rounds
Action: Gas

Capabilities:
Maximum Range: 875yds (800m)
Rate of Fire: Semi-automatic

ABOUT THE AUTHOR

Carl Cart is an author and award winning independent film maker. He lives in rural Southern Indiana in a small cabin with his wife Jennifer and their dog Bob, patiently awaiting the zombie apocalypse.

Carl is also the author of the *ROTTERS* trilogy, and the zombie/comedies *DWARFS OF THE DEAD & DETOUR 366.*

For more information, visit the website www.carlcart.com

CHECK OUT OTHER GREAT ZOMBIE NOVELS

Z BURBIA
by Jake Bible

Whispering Pines is a classic, quiet, private American subdivision on the edge of Asheville, NC, set in the pristine Blue Ridge Mountains. Which is good since the zombie apocalypse has come to Western North Carolina and really put suburban living to the test!

Surrounded by a sea of the undead, the residents of Whispering Pines have adapted their bucolic life of block parties to scavenging parties, common area groundskeeping to immediate area warfare, neighborhood beautification to neighborhood fortification.

But, even in the best of times, suburban living has its ups and downs what with nosy neighbors, a strict Home Owners' Association, and a property management company that believes the words "strict interpretation" are holy words when applied to the HOA covenants. Now with the zombie apocalypse upon them even those innocuous, daily irritations quickly become dramatic struggles for personal identity, family security, and straight up survival.

ZOMBIE RULES
by David Achord

Zach Gunderson's life sucked and then the zombie apocalypse began.

Rick, an aging Vietnam veteran, alcoholic, and prepper, convinces Zach that the apocalypse is on the horizon. The two of them take refuge at a remote farm. As the zombie plague rages, they face a terrifying fight for survival.

They soon learn however that the walking dead are not the only monsters.

CHECK OUT OTHER GREAT ZOMBIE NOVELS

900 MILES
by S. Johnathan Davis

John is a killer, but that wasn't his day job before the Apocalypse.

In a harrowing 900 mile race against time to get to his wife just as the dead begin to rise, John, a business man trapped in New York, soon learns that the zombies are the least of his worries, as he sees first-hand the horror of what man is capable of with no rules, no consequences and death at every turn.

Teaming up with an ex-army pilot named Kyle, they escape New York only to stumble across a man who says that he has the key to a rumored underground stronghold called Avalon..... Will they find safety? Will they make it to Johns wife before it's too late?

Get ready to follow John and Kyle in this fast paced thriller that mixes zombie horror with gladiator style arena action!

WHITE FLAG OF THE DEAD
by Joseph Talluto

Millions died when the Enillo Virus swept the earth. Millions more were lost when the victims of the plague refused to stay dead, instead rising to slaughter and feed on those left alive. For survivors like John Talon and his son Jake, they are faced with a choice: Do they submit to the dead, raising the white flag of surrender? Or do they find the will to fight, to try and hang on to the last shreds or humanity?

CHECK OUT OTHER GREAT ZOMBIE NOVELS

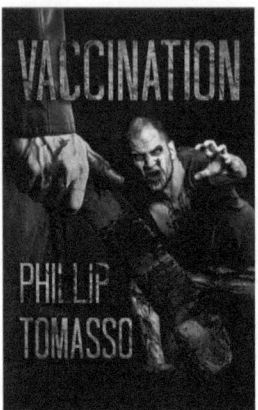

VACCINATION
by Phillip Tomasso

What if the H7N9 vaccination wasn't just a preventative measure against swine flu?

It seemed like the flu came out of nowhere and yet, in no time at all the government manufactured a vaccination. Were lab workers diligent, or could the virus itself have been man-made? Chase McKinney works as a dispatcher at 9-1-1. Taking emergency calls, it becomes immediately obvious that the entire city is infected with the walking dead. His first goal is to reach and save his two children.

Could the walls built by the U.S.A. to keep out illegal aliens, and the fact the Mexican government could not afford to vaccinate their citizens against the flu, make the southern border the only plausible destination for safety?

ZOMBIE, INC
by Chris Dougherty

"WELCOME! To Zombie, Inc. The United Five State Republic's leading manufacturer of zombie defense systems! In business since 2027, Zombie, Inc. puts YOU first. YOUR safety is our MAIN GOAL! Our many home defense options - from Ze Fence® to Ze Popper® to Ze Shed® - fit every need and every budget. Use Scan Code "TELL ME MORE!" for your FREE, in-home*, no obligation consultation! *Schedule your appointment with the confidence that you will NEVER HAVE TO LEAVE YOUR HOME! It isn't safe out there and we know it better than most! Our sales staff is FULLY TRAINED to handle any and all adversarial encounters with the living and the undead". Twenty-five years after the deadly plague, the United Five State Republic's most successful company, Zombie, Inc., is in trouble. Will a simple case of dwindling supply and lessening demand be the end of them or will Zombie, Inc. find a way, however unpalatable, to survive?

CHECK OUT OTHER GREAT ZOMBIE NOVELS

DEAD PULSE RISING
by K. Michael Gibson

Slavering hordes of the walking dead rule the streets of Baltimore, their decaying forms shambling across the ruined city, voracious and unstoppable. The remaining survivors hide desperately, for all hope seems lost... until an armored fortress on wheels plows through the ghouls, crushing bones and decayed flesh. The vehicle stops and two men emerge from its doors, armed to the teeth and ready to cancel the apocalypse.

TOWER OF THE DEAD
by J.V. Roberts

Markus is a hardworking man that just wants a better life for his family. But when a virus sweeps through the halls of his high-rise apartment complex, those plans are put on hold. Trapped on the sixteenth floor with no hope of rescue, Markus must fight his way down to safety with his wife and young daughter in tow.

Floor by bloody floor they must battle through hordes of the hungry dead on a terrifying mission to survive the TOWER OF THE DEAD.

CHECK OUT OTHER GREAT ZOMBIE NOVELS

RUN
by Rich Restucci

The dead have risen, and they are hungry.

Slow and plodding, they are Legion. The undead hunt the living. Stop and they will catch you. Hide and they will find you. If you have a heartbeat you do the only thing you can: You run.

Survivors escape to an island stronghold: A cop and his daughter, a computer nerd, a garbage man with a piece of rebar, and an escapee from a mental hospital with a life-saving secret. After reaching Alcatraz, the ever expanding group of survivors realize that the infected are not the only threat.

Caught between the viciousness of the undead, and the heartlessness of the living, what choice is there? Run.

THE DEAD WALK THE EARTH
by Luke Duffy

As the flames of war threaten to engulf the globe, a new threat emerges.

A 'deadly flu', the like of which no one has ever seen or imagined, relentlessly spreads, gripping the world by the throat and slowly squeezing the life from humanity.

Eight soldiers, accustomed to operating below the radar, carrying out the dirty work of a modern democracy, become trapped within the carnage of a new and terrifying world.

Deniable and completely expendable. That is how their government considers them, and as the dead begin to walk, Stan and his men must fight to survive.

CHECK OUT OTHER GREAT ZOMBIE NOVELS

DEAD ASCENT
by Jason McPhearson

The dead have risen and they are hungry...

Grizzled war veteran turned game warden, Brayden James and a small group of survivors, fight their way through the rugged wilderness of southern Appalachia to an isolated cabin in the hope of finding sanctuary. Every terrifying step they make they are stalked by a growing mass of staggering corpses, and a raging forest fire, set by the government in hopes of containing the virus.

As all logical routes off the mountain are cut off from them, they seek the higher ground, but they soon realize there is little hope of escape when the dead walk and the world burns.

CHAOS THEORY
by Rich Restucci

The world has fallen to a relentless enemy beyond reason or mercy. With no remorse they rend the planet with tooth and nail.

One man stands against the scourge of death that consumes all.

Teamed with a genius survivalist and a teenage girl, he must flee the teeming dead, the evils of humans left unchecked, and those that would seek to use him. His best weapon to stave off the horrors of this new world? His wit.